Prais ... alerie Wolzien
and her novels

"Valerie Wolzien is a consummate crime
writer. Her heroines sparkle as they sift
through clues and stir up evidence in the
darker, deadly side of suburbia."
—MARY DAHEIM

"Wit is Wolzien's strong suit. . . . Her portrayal
of small-town life will prompt those of us in
similar situations to agree that we too have
been there and done that."
—*The Mystery Review*

A FASHIONABLE MURDER

VALERIE WOLZIEN

FAWCETT BOOKS • NEW YORK

A Fawcett Book
Published by The Random House Ballantine Publishing Group
Copyright © 2003 by Valerie Wolzien

www.ballantinebooks.com

ISBN 0-449-00718-9

Manufactured in the United States of America

First Edition: May 2003

10   9   8   7   6   5   4   3   2

This is my twentieth mystery novel. Sometime during the writing of each book, I have been absolutely convinced that I would never finish. I have walked around the house muttering to myself, ignoring my family, eating junk food, and being what my father has always called "an all-around pain in the butt." So I dedicate this one to my husband, Tom, and my son, Trevor, who have lived through it with me. I could never have done it without their support and encouragement.

A

FASHIONABLE

MURDER

ONE

THERE ARE PEOPLE who save all year long for a vacation in New York City. They can be spotted on Fifth Avenue in the summer, nervously clutching their fanny packs, convinced the guy with the nose ring will snatch their traveler's checks the moment they gaze up at the glass skyscrapers. They delay buses as they ask drivers for directions to museums less than a fifteen-minute walk away. They fill the seats of long-running Broadway shows. They eat—and complain—about the overpriced hamburgers in local restaurants. They discover that hours pounding the hot pavement can cause blisters to form in even the most broken-in shoes. They buy cheap T-shirts that will shrink the first time they're washed. They have a wonderful time.

Others tour the city during the holidays. They go to Radio City Music Hall and see the Christmas Spectacular. They visit the tree at Rockefeller Center along with thousands of others, watching the skaters and munching on glazed nuts bought at a corner stand. They shop for presents for family and friends at FAO Schwarz, happily paying twice what they would at the local Toys R Us back home. They take bitterly cold boat rides around Manhattan. They find it impossible to get cabs and walk the streets for hours, lost and freezing. They have a wonderful time.

But this was February. The snow, which had made the city so enchanting in December, had become filthy slush overflowing clogged gutters. City dwellers who couldn't afford trips to warm beaches were either inside hard at work or striding purposefully down the sidewalks ignoring the resort clothing displayed in store windows. Panhandlers, discouraged by the cold, leaned against frozen buildings, not bothering to shake stained coffee cups with a few coins dusting the bottom.

One couple, mother and son, were walking up Madison Avenue, heads butting into the wind. Josie Pigeon was miserable, her shoulders hunched, her normally cheerful face bent into a frown; her unruly long red hair had escaped from her scratchy wool scarf and flew around her shoulders. Tyler, her teenage son, striding by her side, was beaming. "Mom, this is great! I can't believe we're finally here! It's so cool!"

Josie didn't agree. "This isn't cool. It's cold. And wet. Look at this!" She lifted one foot and displayed a soaking wet suede pump. "These are my best shoes!"

Tyler's feet were warmly encased in heavy black Doc Marten boots—a treasured Christmas gift—and he was completely unsympathetic. "Mom! We're in New York City! Who cares about a little snow or ice? Anyway, you can always buy new shoes. Look! There's a shoe store right here!"

Josie glanced toward the window he had indicated. A single shoe was displayed in a space her professional expertise judged to be at least six yards square. Hidden halogen lights caused the burnished Italian leather to gleam from pointy toe to three-inch stiletto heel. "Those shoes probably cost more than I made last month."

"I didn't mean those exact shoes. You'd look really dumb in those shoes."

Josie smiled. "They are pretty stupid looking, aren't they?"

"No way! They're cool. But they're not . . . you know . . . for women like you." Tyler, smart enough to be on the honor roll at one of the most prestigious prep schools in the country, was also smart enough to realize that it was time to shut his mouth.

"I suppose they are about as far from steel toe work boots as it is possible to get," Josie agreed, sighing and looking around at their fellow pedestrians. Many of the women wore shoes similar to those being offered for sale nearby. These women were striding down the concrete, leaping gracefully over icy puddles, long fur coats covering thin stockings and strappy high heels. As she watched, an elegant blond woman hiked a monstrous, bulgy briefcase over her shoulder, and dashed after a speeding taxi. "Beautiful and tough," she added to herself.

"How far is it to Sam's place?" Tyler asked, glancing down at his watch.

Josie knew what he was thinking. "Just a few more blocks north, then we turn right. His building is just east of Park Avenue. Don't worry, we should be on time."

"I hope so. Tony says his dad's on a tight schedule and doesn't like to waste time hanging around."

"I don't think waiting a few extra minutes to meet a houseguest is a waste of time," Josie said grimly. "Tyler, are you sure these people really want you to be with them? You could always spend your vacation with Sam and me. We'd be glad to have you. We could go to museums, shows, the Hard Rock Café. . . ."

"Mom, Tony and I have plans. We're going to be busy working on our extra credit project. We won't have time to hang out at places tourists go! I told you—we're going to spend the next two weeks in the editing room."

"But it's your vacation. You should be getting fresh air and sunshine and . . . I don't know . . . more fresh air and sunshine." Josie had a feeling her argument wasn't too per-suasive.

"We're gonna have a blast. And this could be my big

break. Tony's dad's a very important person in the film industry."

"Your big break?"

"Yeah, it's easier to break into films if you know someone. You know I want to produce."

Josie, who had been under the impression that Tyler's plans for the future centered on a career in architecture, was surprised to hear this. And wise enough not to comment. Her multitalented son had many options. And, if Josie had anything to say about it, he would do lots of things before settling into a serious career track. Her own abrupt entrance into adulthood as a single parent without an education or any marketable skills caused her to value his freedom and education more than she might have done under other circumstances. "That would be very interesting" was all she said.

Tyler suddenly seemed quite interested in a store window they were passing. "Tony said his dad might be too busy to meet us this morning," he mumbled.

"Tyler . . ."

"Taylor Blanco is a very important person, Mom! You don't understand. . . ."

"No, you don't understand. You are not going to spend your vacation with a man who is too busy to bother to meet me for a few minutes—especially since he assured me that he'd be here when I spoke to him on the phone last week."

"But, Mom—"

"I am not going to leave you in New York City alone—"

"I won't be alone. I'll be with Tony. Besides, I'm seventeen years old. Lots of my friends from school live in the city. They're alone here all the time."

"They grew up here. They know the place. They know what to look out for."

"You mean they can tell a mugger from a stockbroker," Tyler said, sounding disgusted.

"I mean they know what to look out for," Josie repeated

in what she thought of as her "no-nonsense, I am the mother here" voice.

Apparently it wasn't carrying across the less than a foot from her mouth to her son's ear. "Mom, I know how to take care of myself! Believe me, I've done much more dangerous things than being alone in Manhattan."

"Tyler, you are not making me feel better."

"I'm just trying to explain."

"Tyler, if Tony and his father aren't—"

"Hey . . . yeah, Mom, whatever. Look. That's him. That's Tony and his father's that man with him—the one on the cell phone." Tyler waved his arms in the air, almost slugging an elegant matron swaddled, from ankle to earlobes, in thick amber fur. "Tony! Tony!"

Josie took a deep breath and turned to see whom her son was waving to. Tony was the new suitemate in Tyler's dorm at school and, while she had never met him, she had heard a lot about him since his arrival in September. Tony, she knew, had his pilot's license and took off for his mother's vacation home on the Outer Banks of North Carolina or his father's place on the dunes in Montauk as often as classes and the required participation in sports would permit. Tony had lived in many countries and was fluent in so many languages that the school had been forced to drop its language requirement for him. Tony's father was a film producer and his mother was an editor at *Vogue* magazine. Josie had lost track of the many stepmothers and stepfathers that seemed to flow through the young man's life. Tyler had hoped to visit Tony in New York City on his way home over Christmas break, but family commitments forced the young man to spend the holiday in a suite at the Hotel Plaza Athenee in Paris. Josie, up to her neck in work, had found it easy to resist feeling sorry for the young man.

Putting together all the stories, Josie had expected Tony to be a blasé, world-weary young man, but the adorable blond boy hurrying toward them, a bright smile on his face, could have modeled as a choirboy on a Christmas card. Josie immediately felt better.

"Mom, this is Tony. Tony, this is my mom."

The young man proved his upbringing, smiling politely and offering his hand. "It's very nice to meet you, Ms. Pigeon. Tyler talks about you a lot."

"I've heard a lot about you too."

"My father is back there . . . on the phone. He's always on the phone. But he should be finished in just a minute." As if to prove him correct, Tony's father hung up and looked around for his son. "Dad! Dad! We're here."

"I am so sorry to be so rude, Josie. You don't mind me calling you Josie, do you?"

Tony's father looked remarkably like Cary Grant; he could call Josie almost anything. "No, that's fine."

"It's great to meet you, but I have to run. My life is a mess, Josie. The movie I'm working on is weeks behind schedule. So I'm not home a lot these days. I've told Tony that he and Tyler are going to have to stay on the set most of the time. I don't want them running loose in New York City. And I've prepared a list of ways for you to reach me—my cell phone, my office phone, the private phone numbers for my personal assistants." He rummaged in the pocket of his sheepskin jacket and handed Josie a sheet of paper. "There are also numbers for Tony and Tyler. I'm giving them both cell phones as well. So you should be able to check in whenever and as frequently as you need to."

"Dad, this isn't necessary. I keep telling you . . . at school . . ."

"You're not at school and I would feel much more comfortable if I know where you are and what you're up to."

"And I agree completely," Josie said firmly. "Tyler has the number of the place I'm staying. If there are any problems . . ."

"I'll call you immediately." Tony's father took the card she had written Sam's number on and smiled at her. "We should be going, boys. I have a late lunch scheduled down at the Union Square Café. If you want to tag along, we should hurry. I hate to keep Julia Roberts waiting."

"Julia Roberts!" Tyler's voice rose to a squeak. "You're going to have lunch with Julia Roberts?"

"Nope, we're going to have lunch with Julia Roberts—if you want to."

"Want to! We want to. Don't we, Tony?"

"Sure do!"

Tony's dad smiled at Josie. "Why don't we all get together for dinner?"

"It sounds wonderful, but I should check with Sam."

"Do that and then call me. If tonight is bad, we can figure out something else. If it's good, how about Indochine at eight? Ready, guys?"

Josie suddenly realized that the limousine standing ready at the curb was waiting for her son and his hosts. She smiled at Tyler, resisting a strong urge to hug him and watched as he handed his duffel bag to the uniformed chauffeur, and, with a grin at his mother, got into the long black car with his friend and host. Tony's father was back on the phone before the car pulled away from the curb.

Josie watched them head downtown and turned in the other direction. Tyler would be fine. He and Tony were going to spend their vacation learning about moviemaking. They had been assigned a report on all they learned. They'd get extra credit and have a lot of fun. She, on the other hand, was going to spend the week helping Sam, her very significant other, pack up his apartment in preparation for putting it on the market. That is, she was going to do this if she could actually find his apartment. She looked up at a street sign. Sixty-three. Time to turn right. She did this, bumping into a woman carrying an elegant briefcase, which felt like steel as it slammed into her shin.

"Oh, I'm so sorry," Josie apologized.

The woman glanced at her and then down at her leg. She brushed her cap of blond hair off her forehead. "Are you all right?" she asked.

"Oh yes. I'm fine," Josie answered. But her assailant hadn't hung around for an answer.

Everyone in the city seemed to be busy, Josie observed, continuing on, this time watching her step as well as looking for the number of Sam's building. This was it, she decided, looking up at a large, dark redbrick building. Brass letters embedded in the pediment over the door spelled out Mentelle Park Apartments. Josie smiled. This was definitely it. She walked up to the steps, pushed open the heavy walnut French doors and stepped into the lobby. Sam had explained the building had been completed shortly after World War I and the marble and brass of the lobby was as rich and imposing today as it had been eighty years ago.

"May I help you?" An elderly man in a quasi-military uniform sat behind a small walnut desk at the back of the room.

"I'm here to see Sam Richardson."

"Of course. You must be Ms. Josie Pigeon. Mr. Richardson told me you would be arriving this afternoon. I believe he said you have a son . . . ?" He peered behind her as though expecting to see someone else.

"My son has gone off with a friend, so it's just me," Josie explained. "I don't suppose you know if Sam's here?"

"Bless me, of course I do. I know more about the people who live in this building than they know I know. The things I could tell you . . ." And he winked at her.

But the elevator doors opened and Sam appeared, putting an end to further confidences. "This is the woman I love, Harold," Sam announced. "She doesn't want to hear a bunch of lies about my past."

"Yes, Mr. Richardson, I hear what you're saying."

"Thank you." Sam put his arm around Josie's shoulder and kissed the top of her head. "Where's Tyler?"

"He took off." Josie smiled. "We met the famous producer and his son as we planned—they both seem very nice—and then they had to run. Lunch with Julia Roberts."

"Sounds exciting."

"We're invited to dinner with them tonight. Maybe they'll bring her along. Sam, I'd really like to get cleaned up. And change my clothes. My shoes are soaked. How much time do we have before we have to meet your mother?"

"A while. She called to say she'd been held up. Apparently Bloomingdale's is having a sale in their women's department. She says she'll be here in an hour or so. Probably wearing a new dress."

"Probably wearing a new dress and carrying a half dozen bags and boxes," Harold interjected, chuckling. "Your mother is one fancy woman, Mr. Richardson."

"That she is," Sam agreed, putting his arm around Josie's shoulders. "Why don't we head on upstairs?"

"Great. It was nice meeting you, Mr . . . ?"

"All the tenants call me Harold and I'd be happy if you did too. Mr. Richardson's women friends have always done so in the past. No reason to change now."

Josie managed to keep a smile on her face. This was one of the things she had been dreading about visiting New York City. "Then I guess we'll see you later, Harold."

"You sure will. I'm on duty until seven."

Josie followed Sam into the elevator and watched as he pressed the button to take them to the fourth floor.

"It's good to have you here." Sam folded Josie into his arms. She wrapped her arms around him, pressed her head into his familiar chest, and wondered if she could survive the next week without going crazy.

TWO

S AM AND JOSIE had been dating for almost four years—
ever since Sam retired from his job as prosecuting attorney for the City of New York, moved to the small barrier
island about a hundred miles from the Empire State Building as the seagull flies, and bought a home to live in and a
liquor store to run. During this time, Josie had heard a lot
about his previous life and more than enough about his previous women friends. She had enjoyed none of these conversations.

And the ones about Pamela Peel had been the worst.
Pamela Peel was beautiful, well educated, and rich. Pamela
Peel was always flying off to spas in the mountains in Mex-
ico, resorts in Thailand, or intimate little hotels in various
capital cities in Europe. Pamela Peel was a successful decorator, a profession which, Josie just knew, she practiced
while wearing elegant little designer suits, high heels, silk
stockings, and, probably, French underwear. Josie was just
guessing about the underwear; Sam had the good taste not to
mention Pamela's unmentionables.

Pamela Peel had been Sam's last significant other. Josie
knew that Pamela had been someone special. After all, he
had let her decorate his apartment. The apartment they were
entering now.

Josie hoped it would be horrible. She knew it would feel
empty since Sam had brought thousands of books, his cloth-

10

ing, his computer, and a few paintings to the island along with what she had come to think of as The Chair. The Chair was cherrywood with a seat upholstered in rich brown suede. The Chair was a work of art, actually signed on the bottom by its maker. It had a place of honor in Sam's living room on the island. It also had a connection to Pamela Peel. Josie wasn't sure what the connection was but she hated it.

Sam opened the door and motioned for Josie to precede him into his apartment.

The foyer was lined with empty bookshelves. Josie followed Sam across a steel gray, handwoven wool runner into a large living room. A pair of charcoal suede couches bracketed a granite fireplace centered on the far wall. A mirror, framed in silver, hung above the fireplace and reflected the pale winter light coming through large windows to the left. There was a massive coffee table, fashioned from slate, in the middle of the floor. A built-in window seat, upon which numerous itchy-looking wool pillows in shades of gray were stacked, completed the furnishings in this section of the room. To the right, a slate-topped table encircled by six black leather chairs indicated that this part of the room was to be used for dining. Josie assumed that the folding doors centered in the nearby wall would lead to the kitchen.

"The bedroom's that way," Sam said, pointing. "So what do you think of this place?" he asked, picking up her small bag and leading the way. Sam had driven to the city, carrying the rest of Josie's luggage in his trunk.

"It's different from your place at home . . . I mean, your house on the island."

"It looked better when my books and things were here, I guess. To be honest, I didn't remember it being this bleak."

"Maybe your taste has changed," Josie suggested, entering the bedroom and gasping.

Sam chuckled. "This I did remember. Hideous, isn't it?"

The bedroom, Josie assumed, would be called minimalist.

A huge king-size bed, flanked by chrome nightstands, dominated the room. A large steel armoire stood on the wall opposite, its open doors revealing empty shelves where a television and tape machine had once been stored. A matching double dresser had been placed under the windows. A massive abstract oil painting hung over the bed. Gray, white, and black paint had been used to ruin a perfectly good canvas.

"Why did you ever buy this?" Josie asked, walking over for a closer look.

"It was a gift."

"Good Lord, from who?"

"Pamela. Actually, she painted it."

Josie looked up at his face. "So you had no choice but to hang it," she guessed.

"Actually, I didn't hang it. She did. Or one of her minions did. I doubt if Pamela actually ever picks up a hammer and smacks nails. She hires people to do that sort of thing."

"People like me," Josie muttered.

"No, Josie, not people like you. You are an independent contractor. Pamela usually hires illegals—men she can boss around and who have no recourse when she expects them to work long hours seven days a week. She avoids hiring young, independent women. She probably thinks they would cause trouble."

Josie, who looked for women just like that when she was hiring her crews, didn't respond. She never knew what to say under these circumstances. She knew Sam was too much of a gentleman to criticize the women he had been involved with before, so much as she would have enjoyed—hell, loved—to trash them with him, she resisted. On the other hand, that was one ugly painting.

"Maybe you should take it down before you try to sell the apartment," she suggested.

"Oh, everything will be gone by then. What I don't take

to the island or Mother doesn't want will be picked up by the Salvation Army."

"Everything?"

"Everything. Unless there's something you want?"

"I . . . What's that?" she asked as a horrible squeal filled the apartment.

"That's what happens when you're not around to tip the superintendent at Christmas. He doesn't take the time to properly fix your intercom." Sam walked back to the front door, pressed the correct button and spoke into the grill on the wall. The voice that came back to him was garbled, but apparently Sam understood the message. "Send them up," he ordered. He was smiling broadly when he turned back to Josie. "We're going to have company. Betty and JJ are on their way up."

"Look, Sam, isn't he the cutest thing you've ever seen?" Josie asked.

"Without a doubt. Why don't we go back into my apartment where we can admire him properly? The hallway can be drafty," he added.

Betty wrapped her arms around her son and pulled him even closer to her chest. "Then let's get inside. JJ seemed to be sniffling a bit this morning and I don't want him to catch cold."

Once safely out of the hallway, Sam relieved Betty of her bags of infant paraphernalia and Josie folded the baby blanket into a nest on the window seat while Betty released her son from his carrier. Once JJ had been settled down in his place, a green plastic elephant–shaped rattle firmly grasped in one hand, the women hugged again.

"You look incredible," Josie cried, releasing her friend.

Betty ran her hands through her gorgeous blond hair and laughed. "You're just being nice. I still have a few more pounds to lose and I need a trim and a facial. And look at my nails." She held out what appeared to be perfectly manicured nails for Josie's inspection.

"They're beautiful!" Josie insisted.

"The polish is chipped." And just as Josie was about to decide that her old friend had changed completely, Betty put her hands down and whooped with laughter. "Listen to me! I sound like one of those I-never-do-anything-to-chip-my-polish women that we were always laughing at on the island! Josie, you must think living in New York has turned me into an idiot!"

Josie grinned at the woman she had known for years. "Well, I was wondering just a bit."

"It's just that I'm nervous. You know, seeing you and Sam again and introducing you two to my little sweetie . . ." She paused long enough to smile down at her baby. "Oh, I'm being an idiot. I'm just so happy to see you again! I love New York and my life here, but I do miss the island."

"What do you miss most? Working long hours at a dirty job for not much pay or living in a tiny little apartment over the garage of a rich person's summerhouse?" Josie asked, laughing.

"I miss running on the beach. I miss seagulls screaming in the wind. I miss the way the salty air smells. I miss sunrise over the ocean. I miss those crumb cakes from the bakery. I miss you, Josie!"

"But you've made friends in the city, haven't you?"

"I have—finally. Great friends from my natural childbirth classes. And JJ and I go to a playgroup. . . ."

"JJ plays with other children?" Josie asked, glancing down at the baby who was happily licking the end of his rattle.

"Well, no, of course, not yet. But early socialization is important and I enjoy talking with the other mothers. Actually, Josie, I do miss the island sometimes, but I love it here. Finally."

Josie, who remembered how lonely Betty had been when she first married Sam's friend and moved to the city, smiled broadly. "I'm glad. I can't wait to see your apartment!"

"Tonight . . ."

"Oh, Betty, tonight we're going to dinner with the father of the boy Tyler is staying with!"

"Why don't we all get together for brunch tomorrow morning?" Sam suggested.

"We're not leaving JJ with sitters yet. Why don't you two come over to the apartment and I'll feed you the best brunch you've ever eaten?"

"You cook?"

Betty laughed. "No, but I'm a New Yorker now. I do fabulous takeout!"

"Sounds great," Sam said. "What time do you want us?"

"Around eleven?"

"We'll be there," Sam assured her.

"You know the address?" Betty stood up and began to gather her belongings.

"Sure do."

"What are you doing? Betty, you just got here!" Josie protested.

"We have our baby yoga class in twenty minutes. Downtown," Betty added, probably noting the surprised expression on Josie's face.

"Baby yoga?"

"Yes. I know it sounds a little silly, but JJ thinks it's such fun and he usually takes an extra long nap after class so that Jon and I get a few minutes to ourselves when he gets home from work. So it's worth going to class for a few reasons."

"And he does seem to be remarkably flexible," Sam said, looking down at the baby who was happily chewing on the chubby big toe on his left foot.

"Isn't he amazing?"

Sam and Josie could both agree with that. "I'll walk you to the elevator," Josie said, picking up the baby chair.

"Great!"

"And I guess I'll answer that phone," Sam said, as its ringing interrupted him.

"See you tomorrow then," Betty said, tightening the last buckle on her son's pack and lifting him up.

The two women walked toward the door. "What do you think of the apartment?" Josie asked her friend before they were even out the door.

"Great apartment. Awful decorating! Didn't you tell me one of Sam's girlfriends did it?"

Josie felt the flood of relief that one woman feels when she discovers that her friends and she are in accord. "Yes. God, she has horrible taste, doesn't she?"

"Hideous! Sam must have been nuts to let her decorate his apartment."

Josie smiled uncertainly. "Or maybe he was nuts about her. . . ." The arrival of the elevator put an end to this depressing thought and to their conversation. With kisses, hugs, and promises to continue their conversation over brunch tomorrow, the women parted.

Sam was hanging up the phone as Josie returned. "Mom just called," he said. "She wants to meet us at some café she's just discovered." He walked over to Josie, put his arms around her, and rested his chin on her head. "I was hoping for a romantic afternoon, but I guess that will have to wait."

"We have lots of time," Josie assured him. "A whole week. We'll see your mom this afternoon, Tyler and Tony and Tony's father tonight, and Betty and Jon tomorrow morning. Then, except for a few meetings with realtors, we have seven whole days with nothing to do."

Sam kissed her unruly hair. "I just hope you're right."

Josie wondered why he sounded so sad.

THREE

INDOCHINE WAS ALMOST empty when Sam and Josie arrived. Sam explained who had made the reservations to the hostess who greeted them rather languidly.

"Oh, he generally arrives a bit later than eight, but I'll show you to the table he usually prefers. If you'll follow me." She strolled between the empty tables and huge palm trees, offering them rattan chairs on the far side of a large round table in the dead center of the room. "Perhaps you'd like something to drink."

"Yes, of course . . . ," Sam began.

"I'll send your waiter over then." The woman turned her back on them and continued her stroll toward the rear of the restaurant.

Sam chuckled. "I guess we're just not famous enough for her to bother with."

"Is this a place where famous people eat?" Josie asked.

"Every place in New York City would like you to believe it attracts the rich and famous, or the rich and infamous, and a table like this is usually reserved for them."

"Why?" Josie looked around. There were smaller tables and there were larger tables, but this one didn't seem so very special.

"This is right in the middle of the room. We can see. And, more important, we can be seen."

17

"What about the famous people who don't want to be seen? The Woody Allen types?"

"They get a table behind one of the palm plants. And the waiters let the diners know that someone famous, someone who prefers some privacy, is eating in the restaurant tonight. They get their privacy and the restaurant gets some status. Works for everybody."

"May I help you? My name is Kirk and I'll be your wait-staff tonight. Drinks? Perhaps something to graze on while you wait for the rest of your party?" Their waiter, a tall, thin young man all in black with his hair caught back in a pony-tail hanging almost to his waist, had appeared.

"Is there a house specialty?" Sam asked.

"We have a delicious house martini, an unusual rum punch, a mango gin and tonic—"

"I'll have the rum punch. What about you, Josie?" Sam asked, interrupting.

"The rum punch sounds delicious," she agreed.

They had eaten lunch at one of Sam's mother's new discoveries. "Just like Paris," Carol had promised. Josie hadn't been terribly enthusiastic. She'd never been to Paris, but if she ever got there, she had no intention of looking for restaurants "just like New York City" or "just like the Jersey Shore." When she was in Paris, she would look for Parisian restaurants. In New York City, she wanted to eat in New York restaurants. Looking around at the palm frond wallpaper while Sam ordered a selection of appetizers, she wondered at the motif.

"It's Indonesian-French," he explained when they were alone together again. "Fusion cuisine is very trendy right now."

"Not very New York City," she said.

"Very New York City. New York is a place that has taken the best from the rest of the world and adopted it as its own. But we'll go to the Four Seasons, the Hudson River Club, or maybe the Gotham Bar and Grill later in the week. They're all very New York."

"I'll gain a ton!"

"So we'll go for long walks in Central Park and burn lots of calories. I really want us to have fun. Remember, the next time we're in the city, we'll be staying in a hotel . . . or at my mother's place."

"I think a hotel sounds just fine." Josie's smile widened. So he was planning another trip here—another trip with her. Then she frowned a bit. But was that what she really wanted?

"If you don't like this, we can order something else." Sam's offer interrupted her musings.

Josie realized that a tall glass filled with a caramel-colored liquid and lots of ice cubes had been placed in front of her. "No, it looks just fine!" A straw piercing a slice of star fruit was stuck in the glass and she picked it up and sucked. The drink wasn't fine; it was exceptionally fine—sweet, delicious, and strong. Carol had insisted that Josie try the salade nicoise for lunch. It had been excellent too, but small. Josie felt the alcohol swim into her brain and blinked. "Wow."

"I hope that means you're having a good time."

"It means I may be drunk before Tyler arrives. And I don't think I want that to happen."

"Sip slowly. And I'll ask for some water as soon as our waiter returns. Besides, it looks like you're not going to have time to get drunk. That is Tyler walking through the door, isn't it?"

Josie looked up. It was Tyler and Tony. She didn't know what surprised her more: that they were both wearing black from head to toe or that they were accompanied by a willowy blond woman. Tiny gold earrings interrupted the black theme that she seemed to have adopted as well. Sam waved and the dark threesome headed toward their table. Tony and the young woman were smiling. Tyler was paying so much attention to the female member of their group that he ran into three chairs and a table on his way across the room. Josie gasped, feeling a pain in her chest. Tyler, her little Tyler, was in love!

"Hi, Ms. Pigeon," Tony greeted them, a wide smile on his face.

"Hi, Tony. Hi, sweetie . . ." Before the endearment was fully formed, Tyler had begun to blush.

"You must be Tyler's mother," the tall blonde said. "I'm Toni. With an I, not to be confused with Tony with a Y. I'm Mr. Blanco's assistant. He was held up on the set and asked that I accompany the boys here."

"Aren't you going to join us?" Tyler asked, still ignoring his mother.

"I would love to, but we're having some problems with the caterers and I'll probably spend the evening making sure everything is set up correctly tomorrow. Who knew that almost half of the local extras we hired would turn out to be either on a macrobiotic diet or vegetarians?" She sighed. "They survived on the fruit platters, salads, and breads today, but I'm trying to get in something with more protein tomorrow . . . but that's not your problem. And I do have something else to do here before I dash." She turned to Tyler. "Do you want to ask your mother or should I?"

"What?" Josie asked quickly. "Is there some problem? Tyler can come stay with us at Sam's place," she began.

"There's no problem at all. It's just that Mr. Blanco was wondering if you would allow Tyler to be in the movie we're filming. He won't have a speaking part, but he'll get decent wages for three days of work and get to see the business from the inside."

"Is Tony going to be in the movie too?" Josie asked.

"Mom, Tony will only do it if I do. So if you don't say yes, he won't get to be in the movie either."

"But I have had other opportunities to be in films," Tony admitted. "Not that this one wouldn't be lots of fun and way cool . . ."

"Are there any contracts involved?" Sam asked.

"Yes. And I have them all right here." Toni pulled a sheath

of papers from her capacious purse and handed them over to Josie.

Josie passed them on to Sam. "Sam's a lawyer," she explained.

"Then why don't you read them through and Mr. Blanco will be able to answer any questions you have when he arrives. I'll see you tomorrow, boys."

The smile on Tyler's face disappeared as her method of address sunk in, but he politely wished her good night and cheered up as she flashed him a winning smile before turning and leaving the restaurant. When he returned his attention to his mother there was a pleading expression on his face. "I'd really like to do this, Mom! Mr. Blanco says there's nothing like being in a movie to find out what the business is really all about!"

"Just let Sam read through the papers," Josie suggested. "And sit down. You must be starving."

"Not really. We're not vegetarians. We've been . . . been grazing all day. You should have seen the food that the caterers brought. There was an entire roast beef! And piles of spare ribs!"

"No wonder the vegetarians weren't happy," Sam muttered, flipping over the page he had been reading.

"Yeah, they were real cranky," Tony said, sitting down in the chair next to Sam. "Perhaps I could fill in a bit until my father arrives."

Tyler sat beside his mother. "There really are some excellent reasons to be vegetarian, you know. It's good for your health as well as kind to the planet."

"Is Toni with an I a vegetarian?" Josie asked.

"She didn't eat any meat today," Tyler answered and then grinned at his mother. "She's one cute chick, isn't she?" he added mischievously. It was an old family joke. Tyler had referred to the girl who sat next to him in kindergarten in that manner on his first afternoon home from school, eliciting a lecture on the proper way to address girls from his stressed-out "my son is old enough to go to school how did this happen?" mother who was busy stuffing him with peanut butter and jam cookie bars.

"That she is," Josie agreed, grinning back. Black clothing or jeans, Tyler was still the son she adored. Although she firmly—and erroneously—believed that she had managed to keep these feelings from him. "So how has your day gone? Did you really have lunch with Julia Roberts?"

As if overhearing this reference, the waiter reappeared at their table carrying a tray filled with tiny plates of food. "Perhaps you would like drinks as well?" he asked, looking at Tony and Tyler.

"Coke with two slices of lemon," Tony ordered.

"Make that two," Tyler added.

"Maybe you both should look at the menu and see if there's anything else you want to order," Sam suggested.

"I know the menu here by heart," Tony said and proceeded to order what sounded to Josie like a feast for at least half a dozen people.

"So you had a good day—besides eating lunch with Julia Roberts?"

"Yeah, really. And," he added before she could ask another question, "we have taken ten pages of notes and are going to start putting our impressions on the computer tonight. Tomorrow we'll take a laptop along with us while . . . well, while we're doing whatever we are doing."

"This looks okay to me," Sam said. "You have to sign it and I'll keep a copy. This way Tyler can be in the movie if the footage they use turns out to have him in it. And, even if he ends up on the proverbial cutting-room floor, he'll be paid three hundred dollars for every day he's on the set."

"Three hundred dollars?"

"Yeah, think how a week like this will build up my college fund!" Tyler said enthusiastically. He could see that he was beginning to win his mother over to his side.

"What is this movie about?"

But the appearance of Taylor Blanco with a gorgeous blonde on his arm prevented Tyler from answering and almost immediately, Josie found herself receiving more attention than she had gotten in her entire life. Waitpersons flocked around them. The owner of the restaurant appeared. The chef popped out of the kitchen to explain the evening's specials in person. Other diners either gaped openly or covertly glanced at them through half-closed eyes. As the evening lengthened and Indochine filled up, the attention continued. But rum, nervousness, and lots of excellent food proved to be too much for Josie and she was exhausted long before midnight.

She and Sam said their good-byes, left the restaurant, and walked into the bitter cold night air. Lafayette Street was bustling. The evening's performance at the Public Theater had just ended, and playgoers strolled by, discussing the night's play. Students from Cooper Union were stamping down the sidewalk, arm in arm, laughing and arguing. Late-night dog walkers gathered around the only tree on the block, chatting and trying to keep their animals from becoming permanently wound up in one another's leashes.

"The city that never sleeps," Sam whispered, pulling Josie close.

"I sure hope that doesn't apply to all of its citizens," Josie mumbled, her speech slurred with fatigue.

"It doesn't. Let's walk a block or two to the west and look for a cab."

"Sounds good to me." She smiled up at him. Their first day in the city had turned out pretty well. Maybe their week together really would turn out to be a lot of fun.

FOUR

"THE DINNER WAS sensational! But it was difficult to eat. Everything was stacked up."

"Stacked up?" Jon Jacobs repeated Josie's words.

"Yeah. I ordered crab cakes as an appetizer and the waiter put down a huge plate with three tiny little crab cakes piled one on top of the other surrounded by three little squirts of sauce—tartar sauce, cocktail sauce, and something else. It was yellow—the third sauce. It tasted wonderful, but I have no idea what it was made from. For my main course I ordered a tuna fillet. The plate it arrived on was even bigger than the first, but the food was jammed together in the middle as though there wasn't any room for it to spread out. There were noodles with tiny pieces of vegetables I didn't even recognize. And then spears of fried sweet potatoes—at least I think that's what they were—were laid on the rice. The tuna had been sliced and piled right on top. It was all delicious, but a little weird.

"And the dessert! Well, the dessert was incredible. I picked the apple tart, thinking of a nice slice of tart with maybe some ice cream on the side. But what came was another large plate, crystal this time. And on it was a little oblong thing that looked like an egg roll; it was topped by a pyramid of cinnamon ice cream which had been stabbed by this sword made out of barley sugar, like those candies we used to get at Christmas. And there was this luscious

24

caramel sauce drizzled over the entire thing. It was all wonderful, but every time I stuck my fork in the food, the entire pile fell down!" Josie suddenly laughed. "Maybe that's the reason they used such huge plates!"

"Well, we're a bit more casual here," Betty said, joining her guests in the living room. She carried a huge tray on which four steaming mugs stood, surrounded by little pitchers of cream and skim milk and tiny bowls of sugar and artificial sweetener. The two couples had finished their brunch, toured the large apartment, admired JJ's new ability to drool and smile at the same time, and then retired to the living room.

Josie was impressed. Betty Patrick, beautiful energetic skilled carpenter had become Betty Jacobs, beautiful domestic mother. Josie, sitting quietly on the couch, little JJ dozing in her lap, wondered if she was capable of making such a big change in her own life.

"So what did you think of the famous movie producer?" Jon asked, passing out their coffee.

"He seems a very nice man. Very low-key," Sam answered. "And his son is a nice kid too. Josie and I felt better after meeting them. It looks like Tyler's in good hands, and we're only a phone call away."

"Yes, but there is one small problem," Josie protested.

"What's that?" Betty asked, taking JJ from Josie and settling him into her arms.

"The girlfriend."

"We don't know that she's his girlfriend. She's starring in the movie he's making. He might just have invited her to dinner," Sam protested and then explained further. "Her name is Suzi and—"

"And she's closer in age to Tyler and his friend than to his father," Josie burst out.

"Welcome to New York," Betty said. "That's just the way

it is in some circles around here. I fully expect Jon to trade me in for a younger model when I pass the age of thirty."

"No way you're going to get out of our marriage that easily," Jon said. "I'm planning on watching you grow old and gray."

Betty grinned. "Old maybe, but not gray. Not if Tina has anything to say about it."

"Who's Tina?" Josie asked.

"Tina does my hair at Elizabeth Arden. She is the enemy of gray hair."

"You're having your hair colored! I thought you looked different!" Josie cried.

"I hope I look different. I spend hours and hours, and hundreds of dollars each month trying to look different." Betty glanced over at her husband and, seeing that he and Sam were starting up a conversation, scooted across the couch closer to Josie. "Do you like it?"

"I love it! It looks natural, like it's sun streaked, only better," Josie assured her, self-consciously smoothing down her own unruly mop as she spoke.

"I was wondering. . . . well, I thought maybe . . ."

Such hesitation was unusual for Betty. "What?" Josie prompted impatiently.

"Well, I have an appointment tomorrow morning—at Elizabeth Arden—and I wondered if you wanted to go with me."

"Oh, Betty, of course. You didn't even have to ask. JJ and I will keep each other company while you become even more beautiful . . ."

"Why is JJ going to be there? Oh . . ." A look of dawning understanding appeared on Betty's lovely face. "Oh, no, Josie. I'm not asking you to take care of JJ. I was hoping you'd come along and get your hair done too. It will be lots of fun and we can visit. What do you think?"

Josie didn't answer Betty's question, but asked one of her

own. "Wouldn't the people there, the women who work there—like Tina—wouldn't someone like Tina . . . I don't know, look down on someone who looks like me? I'm not terribly well groomed."

"In the first place, you look wonderful. You really do! You have natural beauty. And, to be honest, I know exactly how you feel. I felt the same way when I first moved here—like a hick surrounded by all these women who knew how to do things I'd never done. I spent the first six months here afraid of looking like a fool."

Josie nodded vigorously. "Exactly."

"But it was my imagination that had me in a panic. Most people in New York are too busy living their own lives to spend time trashing other people. Of course, every once in a while I run into someone who wants to put me down. The very first charity banquet Jon took me to was in the ballroom at the Waldorf. It's a gorgeous room and the decorations that evening were spectacular—all white candles, white lilies, and crystal. I was blown away. Jon introduced me to one of his coworkers and I said something about the room and asked her if she had ever been there before. I was just trying to be polite, but she used my question as an opportunity to make me feel inferior."

"What did she say?"

"Just that she had been there dozens of times before—that, in fact, everyone she knew had been there dozens of times before. I felt a bit like something that had just crawled out of the gutter and didn't belong in such elevated company. Which is, of course, exactly the way she wanted me to feel."

"Bitch."

Betty nodded. "Exactly. But she's in the minority. And Elizabeth Arden isn't like that. They have new clients coming in all the time—women who are getting married and want to be made over, women who have bought or been given what they call a day of beauty and are getting manicures, facials, massages, hair treatments, makeup design . . . everything. Everyone there is very nice. Hell, they're paid to be nice. Anyway, Josie, I thought we could have fun if we went together."

"Will I come out looking as gorgeous as you do?"

"Even better! Your hair is so thick and long that they can do all sorts of things with it and you have almost flawless skin . . ."

"And about twenty extra pounds, broken fingernails, no makeup . . ."

"You're right! We'll schedule a makeup lesson right after your haircut. And a pedicure as well as a manicure."

"A pedicure! Betty, it's winter! Who's going to see my feet?"

"Sam."

"Yes, but he's used to my naked toenails and callused heels. And won't he think it's odd if I suddenly start acting like a city girl?"

"You don't have to worry about that. Men never really notice the details. He'll think you're looking nice, but he won't realize exactly what's changed. Oh, Josie, please come with me. We'll have fun!"

"Well . . ."

"Great! I'll pick you up at Sam's apartment at eight."

"Sam may have plans . . ."

But at the mention of his name, Sam's attention returned to the women. "If you're going to say nice things about me, you could speak up so I could enjoy it," he suggested, smiling.

"Josie and I are going to—"

"We thought we'd spend tomorrow morning exploring the city," Josie interrupted. "And we wondered if meeting at eight is too early."

"Perfect timing. As much as I'd like to sleep in tomorrow, the real estate agent is hoping to see the apartment at seven-thirty, so we'll have to get up early anyway," Sam said. "Where are you two planning to go?"

"What real estate agency are you using?" Jon asked Sam before anyone had an opportunity to answer his question.

"The one I used when I bought the place. But I'm beginning to think that was a bad idea," Sam answered, returning his attention to his friend.

Josie was relieved, as she really didn't want Sam to know about the plans she and Betty were making. Josie couldn't remember the last time she'd been in a beauty parlor, but she knew enough to know that they weren't even called that anymore. She had been trimming—okay, hacking the split ends off—her hair herself for over a decade. She knew it wasn't chic, but it was cheap. And as for a manicure or a pedicure, well, she had simply never related these things to her life. Every extra dollar she had, she either spent on her son or reinvested in her business, Island Contracting. Once in a while she looked with envy upon the high-maintenance women who lived in the gorgeous houses she worked on, but she had trained herself not to think about what she couldn't have. . . . Except, of course, if she married Sam she could have anything she wanted, within reason. She frowned, pushed her unstyled hair away from her face, and reached for her coffee mug.

"Is anything wrong?" Betty asked worriedly. "If you don't want to go tomorrow, I can cancel my appointment—"

"That's not it . . . exactly." Josie glanced over at the men, now engrossed in a topic New Yorkers always found enchanting: real estate prices.

"Let's put JJ down for a nap," Betty said, standing up suddenly.

Josie knew Betty wanted to talk privately. She agreed and followed Betty down the long hallway to her son's nursery. "This is a gorgeous apartment," she said quietly.

"Yes, we were lucky to find it. Josie, did I say something

to upset you? I mean, you look wonderful. I like your hair, and Sam likes it and . . ."

"It's not my hair. Well, it's not just my hair. I feel weird being here. It feels to me as though a lot is depending on what happens this week."

"What do you mean? I thought you were on vacation. For practically the first time since I've known you, I might add."

"It is. I mean, I'm not working. But I'm not relaxing either."

"I don't understand."

Betty was putting her baby down and had her back to Josie. "Well, in the first place," Josie said slowly, "I think Sam's going to propose . . ."

Betty was a good mother so nothing could cause her to drop her son. But JJ was placed in his crib rather more quickly than was normal. "Josie! That's sensational!" She looked at Josie's face. "It is, isn't it? Josie, you are going to say yes, aren't you?"

Josie was staring at the cheerful mural of a beach scene covering the wall opposite JJ's crib and didn't answer.

"Josie? Isn't Sam the person you want? Is something wrong between you?"

"That's just it. Sam is the person I want. I love him. Nothing has gone wrong between us, but getting married is such a big step. It could change my life."

"And you're not sure you want your life changed."

"There are things I would love to change. When Tyler's at school, I'm alone too much. It would be wonderful to be with Sam all the time. He's perfect for me. The trouble is me. I'm not sure I'm capable of living a different life." Josie suddenly sat down in a rocking chair and sighed loudly. "Sounds stupid, doesn't it?"

Betty was obviously mystified. "I don't understand. Is Sam planning on leaving the island?"

"No."

"Is he going to practice law again?"

"No."

"Are you going to quit running Island Contracting?"

Josie's denial was even firmer than her previous protests.

"So what is going to be different? You and Sam are together all the time anyway. I know you'll miss Risa's wonderful cooking," Betty said, referring to Josie's generous and gourmet landlady, "but—"

"That's just it!"

Betty's gorgeous eyes opened wide and she stared at her friend. "You don't want to marry Sam because you don't want to give up Risa's meals? But, Josie . . ."

"Well, that's not exactly it. That sounds like I'm nuts. And I'm not! It's not just Risa's risotto or her calamari or her spaghetti Bolognese. It's what that apartment means to me. I know it's not well decorated. Hell, it's not even decorated at all. And I really do plan on changing the ugly toilet and sink. And—"

"Josie." Betty reached out and patted her friend's arm. "You don't have to explain. It's not the apartment or the food or even Risa. It's your independence. You're worried about giving up your independence."

"Am I being stupid? I worked so hard to get where I am. And once I'm Sam's wife, it won't be the same. I'll be responsible for him. He'll be responsible for me. It won't be the same."

"It may be better," Betty said gently.

"I know. It probably will be better, but . . ."

Betty smiled. "You have to do what makes sense to you."

"I know that too." Josie brightened up. "And he might not even ask me. I've been here for less than a day and Sam seems sort of distracted. Most of what he talks about when we're alone is the women in his past—"

"What?"

"Yeah. One Pamela Peel in particular. She's a decorator."

"Oh, I know who she is! Everyone on the Upper East Side knows who she is! She's famous."

"She's just an interior decorator," Josie said slowly. "Maybe we're talking about a different person."

"Pamela Peel is half of Henderson and Peel. They're the hottest decorators around. Everyone wants them! They probably have a two- or three-year waiting list. And in this economy that's a big deal!"

"And she's beautiful and rich, right?"

"Well, she should be rich. She's certainly successful. And adorable more than beautiful. She has this gamine look. A cap of shiny blond hair. Blue eyes. Gorgeous skin. And she's thin and sort of athletic looking. I've heard that she reminds people of Tinkerbell. You know, Peter Pan's fairy."

"Sounds like a lot of the women I've passed on the street in the last twenty-four hours," Josie said bitterly.

"Oh, but she's not ordinary. Her photo is always popping up in the Styles section of the Sunday *New York Times* and there's actually a big article about her in this week's *New York* magazine. Her photo is on the cover and everything!"

"You're not making me feel better."

"No, I guess not. I'll stop talking about her."

"I wish I could stop thinking about her. It's just that as long as I'm in the city, I'm staying in an apartment she decorated, sleeping in a bed she picked out, and . . . Oh, I don't know. I came to New York to be with Sam while he cleaned up his apartment before putting it on the market. I thought of this trip as a time for him to be disconnecting from his past. But it's not working. Sam's not leaving his past behind. In fact, I feel as though I'm somehow slipping into it."

"Listen, you came to the city worried about Tyler. You have very legitimate concerns about what marriage to Sam might mean. And everything here is new to you. There's a lot coming at you in a short time. Sam told Jon that he'd gotten tickets to that hot new Broadway show. Go have a long, relaxing dinner and then enjoy the show. You'll feel better after a good night's sleep with the man you love."

Josie snorted. "Well, maybe. But I'd feel a whole lot better if Sam and I weren't sleeping in a bed that Pamela Peel picked out for the two of them."

FIVE

BUT JOSIE WAS to learn that sleeping in a bed another woman had picked out is not the worst thing that can happen to a couple. Sleeping in an apartment with a dead woman in it topped that particular list.

The crime scene team had just left Sam's apartment when Harold called to announce Betty's presence.

"Send her up," Sam ordered the doorman. He flicked off the intercom and turned to Josie. "I'm sure Betty will understand if you cancel your plans. The detective said they were finished here. You may as well go back to bed."

"No way!" Josie protested, yawning. "I'm exhausted, but I can't imagine sleeping now, can you?" She waited a while, but apparently Sam thought hers had been a rhetorical question. "Do you want to do something together? Why don't we go for a walk?"

"No. There are people I should call . . ."

Betty arrived at their door before Sam finished his sentence. Not that Josie thought he was going to finish it; his attention had drifted off as he was speaking.

"You're not even dressed!" Betty announced as though Josie might not be aware of the fact that she still had Sam's robe wrapped around her.

"I know. We found a body last night."

"You what?"

Josie glanced over at Sam. He had wandered over to the

window and was staring down at the street. She looked back at Betty. "Come into the bedroom with me. We can talk there."

Neither woman said anything until they were alone together.

Betty got right to the point. "Whose body?"

Josie didn't answer immediately and when she did, she spoke slowly and deliberately, pronouncing each syllable clearly. "Pamela Peel."

"Who the hell is . . ." A look of understanding washed over Betty's face. "Oh my God! Sam's old girlfriend. We were just talking about her yesterday. Henderson and Peel, right?"

"Well, now just Henderson, I guess."

"Where did you find her?"

"In the space underneath the window seat . . . in the living room. She had been strangled. The cord was still around her neck."

"For a curtain?"

Josie looked up at her friend, a perplexed expression on her face. "Why are you talking about curtains?"

"You said there was a cord around her neck. I thought a cord from a curtain. Since she was underneath the window, right?"

"I guess. I don't know what sort of cord it was or where it was from. I just know that it was used to kill her." Josie sat down on the bed and looked around the room. "She decorated this room."

"Really? It's not very attractive, is it?"

"It's ugly," Josie said flatly.

"The padded walls are particularly unappealing," Betty said, walking over and patting them.

"Yeah, soundproof. On the other hand, maybe they were put up for practicality instead of decoration. Maybe Pamela Peel was particularly vocal in bed," she added ruefully.

"Not anymore," Betty reminded her.

"Yeah, I know," Josie admitted. "I'm not being very nice about her, am I?"

"Well, she was just killed. . . ."

"I know. I think the policeman thought it was a bit strange to dislike someone I'd never even met."

"And why does a policeman know anything about your feelings?"

"Betty, Pamela was murdered. Of course there were policemen here. And . . ." Josie paused before continuing. "And it was in the middle of the night when we found her body. I wasn't thinking. When a seemingly sweet policewoman and her partner gave me a cup of hot tea in the kitchen and asked me how I felt about finding Ms. Peel's body, I told them. Stupid, right?"

"Josie, murder is nothing new to you. You know better than to make yourself the primary suspect in a murder investigation."

"I did tell them that I'd never met Pamela Peel," Josie protested. "Oh hell, I just wasn't thinking about much except Sam."

"What about Sam?"

"He looked so miserable, so unhappy, so devastated . . ." She took a deep breath, pushed her hair back over her shoulders, and said the words she didn't even want to hear. "So much like a man who had just discovered that someone he loved had died."

"Oh, Josie." Betty sat down on the bed next to her friend. "You know Sam loves you."

"I do, but you know what else? I feel as though I've been competing with Pamela Peel for years. Sam is always mentioning her, along with the other women he dated. You know Sam."

Betty nodded.

"But Sam's mother once said something I've never been

able to forget," Josie continued. "She said that everyone they knew was shocked when he moved to the island. Apparently everyone thought he was going to marry Pamela Peel and settle down. Everyone including Carol," Josie added.

"Sam's mother is one of the most flamboyant women I've ever met. I can't imagine her being fond of a woman who decorates an apartment to resemble a gray flannel suit." Betty got up and began to rummage in an open suitcase that was lying on the steely dresser.

"What are you doing?"

"Finding you some clothing. You'll feel better after you get dressed."

"I suppose. I tried to talk Sam into going for a walk with me but he said something about making phone calls."

"Then he doesn't need you and you'll feel much better after a haircut." Betty put down the cotton sweater she had pulled out of the suitcase. "I wonder if we should schedule a facial too . . . or maybe a massage. They're both really relaxing. What do you think?"

"Betty, you don't think I'm going to go to the hairdresser now, do you?"

"Why not? You said Sam had things to do, right?"

"Yes, but—"

"And the police had finished here and they haven't asked you to hang around either, right?"

"Yes, but—"

"So you really don't have anything else pressing to do, do you? Unless you think saying things to the police that will force them to include you in their list of potential suspects is something you might pursue further. . . ."

"Of course not! I just don't think getting my hair cut while Sam is obsessing about his long-lost love is a good idea."

"Got a better one?"

A tiny smile slowly spread across Josie's face, causing

her to crinkle her freckle-covered nose. "Nope. But I do have to be absolutely sure Sam doesn't need me."

"Get dressed and we can ask him."

"Okay, but I should wash my hair before we go."

"Josie, in less than an hour someone is going to wash your hair for you." Betty raised her hand to prevent Josie from answering. "Look, I know just how you feel. I always used to try to look my best before going too. These spas and salons can be intimidating. But, believe me, there is no reason to wash your hair. Or put on makeup, unless you really want to."

"I have to admit I really don't feel like getting all dressed up."

"Then don't. We'll have a few highlights put in your hair. They'll give you a robe to protect your clothing." She tossed the sweater to Josie. "You can wear this."

Josie felt there was just too much coming at her too quickly for her to deal with in her sleep-deprived state. "Do you really think I should leave Sam alone?" she asked, picking up the sweater from where it had fallen on the bed.

Sam himself answered that question for her, sticking his head in the door to make an announcement. "Josie, I've got to go out. I'll be back by dinnertime."

"I . . . you're what? Where are you going? What about the police? What if they come back?"

"They're done here. The team that showed up were old friends of mine back in the days when I was prosecuting for the city. They did a thorough investigation—but, perhaps, not as thorough as if they hadn't known me. They have everything they need. I can't imagine that they'll be back.

"Anyway, I left keys for you on the coffee table. The silver one opens the apartment door. You and Betty have a great day exploring the city. I'll see you tonight." His head vanished and a few seconds later the front door slammed.

Josie ran from the bedroom with Betty close on her heels. They found themselves alone in the apartment.

"He's gone!" Both women looked around as though expecting Sam to materialize in the corner or suddenly appear sitting on the couch. "I can't believe he's gone," Josie repeated, obviously bewildered.

"I thought you said he had some phone calls to make."

"That's what he told me. I never expected him to dash off like that." Josie frowned. "I don't know what to do."

Betty took over. "Get your haircut. It's the New York City woman's response to crisis. Besides, what else do you have to do today? You don't want to hang around here, do you?"

Josie glanced around the dreary interior, now liberally doused with fingerprint powder. "I sure don't. Let's go."

Elizabeth Arden's Red Door Spa and Salon on Fifth Avenue was well known all over the world. Probably millions of women had walked through the door and into the inner sanctum dedicated to beauty during the many decades it had been in existence. And certainly many of them had been less than chic when they arrived, but Josie, looking at the other women zipping in and out of the small street-level shop, couldn't imagine that any of them could look any smarter than they already did.

"The elevator's in the back." Betty nudged her forward. "We're going to the second floor."

"Oh . . . okay." Josie, who had been reaching out for a tiny bottle of pale green liquid, moved forward.

A thin young woman sporting an asymmetrical haircut bent her perfectly outlined lips into a half smile. "We have numerous displays of that product on the upper floors. You'll be able to buy anything you want after you get your hair done," she assured Josie.

Josie merely smiled back and hurried after Betty.

The elevator walls carried advertisements for the various

spa services, but Josie was still trying to figure out what lava rocks had to do with beauty when they arrived at their floor.

"Back there." Once again Betty pointed out the way and once again Josie followed, feeling like a kid on the first day of kindergarten. Three gorgeous blondes, giggling shrilly, brushed by them in the hallway. "I could have killed her," one of them announced as she passed. Josie swung around and stared.

"Come on, we're late. And they're not talking about Pamela Peel," Betty insisted, pulling on Josie's sleeve.

"How do you know?"

"Josie, this is a huge city. What are the odds. . . ? Oh, thank you." Betty interrupted herself to accept a shiny brown robe from the coatroom attendant. "She needs one too," she added, nodding to Josie. The gray-haired attendant handed Josie a wooden hanger with her robe hanging from it. A red plastic disk with number seven stamped on its surface was tied to the hanger.

"Thank you," Josie said, smiling vaguely and following Betty down another narrow hallway, this one lined with curtained booths like a department store dressing room.

"Take off your sweater and put this on," Betty ordered.

Josie did as she was told, thinking about how her previous relationship with Betty had changed. In the past, Josie had always been in the dominant role: as older woman, as employer, as the one with the more stable lifestyle. Now Betty was in charge and Josie followed.

Not that there was a lot of time to think about any of this. Betty was urging her out of her dressing cubicle before Josie had managed to figure out if it was possible to tie the robe about her in a manner that made her look a bit less like a chunky upright summer sausage. Betty, not surprisingly, looked elegant.

As did everyone else, she realized, looking around. Everyone else seemed to have freshly washed hair. Everyone else was wearing more makeup than Josie even owned. No one else looked like a meat by-product.

". . . on the hanger . . . keep . . ."

"Excuse me?" Josie discovered the woman who had given her the robe standing by her side, one hand extended.

"She wants your hanger," Betty explained, giving hers away. "Keep the coat check. And keep your purse," she added as Josie started to drape the strap over the hanger.

"Oh . . ." Josie fumbled around until she had followed Betty's directions, smiling awkwardly at the woman trying to help her.

"Have a nice time," the coat check lady said with a big smile, grabbing the hanger when Josie had finally gotten everything in order.

"Yes, I'll try." Josie followed Betty out to the main area of the salon.

SIX

"**A**ND WHAT ARE we going to do here?" Two elegantly shaped eyebrows disappeared beneath thick bangs. Ten polished fingertips lifted Josie's mop of red hair off her neck and then allowed the tangled curls to flop back onto her shoulders. "Just a bit nineteen-eighties . . . perhaps you're ready for a change? A more grown-up look?"

Josie frowned at the woman in the mirror. Now she knew why she was in the robe. Dressed in street clothes, she could have stood up and marched right out the door.

"We can, of course, just wash and trim. But you have such an abundance of hair; it's a shame not to take advantage of it. Many of my clients would give almost anything for raw material like this."

Well, that was better. "I think . . . ," Josie began.

"Josie leads a very active life. She needs something easy to take care of." Betty spoke up from the chair next to Josie's.

"Well, we can do that, of course." Josie's hairdresser, who had introduced herself as Mia, bit her bottom lip and frowned. "I think something slightly shorter. And perhaps some highlights around the face. Of course, nothing that looks artificial. Just a few streaks as though the light is falling naturally from above."

"I . . ."

Betty spoke up before Josie could protest. "Excellent. And maybe three or four inches off."

"Three or four!"

"Why don't I start with the highlights and we can figure this out as we go along?" Mia suggested, raising her seductively calm voice above Josie's protests. "I do see a lot of split ends. Certainly you want those removed?"

"Excellent idea," Betty agreed. "Now about those highlights: Do you think maybe more than one shade . . ."

Josie looked in the mirror from her friend to her newly acquired hairdresser; they were speaking a language she didn't understand.

"Certainly, and we could add a glaze after the wash. It might tone down the color a bit as well as add some extra shine."

"But that wears off in time. I think of Josie as . . ."

Josie relaxed, deciding there was no reason to think of herself—or for herself. She'd leave the decisions up to the pros. It was hair. Whatever was cut off would grow back. And there really wasn't any way they could make the color more outrageous than her genes had previously determined. She sat back, watched the activity around her in the mirror-lined walls, and, surprisingly, began to relax. Pamela Peel was dead. There was nothing she could do about it. She would let the police worry about what had happened and take some time to enjoy herself, as Betty insisted.

She had never seen or heard so many handheld hair dryers in use simultaneously. Josie started to calculate the total wattage, but gave up when she realized the numbers were too large to manipulate without pencil and paper. Besides, if she were going to count wattage, she would have to add in all those curling irons and those odd halo lighting things standing above the heads of some clients. She gave up, smiling nervously at the woman sitting across the aisle from her.

Her smile was not returned—or even noticed. The client and her hairdresser were engrossed in conversation.

"I told her it would never work. But did she listen to me? Of course not! I know he had an excellent career. I know he was respected all over the city. He's good-looking . . . for a man his age; he's fabulous looking, in fact. But he didn't stick around, did he? And I told her that's what was going to happen."

Josie smiled for the first time since sitting down in the chair. In a spa, salon, beauty parlor—no matter what it was called or where it was located—the subject of men always came up.

"Now, of course, there's nothing I can do to help her." The conversation ended as the last spritz of hair spray glued the last curl in place. The women hugged, pecked at each other's cheeks, and parted. Josie was fairly sure she'd seen a folded-up bill pass between client and hairdresser, but couldn't be absolutely sure. Tipping! She and Betty hadn't discussed tipping! On the other hand, she might not like the way she looked. . . .

"Seems as though most everybody's talking about the same thing today." Josie's hairdresser had disappeared with a comment about mixing something up, and the woman busily covering Betty's gorgeous hair with beige sludge chatted as she worked.

"Really?"

Josie got the impression that Betty wasn't terribly interested in talking. She was staring at her hair with a slight frown on her lips.

"Of course. How often is it that one of your clients is murdered?"

Betty chuckled. "Well, if you're Josie . . ."

"Now that's not really true. . . ." Josie's hairdresser returned and interrupted her protest. "What is that for?"

Mia looked down at the tray she carried. Three little

bowls containing three darker colors of sludge sat in the middle of it. "Just a little highlighting. If you've changed your mind, I can always . . ."

Betty spoke up. "She hasn't changed her mind."

"No, I haven't," Josie admitted. She hadn't made it up either. In fact, she was beginning to wonder if she even had a mind. A few hours ago she had found a body. And here she was getting her hair done. Mia stood behind her, a gloppy paintbrush in one hand, a comb in the other; the smile on her face was beginning to look a bit forced. It was now or never. Josie took a deep breath. "Go ahead."

It took less than half an hour to cover the crown of Josie's head with small squares of foil. Conversation swirled around her. Husbands were discussed as well as lovers. Children at prestigious prep schools and colleges. Children who weren't living up to parental expectations. Shopping. Trips to exotic—and warm—parts of the globe. Designer clothing. The stock market. Jobs. Parties. Weddings. The prices of apartments. Condo boards. Once in a while someone actually mentioned hair. But Josie strained her ears, hoping for more news about the woman who had been murdered.

When enough hair dryers had been stilled for her to make out more than a few words at a time, the name she did hear was even more familiar than Pamela Peel's.

"What I want to know is what Sam could possibly have been thinking!"

Josie swung her seat around to see who had asked that question. Unfortunately, the small metal stand holding the various hair dyes, combs, and extra foil squares was in her way. As it crashed to the floor, hair dryers were switched off and people stopped what they had been doing and turned to stare. But it took just seconds for professionalism to reassert itself. Women who had been delivering coffee, tea, and tiny pastries to the customers dropped what they were doing, grabbed mops and brooms, and had the floor clean in minutes. The woman who had greeted Josie and Betty upon their arrival appeared on the scene to make sure no one had been hurt and ended up assuring Josie that there was no need to apologize. This type of thing, she claimed, happened all the time. Josie doubted it, but she appreciated the attempt to put her at ease. She was still apologizing profusely to everyone nearby when Mia, assuring her all was well, led her to the shampoo sinks on one side of the room.

Betty was already there, seated in a reclining chair, her long legs propped up on a wide comfy footstool, a smile on her face as her scalp was massaged. Josie moved beside her, managing to bump into her friend's arm on her way to her seat. "Sorry."

Betty opened one eye. "What happened? What was all that noise?"

"I knocked over the bowls of bleach—"

"Coloring. Not bleach," Mia corrected. "We're not using bleach on your hair."

"Whatever it was, it all hit the floor, thanks to my clumsiness."

"No, no! It was not your fault!" Mia protested. "This place is too full, too cramped. People are always knocking things over. Lean back."

Josie did as she was told and felt warm water run over her hair as Mia pulled the foil squares out and dropped them into the sink.

"You'll never guess what I heard!" Betty hissed above the sound of running water.

"You'll never guess what I heard!" Josie hissed back. "Would you believe that someone was talking about someone named Sam?"

"Sam? There must be thousands of men named Sam in this city," Betty reminded her. "I heard something about Pamela Peel. The woman getting her hair washed behind me—"

"Are you two speaking of Pamela?" An elegant silver-haired woman peered through gold-rimmed glasses at them.

"Well, yes, we were," Betty admitted. "You see, my friend here—"

"Oh, you are friends of dear Pamela."

"Not really. We are . . ." Josie paused, trying to describe their relationship with the dead woman. "She decorated a friend of mine's apartment . . ."

"You are clients of Pamela. Well, so many people are, aren't they?"

"That's what we've heard," Betty replied. "How do you know her?"

"I'm her aunt. Well, her unofficial, unrelated aunt. We've been friends forever and she's always introduced me as her aunt."

"Have you heard about . . . from Pamela recently?" Josie asked, as her head was released from the basin, her hair wrapped in a thick towel, and she was allowed to sit up.

"No, dear Pamela is sometimes just a bit naughty. She doesn't spend enough time with her family, I'm afraid. She's horribly, horribly busy, of course. What with her work and her social commitments. You can read all about it in this week's *New York* magazine, you know."

Josie glanced over at Betty. It was obvious that this woman had no idea her beloved niece was dead. "Well, we really didn't know her," Betty said hastily.

"Perhaps you will have that opportunity in the future. Do you attend Junior League events? Or perhaps you're involved in the Lighthouse for the Blind annual benefit sale?"

"No. You see, I have a new baby," Betty added.

"And your nanny takes weekends off. How unfortunate. These young women have no idea what hard work is. When I was a child, my nanny was never ever allowed to interfere in the life of the family. When my parents wanted to go out, they went, always knowing that there was a reliable person at home to take care of my sister and me."

"As you say, things aren't exactly like that these days," Betty agreed.

Josie wondered if this woman had been raised on a different planet or perhaps in a different—and wealthier—solar system. "Not everyone is fortunate enough to have someone else raising his or her children," she said, remembering Tyler's infancy. She had been forced to leave him to go to work during the day, but she had never had the luxury—or the desire—to leave him to socialize in the evenings.

"And not everyone wants someone else to raise their children," Betty added flatly.

"No? Well, you young mothers always seem to feel you know what's best. Time for my manicure." Pamela Peel's unofficial aunt, apparently deciding further conversation would be a complete waste of time, turned and walked away, waving ten perfectly oval and polished nails in their direction.

"She needs a manicure?" Josie asked no one in particular.

"She gets a manicure every week, whether she needs it or not," Mia answered. "She's one of our regulars." She picked up a pair of scissors and began to snip at Josie's damp hair.

"Do you have many people like that?" Betty asked.

Josie, noting that Betty was losing her hair a fraction of an inch at a time while Mia was lopping off her own curls in half-foot-long sweeps, didn't pay much attention to the answer.

"Oh, yes. Of course, Pamela Peel used to come here, but she followed her hairdresser."

"Pamela Peel? The decorator?" Josie asked to make sure they were talking about the same person.

"Yes."

"What do you mean, she followed her hairdresser?" was Josie's second question.

"The person who did her hair left for greener pastures and Ms. Peel followed close behind," Mia explained. "It happens all the time."

"Maybe that's a good thing now," Betty's hairdresser said, standing back to admire her own work.

"Why?" Josie asked.

"Maybe a bit more off on the left side" was Betty's contribution to their conversation.

"There's a rumor going around that she's dead," Mia said quietly.

"Murdered," Betty's hairdresser added.

"We heard that too." Betty spoke up when Josie didn't respond.

Josie, realizing Pamela Peel's body had been discovered less than twenty blocks away, was amazed that the news had traveled so quickly. "How did you hear about it?" she asked, hoping Mia wouldn't be surprised by the question.

Apparently not. "Everyone was talking about it when I first arrived this morning. I don't know exactly who heard about it first. I suppose it was on the radio or something. She is pretty famous. At least in this part of New York."

"And when I was getting some coffee earlier I overheard someone saying that her boyfriend was going to be arrested for her murder. . . ."

"Her boyfriend?" Betty asked, sitting up straighter in her chair.

"That's what I heard."

"Do you know his name?" Josie asked. "Could it have been Sam?"

"I suppose so . . ."

SEVEN

JOSIE AND BETTY were back on Fifth Avenue before their hair spray had dried. "Where do we go? Where do you think Sam is?" Josie asked frantically, looking up and down the sidewalk.

"I have no idea . . . Oh, excuse me." Betty bumped into a man rushing by, cell phone to his ear. "Is your cell phone on? Why didn't Sam call?"

Josie rummaged in her purse. "I thought . . ." She was so upset that her hands were shaking, but she managed to press the correct buttons. "Two messages. There are two messages. Probably from Sam. Just wait one minute." She pressed the buttons required to retrieve her messages and listened intently. "The first is from Tyler. He's fine, may need more money . . ." Impatient, she pressed some more buttons and listened, a frown on her face.

"What? What is it?"

"He says not to worry. He got an advance on his salary."

"Why does Sam need a loan?"

"It's Tyler, not Sam. Both calls were from Tyler." For the first time in her life, Josie ignored an opportunity to worry about her son. "Betty, where could Sam be? Who are you calling?"

"The person we should have called first. My husband. He's one of Sam's best friends and he's a defense attorney.

Sam's a smart man. If the police are going to arrest him, he would have called Jon first. . . . Damn!"

"What's wrong?"

"Battery's dead. Give me your phone." It was in Betty's hand before the words were out of her mouth. "Damn," she repeated, staring at the keypad.

"What's wrong now? Why aren't you dialing?"

"I can't remember his cell phone number. It's on my auto dial at home and on my cell and I . . . wait, let me think for a second . . . Okay, got it, I think . . . at least . . ."

Just when Josie had decided that she could no longer resist screaming, Betty got through.

"Jon . . . Yes, hi . . . Yes, we heard . . . At Elizabeth Arden . . . Oh, well, that's a huge relief. . . . Yes . . . Why not? Oh . . . well, okay, but I don't think she's going to be very happy about it. . . . Okay, we'll wait at home. Love you. Bye."

"He's seen Sam?"

"He just left him at the police station and he says everything is okay."

"What? Why were they at the police station? Why did he leave him there?" Josie shrieked, backing into a woman carrying three large bags from Bergdorf Goodman. "I'm sorry!"

"Why don't you watch where you're going? You could hurt someone!"

"She said she was sorry!" Betty grabbed Josie's arm and pulled her to the side of the sidewalk. "Listen, Josie, our information's wrong; Jon says Sam wasn't arrested. He was asked to come down to the police station and make an official statement. That's what he did—after calling Jon. No smart lawyer is going to be questioned by the police without another lawyer present. Anyway, Jon stayed with him during the questioning and then left. Sam was waiting around for his statements to be typed up and then, after checking them over, he'll leave. Let's go back to my place. We can figure out what to do when we get there." She raised her arm to flag a cab.

"I think I should go back to Sam's. I want to be there when he comes home."

"Josie . . ."

"Betty, I'm going to go back to Sam's apartment." Josie had been Betty's boss for almost a decade. She knew the tone of voice to use to get her point across.

"But you'll call me the second you hear anything," Betty said.

"Of course."

"And, Josie . . ."

"What?"

"Your hair looks wonderful."

"I just hope Sam gets to see it." Josie's answer was grim. She turned and walked up Fifth Avenue. Her mind was as chaotic as the midday traffic. At Fifty-fifth Street a taxi, swinging around the corner, almost ran over her toes. Josie scowled and continued on. The sign said Walk; she had the right of way. She stomped down the sidewalk, ignoring shopping bags that nicked her legs, brushing by women in full-length furs and men in immaculate trench coats, Burberry scarves wrapped around their necks, briefcases firmly tucked under their arms. She detoured around an elegant young couple in matching black leather staring at the display of diamonds in Cartier's windows. The woman already sported a pretty large diamond—pierced onto her left eyebrow. A block later a group of noisy high school students had taken over the sidewalk; giggling, pushing, and shoving one another despite their teacher's attempts to convince them to line up for a group photo beneath a sign indicating that they were at Fifty-seventh Street. Josie passed them all, pausing only when she came to FAO Schwarz.

There was very little about New York City that she remembered from family vacations when she was growing up, but a visit to this store was printed on her mind. She had wanted—desperately wanted—a massive stuffed St. Bernard. Her parents, always practical, had refused to spend hundreds of dollars on such a thing and she had gone home with a red plastic pencil case; it had fallen apart the first day of the new school year. How long, she wondered, would that stuffed dog have lasted?

She tripped on a chunk of uneven sidewalk and stopped wondering about the past. She would have fallen on her face if a young man hadn't grabbed her, set her upright, and hurried on his way without giving her time to thank him for his good deed. Realizing there might not be a Good Samaritan waiting for her on every block, Josie marched on, paying more attention to what she was doing. She had to get to Sam's apartment. Sam would be waiting at his apartment. Once she saw him, once she talked to him, everything would be okay. By the time she arrived at Mentelle Park Apartments, she was almost running. She pushed through the double doors into the lobby.

The doorman, Harold, was on the phone and Josie hoped she would get by with just a wave, but he hung up as soon as he saw her. "Miss Pigeon. Your timing is perfect. Mr. Richardson will be relieved that you beat the crowd."

"What crowd?"

"He'll explain. You hurry right on up. You can depend on Harold to protect you."

Josie didn't understand but she didn't care. She was finally going to see Sam. She trotted into the elevator and pressed the correct button. And gasped as the doors closed.

The elevator was paneled in walnut burl. And set in that burl were four pairs of mirrors. Josie was presented with eight images of herself. She looked around. She moved a bit to the left. And then a bit to the right. She moved forward and then back. She couldn't believe it. She really looked wonderful. Mia had tamed her red hair into a shoulder-length bob. It was perky without being adolescent, mature without being matronly. She tilted to see the highlights on top. They really did look natural and even elegant. Josie smiled as the elevator stopped. The doors slid back. And she ran straight into Sam Richardson's arms.

"Sam!"

"Josie! Thank God you got back before they arrived!" Sam's quick release was completely unsatisfactory—as was his next action. Sure he had lost an ex-girlfriend, sure he was in that ignoble position of helping the police with their investigation, sure he had a lot on his mind. But how could he ignore her new look? And was it necessary to grab her arm and hustle her through the hallway and into his apartment without any explanation?

"Sam? What's going on?" she asked as he locked the door behind them.

Sam slammed the last dead bolt in place and turned to her. "If anyone knocks, we ignore it. I know Harold thinks we can rely on him to keep the horde out of the building, but I'm not so sure."

Josie was completely mystified. "What horde?"

"Reporters and photographers."

"Because of the murder?"

"What else? Pamela wasn't really rich and famous, but she worked for the rich and famous and that's all the local press are interested in. God, I hope her murder isn't picked up by the tabloids."

Josie ran her hand through her hair—with some difficulty due to Mia's fondness for hair spray—and glanced around the room. Nothing seemed to have changed since she left a few hours ago. She looked at Sam. He'd changed. She wasn't sure just how, but he had definitely changed. "We heard that you were arrested, but Jon told Betty that wasn't true."

"No. Just brought in for questioning. Any arrest will come later."

Sam's last sentence was spoken almost under his breath and Josie stared up at him. "Why would they arrest you?"

"In the first place, I didn't say they would, but you have to realize, Josie, that there are lots of reasons to look at me as the most likely suspect." He sat down on a stool by the counter that separated the kitchen from the dining area and folded his hands in his lap.

"What reasons?" Josie asked quietly.

"Well, her body was found in an apartment I own—"

"But you don't live here anymore. Maybe the person you were renting this place to killed her."

"The person I rented this place to hasn't lived here for three months. He was transferred to Singapore in the late fall. And there's no reason to assume he knew Pamela. Besides, I doubt if finding the body here is all the police are considering."

"What else?"

Sam got up and walked to the window. "Well, remember we went together—were a couple—for over a year. There are a lot of people who knew the two of us and knew about our relationship."

"So what? You've had relationships with lots of women!" Certainly too many for Josie's taste.

"But Pamela was different."

This was something she certainly didn't want to hear. "What do you mean?" Josie asked.

"She . . . I . . . we used to argue a lot. Everyone knew it."

Josie didn't know what to say. "That doesn't sound like you" was all she came up with.

"I know." Still looking out the window (avoiding her eyes? Josie wondered), he continued his explanation. "Pamela and I weren't good for each other. I mean, we didn't bring out the best in each other."

"Which is why you argued," Josie guessed, hoping to keep him talking.

"I suppose. To tell the truth, I have no idea why we were always disagreeing. Hell, I have no idea why we got together in the first place."

"Love at first sight?" Josie almost whispered the words, half of her hoping Sam wouldn't hear and the other half hoping Sam would hear and deny the truth of her suggestion. But Sam didn't respond the way she wanted him to. He didn't respond at all.

Finally Josie couldn't stand the silence. "So what if people knew you and Pamela Peel argued. She may not have gotten along with a lot of people. It's not reason enough to arrest you for murder."

"There's more . . ."

"What? Sam, what is it that you're not telling me?"

Finally he turned from the window and looked at her. "Josie, I can't tell you any more than this. Really, I can't."

"But—"

"You're going to have to trust me. I . . . I can't say any more about this."

Josie blinked and turned her back to the room. She couldn't believe Sam was saying this to her. Her Sam didn't say things like this. Other men did. Her girlfriends had husbands and boyfriends who said things like this. And when they told Josie about it, her response was always the same: Dump him. But not her Sam. He wasn't like this. And she sure wasn't going to dump him. She blinked back the tears beginning to spill out of her eyes. She had no idea what she was going to do. She looked around the apartment. She hated everything about it: the color, the uncomfortable furniture, and the way the large area had been broken up into small, awkward spaces. But most of all she hated the woman who had decorated it. And what that woman's death was doing to her Sam. She took a deep breath and turned to him.

Sam was staring out the window again, his back to her so she couldn't see the expression on his face. Josie thought for one minute. She had to be sure about the decision she was about to make. Once made, it couldn't be changed. "Sam."

He didn't move and, for a moment, Josie wondered if he had heard her. Then, "Yes?"

"Sam, I know you didn't kill Pamela Peel and I wish you would tell me whatever it is that you're not telling me." She stopped, taking a deep breath before continuing. "But I trust you. So tell me what you want me to do and I'll do it."

Finally he turned around and looked at her.

"Thank you." He took a deep breath and Josie realized he had been near tears. "This is a horrible situation and it may become even more horrible very shortly. I don't know what people will say. I don't know what you're going to hear, whether it will be lies or truth. This is not going to be easy, you know."

"I know. And it doesn't matter."

"Your faith in me is the only thing that will get me through this."

Josie moved across the room and flung herself into his arms. But even as she was finding the comfort she desired, she wondered where she was going to find the strength to get through this herself.

EIGHT

NEW YORK CITY has a restaurant on every block. There are even areas where the restaurants outnumber all other businesses. So an empty refrigerator isn't a problem. But, in Sam and Josie's case, getting to the restaurant without drawing unwanted attention from the journalists who had gathered outside of Mentelle Park Apartments was. At least that's what Josie had assumed. Her assumption was wrong.

"We'll use the tradesmen's entrance."

"The what?"

"I'll show you. Just let me call Harold and make sure the doors are unlocked."

Josie, who hadn't been in the apartment long enough to remove her coat, waited silently while Sam called down to the doorman and pulled his Burberry from the stainless steel armoire by the front door. Watching him, Josie smiled sadly. Leave it to Sam to be neat even in a crisis.

"You know, I should call Jon and let him know where I'll be before we leave."

"You have your cell phone, don't you?" Josie reminded him.

"Yes, but I don't want anyone to overhear my conversation. This will just take a few minutes."

Sam's phone call did take only a few minutes. But he spent them on the extension in the bedroom and to Josie it was an awfully long time to wait and wonder what was going on—and why he wasn't sharing it with her. Well, she had other things to worry about. She rummaged in her purse and pulled out her cell phone. Time to check on Tyler. And, perhaps, she had better tell him about the murder before he heard about it on the news.

"Tyler, this is your mother. Please give me a call when you have a moment free. Sam . . ." She paused, wishing she had had the sense to think of what she was going to say before dialing his number. "There are a lot of things going on here that you might want to know about. Love you, hon. I hope you're having a good time. Hi to Tony and his father." She pressed the button to hang up and wandered over to the spot by the window where Sam had stood. Looking down, she realized that the peaceful scene she had pondered last night had disappeared, that mayhem seemed to be the order of the day. She counted four television microwave vans, aerials up.

Josie turned from the window and wandered around, once again examining the apartment. She had wondered sometimes why Sam had arrived on the island with so little in the way of personal belongings. Aside from clothing, some paintings, his computer, an incredible collection of books, and one comfortable chair, everything in his beach house was new. But this apartment didn't seem to be missing anything. There were lamps on tables. Monochromatic photographs framed on the walls. There were even small appliances on the kitchen counters. Josie shrugged. Maybe all this was expected when an apartment was put up for rent in New York City. Certainly most houses on the island were rented furnished. On the other hand, these things had been chosen and purchased by Pamela Peel. If she had been the love of his life, wouldn't Sam have brought some of it to the island to remind him of her? Josie ran her hand along the top of the gray suede-covered couch and wondered exactly who had ended their relationship. He had once told her that the decision was mutual, but were these things ever completely mutual? Wasn't it likely that one person was more involved than the other? And wouldn't that be important for her to know if . . .

Josie paused for a second, hand clenching the leather, lips pursed. She took a deep breath and finished her thought: If she was going to investigate Pamela's murder.

When Sam reentered the room, only a few minutes later, there was no longer an *if* in that sentence. She was going to investigate. Period. She had to help Sam. And, she realized, she had to help herself; she needed to know the truth.

"Ready to go?"

"Yup. I'm starving."

She was rewarded by a brief smile on Sam's face. "Some things never change." He opened the door for her and she walked through it, turning toward the elevator.

"No, this way." Sam pointed her in the opposite direction. They went down the corridor and through an unmarked door. Here the wall-to-wall carpeting was replaced by ugly, worn linoleum and three large plastic recycling containers almost blocked their way. They continued on, passing a garbage chute, and walking through another unmarked door leading to another elevator. Sam pressed the down button and the doors slid open immediately. This elevator wasn't paneled in expensive hardwood nor were there any mirrors. It was metal lined and the metal was liberally covered with dings and scratches. "This is the way the furniture travels in and out of the building," Sam explained. "And, of course, tradesmen use this elevator too."

The elevator moved more slowly than the one routinely used by residents so Josie had a few minutes to consider the fact that, if she had located her business in New York City, she'd be traveling in this elevator with its damaged walls rather than in mirrored luxury.

"This building is unusual in that it shares a basement with the building next door," Sam explained.

"So?"

"So we're going to go out through their basement and enter the street not from behind Mentelle Park but from the side of Tanbry Towers, our neighbor."

"You're saying that the press won't notice us."

"Not if we're lucky. So what do you want for lunch?" Sam asked as they negotiated their exit toward the street again.

"I don't care. Whatever you want."

"There used to be a nice spot a few blocks over. La Belle Jardin. It's a traditional French bistro."

"Sounds fine."

"Of course it may no longer be there. Restaurants come and go in this town."

But La Belle Jardin was exactly where Sam had left it and the maître d', apparently thrilled to see an old customer, ushered them to the best seat in the house and then dashed off to get a complimentary bottle of wine.

"That's amazing," Josie commented, looking around the charming bistro. It was decorated to resemble a French farmhouse, with massive bouquets of flowering branches standing on tables scattered about. Inside this cheerful room, it was possible to forget the slushy streets outside.

"What is?"

"You haven't been here for how long? A couple of years?"

"At least."

"And there are millions of people in the city; it's actually possible that thousands come here to eat every year."

"So?"

"He remembers you."

"Carl probably remembers many good customers. It's part of his job. Besides, Carl and I share a passion for wine.

In fact, I was sitting in this very spot when I made up my mind to retire and go into the wine business."

Josie smiled. "I'm glad you did."

Sam smiled back at her and picked up the menu.

Josie did the same. But for once she wasn't thinking about food. She was wondering how long Sam was going to avoid talking about the murder. It seemed she was going to be the one to raise the topic. "Sam, are the police . . ."

"Josie, I'd really rather not talk about all that in a public place."

She looked around. It was true that the tables were close together, but there was no one on either side of them and the table itself was tiny. If they leaned toward each other, certainly no one would overhear their conversation. But she couldn't force him to talk about it. "Okay. So what do you want to do this afternoon?"

Sam put down his menu. "I think I should spend some time with Jon. We have things to go over. Just in case."

"Oh . . . well, then I guess I'll go back to the apartment . . ."

"Josie, you're in New York City. There are stores, museums, and lots of things to do. I hate to think of you sitting in that hideous apartment waiting for me to come home. It isn't like you."

"I guess not." Josie picked up the large menu and hid behind it. Sam was wrong. This was like her. Not like the Josie Pigeon she had become. But like the Josie she had been when she was young and insecure. She'd worked hard to become self-sufficient and confident. Of course, sometimes she didn't feel that way at all.

"Why don't you call my mother? She would love to show you around."

"What a great idea!"

Sam looked up, obviously startled. "Really? I mean, Mother can be rather—"

"Sam, your mother loves this city. Who would be a better person to show it to me?"

"Well, Mother loves Saks, Bergdorf's, Bloomingdale's, and Barney's, but—"

"Perfect. I promised myself some new shoes. This way I can shop and see the city at the same time."

Sam still looked doubtful. "You know how Mother likes to . . . to share her opinions."

"Sam, we'll be fine together. We get along at home, why not here?"

"I guess. But there is one thing."

"What?"

"She may not have heard about Pamela's death. In fact, I'm sure she hasn't heard. She would have come over or at least have called if she knew."

"So? Do you think I should be the one to tell her? I mean, I don't think I should spend the afternoon with her and not mention it. That would seem a little odd."

He didn't answer right away. "I could call her . . ."

To Josie, his answer didn't sound overwhelmingly enthusiastic. "If you don't mind me being the one to tell her, I don't mind doing it." Besides, their conversation was finally heading in what she considered the right direction.

"She never admitted it, but I'm not sure she liked Pamela," Sam said slowly. "So don't be surprised if she isn't terribly upset. But I don't want her to start worrying about me."

"You mean about you being upset or about the possibility of the police thinking you killed her." Josie found herself unwilling to say the dead woman's name.

Sam gave her a strange look. "Josie . . ."

But the arrival of the wine interrupted their tête-à-tête. For once, Josie was glad Sam made such a big deal about tasting the vintage. It gave her some time to think and plan. Spending the afternoon with Carol was a golden opportunity. Especially if Carol thought her darling son was a murder suspect. Josie

knew she would learn a lot. She just hoped she would learn
enough to start in the right direction.

"Josie." Sam pointed to the full wineglass in front of her.

She took a sip and smiled. "Delicious." She knew it was
the only response necessary as Sam could find more to discuss in one glass of wine than she could possibly imagine.
And attempting to join in would be impossible. To her wine
was either delicious or not worth drinking. She had explained this to Sam early in their relationship and she hadn't
been bothered with questions about finish, legs, or bouquet
ever since. She listened to the conversation, smiled when she
thought a smile was appropriate, and frowned when she forgot she was supposed to be enjoying herself. When their
waiter appeared, she and Sam both ordered and then she ex-
cused herself and headed off to the ladies' room.

The door was still swinging closed as she pulled her cell
phone from her purse and started to dial. Tyler first. Once
again, he didn't answer and Josie's second message was almost identical to her first. Betty was the second person she
called.

"Hi, Betty, I . . . well, to tell the truth, he didn't notice. No.
Really. No, I didn't touch it! Yes. Well, maybe he has more
important things on his mind. . . . Betty, don't worry about it,
I like it. That's what's important. Listen, that's not why I
called. Sam and I are having lunch. In a French place over on
Madison . . . La Belle Jardin . . . Betty, you're not listening to
me! He's going to see Jon after lunch. Yes, they're meeting.
Yes . . . Why not? You're sure? Well . . . okay. Did Jon say anything to you yet?" Josie sighed. "You'll tell me when he does,
won't you? Yes, same here. Thanks, Betty. Bye."

Josie stared at her reflection in the mirror. Something was
going on. Tyler wasn't answering her calls. That was a worry.
But she was even more worried about Sam. Of course, he
hadn't killed Pamela Peel. But there was something he
wasn't telling her.

NINE

SAM'S MOTHER APPEARED along with their dessert. Josie had talked Sam into ordering crêpes suzette. But Carol Birnbaum was sizzling at least as much as the buttery concoction they were consuming. She didn't enter the restaurant as much as fly in, mink-covered arms spread wide, eyes dilated, in the middle of a sentence.

" . . . what you thought you were doing. Did you think I wouldn't hear?"

Sam jumped to his feet. "Mother—"

"Mother? That's all you have to say? I have to hear about Pamela's murder from a woman I cannot stand? You can't pick up the phone and let me know what's going on?"

"Mother—"

"You call me up and ask me how I'm doing, what's happening in my life as though nothing unusual is going on and never mention Pamela's murder!" Carol glanced at a waiter hurrying toward their table. "Bring me crème brûlée and an espresso with artificial sweetener," she ordered and he turned and dashed back toward the kitchen. "Josie, you poor thing, how are you? Just like Pamela to ruin your lovely week in New York City."

"Mother, I don't think Pamela . . ."

"What are we going to do about all this? I can't imagine that you won't be a suspect unless the real murderer is quickly discovered. I really believe—"

"Mother, everything is just fine. It's true that Josie discovered Pamela's body in my apartment—"

"In your, her body . . . Josie discovered . . . I didn't know that. I just heard she had been killed." A very attentive waiter had pulled a chair over from a neighboring table and Carol flopped down in it. "Tell me. Everything. From the beginning," she demanded.

"Mother . . . "

Josie decided she couldn't let this go on any longer and interrupted Sam. "I couldn't sleep and got up in the middle of the night and went into the living room. I was looking out the window, watching the traffic and people walking their dogs, and I remembered that Sam had told me there were—"

"That there might be," Sam corrected her. "I told you that there might bc . . ."

". . . binoculars in the window seat," Josie finished his sentence, glancing over at him. Why did he think that distinction was so important? "Anyway, I found Pamela Peel. Well, I found a dead woman and then, after I yelled and Sam came in, I found out that she was Pamela Peel. She was strangled."

"I called the police right away." Sam picked up the story. "Luckily, I knew the detective who came out. He had been on a lot of cases I prosecuted back when I was working for the city. Anyway, he and his colleagues asked Josie a few questions, and the techs took their photos, collected fingerprints, DNA, whatever they could find, and then they removed . . ." Sam floundered for the first time since beginning his explanation, but he quickly regained his composure and continued. "They removed the body and then asked me if I would stop down at the station and answer a few questions later. I did. They did. And then Josie and I came here for lunch."

Josie knew large parts of the story had been omitted. From the expression on Carol's face, she was fairly sure

Carol knew too. So she was incredibly relieved when Carol turned to her and didn't ask another question. "Your hair looks wonderful, dear."

Josie grinned—and not just with relief. "Thank you. Betty took me to Elizabeth Arden this morning."

"Who cut it?"

"Mia." Josie took a bite of her crêpe before continuing. "You know, Carol, I was wondering if you might help me look for shoes this afternoon."

Carol automatically lit up at the thought of her favorite activity. Then her smile faded and she looked over at her son. "Is Sammy going to accompany us?"

"No, he . . ."

"Good. Sammy didn't like shopping when he was a little boy and, I'm afraid, he didn't improve in that respect as he got older. We'll do much better on our own." The waiter placed her order before her and she picked up her spoon and tapped on the crackled caramel surface. "Now where should we start? Barney's? Saks? Bloomingdale's?"

"Wherever you think," Josie answered, knowing that it didn't matter whether or not she could afford to shop in these places. She had no intention of buying anything.

"My suggestion is to start at Saks." Carol looked down at her tiny gold watch. "I hope we have enough time. Shoes can be very difficult. Just let me taste this custard. I really only want a taste. That usually satisfies me."

Josie, who was rarely satisfied until she had a clean plate before her, scarfed down the last of her food and hopped up. "That's fine with me. Sam?"

"Let's meet back at the apartment for drinks around five," he suggested. "I don't know about whether you want to join us for dinner, Mother, but—"

"Drinks will be fine. I have a date tonight." His mother interrupted what promised to be an unenthusiastic invitation. "Now, don't worry about us. Josie and I are going to have a wonderful time." She put her arm around Josie's shoulder and Josie discovered herself being led with surprising force toward the door. She grabbed her coat and was still slipping her arm into the sleeve when they arrived on the street. "Now tell me what the hell is going on. And don't give me any more of that protecting mother stuff that Sam's been shoveling my way."

"I'm afraid the police might think Sam killed Pamela Peel," Josie blurted out.

"Of course they do. She was found in his apartment, after all. Now what are we going to do about it?"

Josie stopped in the middle of the sidewalk and turned to Carol. "I was thinking . . . well, to tell the truth, I was thinking of investigating on my own. Do you think I'm being foolish?"

"No, I think you're being smart," Carol said. "Now we can walk and talk at the same time, so you can tell me everything."

"I don't know everything. That's the problem. Sam . . . well, Sam doesn't seem to be entirely truthful with me," Josie added reluctantly.

Carol stopped so quickly that a deliveryman, who had been hurrying behind, crashed into them, dropping his boxes and cursing. "Ignore him," she suggested, scowling over her shoulder. "We have much more important things to worry about. Now what exactly has been going on? Sammy's an honest man so what you just said has me incredibly worried."

"He just told me that he was going to see Jon Jacobs after lunch, but I spoke with Betty—you know, Jon's wife—and she told me that Jon is in court trying an important case all afternoon. So he lied about that and—"

"Professionally? Sammy thinks he needs Jon to help him out professionally? Isn't Jon a defense attorney specializing in criminal cases?"

"Yes, and Jon was already at the police station when Sam was being questioned earlier."

Carol frowned and turned and walked into the wind, her head down so Josie couldn't see her face. "This is very bad news. Start at the beginning and tell me everything. Absolutely everything. Even what Sam doesn't want me to know."

"The problem is that Sam doesn't want me to know some things either. Anyway, I got up last night. . . ."

The tale, interrupted frequently by questions that Josie couldn't answer, took them to within a block of Saks. "Perhaps we should stop in and offer up a prayer or two," Josie suggested as they passed St. Patrick's Cathedral. She was only half joking.

"Sammy will be fine," his mother stated flatly. "He has us working on the problem."

Josie smiled broadly for the first time since happening on Pamela's body. She had never really been sure what, if anything, Carol thought about her. This vote of confidence was unexpected and deeply pleasing. But there wasn't time to wallow in her feelings. Carol had achieved her objective. She pulled open one of the swinging doors and pushed Josie ahead of her into Saks Fifth Avenue. Josie blinked in the brightly lit warmth. Even the air smelled rich. She took a deep breath and sneezed.

"Oh, my dear, I hope you're not getting a cold. We have so much to do. Shoes are on the fourth floor. This way."

"I thought we were talking about the murder. Pame—"

"Hush!" Carol pulled Josie to her side and hissed in her ear. "You can talk about murder all you want, just don't mention that woman's name! Who knows who might overhear us."

Josie looked around. "Why do you think anyone listening might be interested in her?"

"Because this is her stomping ground. People who shop

here might know her and almost certainly have heard of her. That's why we're here—besides looking for shoes for you."

"Oh, but I really don't need shoes."

Carol looked down at Josie's feet. "Josie, dear, you do need shoes. Badly. And, don't worry; this is my field of expertise. I can shop in my sleep. We'll talk and buy you something more . . ." She paused as if looking for the perfect word. "More suitable for walking up Fifth Avenue."

"But I—"

"Now, the first thing we might investigate is what Pamela Peel was doing when she was killed. Tell me, what was she wearing?"

"What was she wearing?" Josie couldn't believe she hadn't misheard the question.

"Yes, what was she wearing? We might be able to figure out what she was planning on doing when she was killed by what she was wearing."

Josie supposed that made some sense. "Um . . . let me think. A dress. Short, but the sleeves were long. It was black," she added, triumphantly sure of something.

"What fabric?"

"I have no idea."

They were wandering through the crowded aisles, Carol stopping occasionally to pick up a small object like a scarf only to put it back down on the counter, rejected, before moving on.

Josie was trying to concentrate on Carol's questions while watching the action. Was it possible that every woman in New York City was trying to improve her appearance? The back third of the large store's main floor was dedicated to cosmetics and it was jammed. Makeup was being applied to customers who seemed to think nothing of discussing moles and wrinkles in front of a crowd of strangers. Thin, young women smilingly offered samples of exotic perfumes. Hundreds of dollars' worth of creams were being sold by the ounce in containers that looked as though they had been fashioned from rock crystal. If Josie was overwhelmed, apparently Carol was right at home.

"Oh, dear, if you could just wait a second. I'm almost out of my favorite eye cream and it seems to be on sale."

"Of course. I'll just look around a bit." Josie stared at the hundreds of products crowded together on glass countertops. She had no idea where to start. It wasn't that she didn't use creams or lotions. But she bought hers at a drugstore and, generally, used whatever had been on sale when she was shopping. And, to tell the truth, she found that to be confusing enough. It seemed as though every few months there was a new ingredient, which promised eternal youth, and Josie felt it would be foolish not to try it and almost always ended up buying more than she needed. But her splurges were limited by the store's small selection. Here a woman could buy hundreds of products and spend thousands. . . .

The reappearance of Carol, a large shopping bag dangling from one hand, cut into her musings. "Okay. I'm ready. Now have you been trying to remember more about P . . . about that outfit we were discussing?"

But Josie was focused on the bag. It was huge. "I thought you were buying eye cream."

"Yes, dear, but the entire product line was on sale. And then they had this wonderful premium, a little travel bag. Not that I need a travel bag and the lipstick sample is always so dreadful, but . . ." Carol ended her explanation and looked at Josie. "You didn't buy anything?"

"No. I didn't even look."

"Good heavens, you do have an amazing amount of self-discipline. Well, let's head on up to shoes. Although perhaps we should stop on the second floor and look at dresses. Something there just might remind you of that dress we were discussing and it would be so helpful in our investigation if we could pin down what she was wearing."

"Carol, I really don't think I can help you there. I recognize denim, of course. But frankly, I can't tell the difference between silk and polyester without reading the label. I've even been wondering if maybe the dress was black. It could have been navy. . . ."

"No, not navy. Not this time of year. Definitely not navy."

Josie couldn't imagine why not, but Carol seemed so positive that she didn't argue. She followed Carol to the escalators and stepped on, glancing back at the bustling floor as they rose. To Josie, Saks Fifth Avenue was a foreign country. How was she going to find anything to help Sam here?

Carol insisted they sweep through the designer clothes on the second floor and Josie trotted behind without protest. At first glance, there appeared to be dozens of black dresses. By the time they had traversed the entire floor, she had upped her estimate to hundreds. And it wasn't surprising. More than half the well-dressed shoppers were in black—dresses, shoes, suits, slacks, coats, boots, purses. Black was the dominant color. The only person in navy was a toddler, who was hanging on to his mother's hand whining. He was the exception in another way as well: everyone else seemed to be having a sensational time.

Josie wasn't exactly happy, but at least she and Carol were on the same track. That is, they were on the same track until they walked into the shoe department. Once surrounded by so many shoes, Carol was energized. She was going to find new shoes for Josie and she wasn't going to accept no thanks as an answer. Josie could not believe the prices. If there was a pair of shoes costing less than $150 she couldn't find it. Most of the shoes were well over two hundred. After turning over a pair of simple black flats and discovering that they cost almost four hundred dollars, she stopped even bothering to look. She wasn't going to buy shoes here. She would browse, be nice to Carol, and refuse to buy. That was all there was to it.

Unfortunately, she should never have told either Carol or the salesman her shoe size. In minutes Josie was sitting in a small leather-covered chair surrounded by shoes of all types. They were all expensive. They were mainly uncomfortable. They were entirely inappropriate for the life Josie led. Besides, they were wasting time. They should be looking for the murderer. They should be investigating Pamela Peel's life. They should . . . Josie suddenly stood up and pointed.

"Those shoes over there. The ones with the silver flowers on the heel. Those are the shoes she was wearing!"

TEN

"**A**RE YOU ABSOLUTELY sure?"

"Carol, I know I have no fashion sense. I can't tell an Armani from a Donna What's-her-name, but these are the shoes that Pamela Peel was wearing. I'm positive. They're exactly the same. There's a flower on the heel, and that's not all," she added before Carol could inform her that flowered high heels were all the rage this winter. "I noticed the little butterfly on the flower—it has rhinestone eyes. There can't be a whole lot of shoes like these!"

Carol picked up one of the shoes and examined it carefully. The black stiletto heel was elegant and expensive. "I think you're probably right about that." She looked up at the man who had been helping them. "Do you have any idea how long this shoe has been on display?"

"I'm not positive. We carry that style in white as well as black—"

"Is there anyone who knows exactly how long this shoe has been available to your customers?" Carol interrupted.

"I could check with our buyer. . . ."

"I'd appreciate that. And if you're going into the back, could you bring out those Ferragamo slides? Size nine and a half."

"Excellent. And I'll bring those shoes too. In a size . . . ?" He left it to them to fill in the blank.

"Seven and a half," Carol suggested.

Josie was still busy examining the pumps. "They're silk, aren't they?"

"Yes, and very elegant. I think we can assume that Pamela was killed when she was dressed to make a good impression."

"Why do you think so?"

"Dear, the outfit that goes with these shoes isn't something she would wear to lounge around the house, or to visit clients. Although it's just possible she would have worn it for an evening at home. . . ."

"An evening at home?"

"Yes. Perhaps she was giving an intimate dinner for a few friends, or perhaps just some special man. She might have worn a dress and high heels. Although, of course, something like silk pajamas and sparkly slides might have been more appropriate if she wasn't going to leave her apartment, but maybe it was a big party with lots of guests and she wanted to be prepared if they all decided to head out on the town afterward."

The return of their salesman put an end to Carol's speculation. "These are for you," he said, dropping a box at Carol's feet. "And these are for you."

Josie was surprised to find her old shoes being pulled off her feet and the silk high-heeled pump with flower and butterfly being slipped on.

"How do they feel?"

"I . . ."

"Perhaps you should stand up."

"If I can." Josie clutched the arm of her chair and staggered to her feet. Her toes were pressed into something resembling a flying wedge; her heels were held high in the air.

"There's a mirror over there."

Josie tottered over to the mirror and peered in, expecting nothing. What she discovered was someone else's feet—and ankles and calves—on the bottom of her legs. And these unfamiliar body parts looked wonderful. She turned and looked at Sam's mother.

"Amazing what an elegant pair of shoes does for one, isn't it?" Carol asked with a knowing smile.

"I guess so . . ."

"And remember they come in white. So perfect for summer social commitments," their salesman jumped in.

Josie frowned. She couldn't imagine wearing these to the island's Fourth of July sand castle contest, or the Memorial Day end-to-end run, or the Labor Day decorate-your-boat water parade. And that had been the entire list of her "summer social commitments" for as long as she could remember.

"You know, those shoes in white would be lovely with a simple wedding dress." Carol sounded wistful.

"Oh, you're getting—," the salesman began.

Josie nipped that one right in the bud. "No, I'm not. Did you find out how long the shoes have been in stock?"

"Oh, they're quite new! Part of our early summer collection. Pat says they've been on the selling floor less than two weeks."

"Really?"

"Pat is your department buyer?" Carol asked for clarification.

"Yes. And she's just wonderful. We always carried the most amazing shoes, but since she came on board two years ago, well, let's just say we don't have those end of the season duds to get rid of."

"And she's sure that if anyone bought these particular shoes here, they did it sometime in the past two weeks."

"Yes, definitely. Of course this model may be carried in other stores in the city and probably in Saks's suburban branches. . . ."

"I think we can forget about the suburbs," Carol said. "Do you happen to know if other city stores would have carried that style earlier than Saks?"

Her question seemed to offend the man. "Madam, Saks Fifth Avenue—"

"Of course, you always have the very latest," Carol agreed with what he was about to say.

Meanwhile, Josie was still admiring her feet. Carol noticed. "Those shoes really are lovely, dear."

"Yes, they'd be perfect—except that I like to walk a bit and I can hardly hobble in these without my toes screaming in pain."

"You'd be amazed how quickly you forget that."

Josie sat down and removed the shoes. "I always notice when my feet hurt," she stated flatly.

"We have many styles designed for comfort," the salesman said, reaching for some examples on a nearby table. "These are from France and they're known for their comfort. And the shoe on display just happens to be in your size."

"They're neat," Josie admitted.

That was all the encouragement the man needed. He was slipping the shoes onto Josie's feet before she could protest. "Stand up and walk around," he suggested.

"They're wonderful!" Josie said, walking to the mirror and back to Carol. The shoes were beige suede set on soft black rubber. They were as comfortable, maybe even more comfortable, than plastic flip-flops.

"We'll take them in beige and black," Carol said, opening her purse and reaching for her wallet.

"Carol . . ."

"They're my gift to you, dear. And this isn't really the time or place to argue."

"But—"

But Carol was on to another thought. "Where are the personal shoppers located?" she asked their now beaming salesman.

"Oh, our One-on-One personal shopping service is on the fifth floor, but I could show you other models—"

"You've been wonderful and I can't tell you how pleased we are with our shoes, but I would like to talk with someone about . . . about a new fur coat," Carol concluded with barely a pause.

"Well, I'm sure they will be more than happy to help you up there. If you'll just wait here a moment, I'll be back with your purchases and your card."

Josie watched the man as he walked away and then turned to Carol. "I really can't let you buy—"

"We'll discuss this later, dear. Right now we need to figure out a strategy."

"What sort of strategy?"

"We need to find out if Pamela Peel used a personal shopper here. I don't think we can just walk up and ask, but we do need to find out."

"Don't you think you might be becoming just a bit obsessed with that dress?"

"What dress, dear?"

"The one Pamela was wearing."

"Oh heavens, I'm not thinking about that anymore. We know she was dressed up for a fairly formal event. So she must have been killed in the evening or getting ready for an evening event. It seems to me that we've learned something very significant."

"So why are we looking for a personal shopper?" A dreadful thought occurred to Josie. "Carol, I don't need anything else."

"Oh, my dear, the shopper is for information. Not for you. Some personal shoppers know the most amazing things about their clients. Where they go. What they do. And, frequently, who they are going and doing with and when and where. This woman just might be a veritable font of information of the type we're looking for."

"Oh . . ."

"Of course getting her to share the information may be a

bit difficult, but since when has that stopped two determined women like ourselves? Ah, here's our nice salesman, back so quickly."

Carol took the charge receipt and signed it, turning her back on Josie as she did so. "I am going to pay for my shoes," Josie said.

"We can talk about that later, dear. Thank you so much. You've been a big help," Carol added, smiling to the salesman and handing back the receipt. In return, she was given two big shopping bags. "If you'll take one, I'll handle the other," she said, passing a bag over to Josie.

Josie looked down. "There are four shoe boxes."

"Only two are for you. I just did a bit of shopping while you were admiring that first pair of shoes. Now let's go on upstairs. I've had an idea that just might get us the information we need."

Josie hurried after Carol, trying to remember when Carol had found the time to try on and purchase two pairs of shoes. They arrived at One-on-One, Saks Fifth Avenue's shopping service's offices, before she could figure out an answer.

"Okay, now just follow my lead." Carol brushed her hair off her forehead, straightened her shoulders, and walked through the door, a wide smile on her face. "Good afternoon," she said loudly.

A young woman with an immaculate shiny straight bob looked up from the work on her desk. "May I help you?"

"Yes, we have a special problem. Something I hope you might be able to solve."

"Of course, helping customers here at Saks Fifth Avenue is my job. If you will just tell me what you need."

"A friend of ours—a very good friend of ours—is having a birthday and we're shopping for her present."

"Helping people buy gifts for their family and friends is a large part of my job, so if you'll just tell me a bit more about your friend. Her age. What sort of things she likes . . . I assume this is a woman we're talking about?"

"Yes, but, you see, we thought you might be able to tell us what to get her. Since we understand she was . . . she is one of your clients. Pamela Peel."

"I don't believe I've worked with anyone with that name. But, of course, someone else in this department might have done so. If you have a moment, I can check our files."

"Excellent. We would appreciate that."

The woman turned to the computer sitting on a console behind her desk and began to type. "Peel with two e's?"

"Yes, exactly."

"Her name isn't here," she repeated after a few minutes. "But you know, it does seem familiar for some reason. Perhaps I could check with my colleagues and   "

"No, that won't be necessary." Carol poked Josie in the side and nodded at a small coffee table near the door they had come in. The current copy of *New York* magazine lay there. On the cover was a photo of an attractive gamine blond woman smiling at the camera. She was sitting on a chintz couch in a room filled with antiques, artwork, and accessories. The headline identified her as the beautiful and talented Pamela Peel. So now they knew why Pamela's name seemed familiar.

"I think we probably should stop taking up your valuable time," Carol went on, tugging gently on Josie's sleeve. Josie didn't answer, but continued to stare at the photo.

"But I'd be happy to help you shop for a gift. If you would just tell me more about this woman, I'm sure we can find something suitable. . . ."

"No, we're in a hurry. I'm sorry we wasted your time." Carol grabbed Josie's arm more forcefully and edged her out the door.

Josie waited until they were alone to speak. "So who are we going to see now?" she asked, when they were on the down escalator.

"Who?"

"Yes, there must be lots of people. Women friends. Boyfriends. Colleagues."

"But, my dear, why would they tell us anything?"

"Because they will want her murderer to be found."

"The police will probably arrest Sammy for her murder. He's not a part of that group. I suspect most of them will be perfectly happy with that scenario."

"You mean they're the type of people who won't care if the wrong person is arrested?"

"No, I mean they're the type of people who will leave all that to the police. They'll talk about it over lunch and dinner and in intermission at the theater. But they'll talk among themselves. A stranger claiming to be investigating the murder will . . . well, I don't know what they would think of you being involved. I, of course, will just be written off as a hysterical mother. You, well . . ."

"You don't see me being accepted in Pamela Peel's circle," Josie said flatly.

"Frankly, my dear, I doubt if they would confide in you. And that's what you're looking for, isn't it? You want them to talk to you about Pamela and her life. Of course, with that new hairdo and just a bit more shopping . . . You know, I have an idea. An excellent idea!"

"Does it involve buying more shoes?" Josie asked.

"My dear, this time we're going to buy you a completely new look! But first I must call my dear friend, Sissy Austin. She was going to be interviewing Shep Henderson for a possible decorating job. If things go as I hope, this time tomorrow morning you'll be meeting the person Pamela Peel has been working with for years. You're going to interview Shep Henderson yourself!"

ELEVEN

CAROL REMOVED HANGER after hanger of slacks, shirts, sweaters, and jackets from walls lined with clothing, dumped the pile in Josie's strong arms, and guided her to a nearby dressing room.

"Perhaps Madam needs some help," a saleswoman suggested, dashing after them.

"No, I think . . ," Josie began only to be interrupted by Carol.

"Yes, we do. Could you find a skirt to go with this sweater, a pair of pants—camel perhaps—that would blend in with the heather of the jacket, and a white cashmere turtleneck, hip length? Size eight." She pushed Josie into a large dressing room before she could protest.

"Carol, I wear at least a twelve. . . ."

"That's fine. If she actually finds what I asked for in an eight, we can always send her back for a larger size. I just didn't want anyone hanging around, pestering us, and listening in on what we're saying. Now, I think the black silk slacks and the red shirt first."

"You could tell me about Pamela while I try on clothing," Josie suggested.

"Yes. Not that I know all that much about her, but I'll tell you what I know."

"From Sam?"

"From Sammy and other things. You see, Pamela Peel had

been on the edge of my vision for a while. One of my dearest friends, before she moved to La Jolla and became a New Age nut, had her apartment done by Henderson and Peel, and she used to rave about Pamela Peel. And I read *Women's Wear Daily*, the Style pages in the *New York Times, Vogue* . . . whatever. Let's just say before I actually met her, I knew of her. And so I was very surprised when Sammy told me he and Pamela were dating."

"Why? I thought Sam dated dozens of women."

"Oh, my dear, he did. But none of them were celebrities and he never made a big point of introducing me to them. I mean, he would bring them over to my house for holidays, parties, whatever. He was never without a date. But he had never made a special point of me getting along with his dates. They were just dates. I knew from the very beginning that Pamela was different."

Josie, her head inside a fabulously heavy silk pullover, appreciated the privacy the situation afforded. She knew Sam had loved Pamela. She was just a bit surprised at how painful it was to hear about it. "Why?"

"Well, he made such a big deal about us being friends."

"What sort of big deal?"

"Well, he invited us both to the Rainbow Room one Friday night. The Rainbow Room is one of the only places in the city to still have ballroom dancing. I adore it. And Sammy knows I adore it. He said I wasn't to bring a date along. That he wanted to have his two best girls to himself . . . Did you say something?"

"No. Go on. I was just trying to reach that tiny button behind my neck."

"Turn around and let me help," Carol ordered before continuing her story. "Well, it was an incredible evening. Vintage champagne, fabulous food, a view to die for . . . What more could anyone ask. We ate dinner and Pamela was at her best—gracious, charming, beautiful, and attentive to me.

After dinner, we talked more over brandy. Sam took turns dancing with Pamela and me. It was such a special moment that it wasn't until I arrived home—no, actually when I got up in the middle of the night to go to the bathroom, that I began to feel uncomfortable."

"Why?"

"They didn't belong together."

"What?"

"Pamela Peel was using my son. Oh, I didn't realize that right away, of course. But that night, when I thought it all over, I realized something was wrong. At first glance, it had all gone so well. Sammy was so charmingly attentive to me and to Pamela. And Pamela was so obviously making an effort to make a good impression on me. But something felt wrong. I just had a hint of it then. And I convinced myself that I was imagining things, making up problems where none existed. I had been waiting so long for Sammy to settle down. I wanted him married. I wanted grandchildren. But my instincts told me something was missing. I should have listened to them."

"What happened?"

"For a while, nothing. Sammy and Pamela became a couple. You know the way that works. You're seen together out in public. Then people begin to invite you both places. It was only a few months before there were hints about an engagement. I remember Sammy gave a huge party the week before Christmas. I think everyone he'd ever known was there. And I'm sure at least half of them were expecting an announcement of some sort."

"What sort?"

"An engagement. Or maybe that they would announce their marriage. At Sammy's age there's no reason for a big wedding with the blushing bride all in white—unless the bride wants one," Carol added hurriedly. "You know I think the bride should be the one to decide on these things."

"I guess." Josie seemed to be moving further and further away from this sort of thing in her own life. "So tell me about that party."

"Well, it turned out that Sam did make an announcement—no, I'm wrong about that. Pamela made an announcement. She told everyone that Henderson and Peel was going to redecorate Sam's place. I don't know about the rest of the guests, but I assumed that meant she was going to move in with him. I was a bit surprised. It's not a terribly big apartment. In fact, if I had thought the whole thing through at the time, I would have realized that there was no way Pamela would even consider moving in with Sammy. Her shoes alone would have filled both his closets. Anyway, they were a couple. And Sam trusted her to redecorate his apartment."

Carol frowned, but whether it was a response to a distasteful memory or the sight of Josie's thighs in the low-riding silk pants, Josie couldn't guess.

"So what happened next?" Josie asked.

"The apartment was redecorated. And I know I'm not the only person who thought it was not an improvement. Sammy's place had had a kind of rough charm. Over the years, he bought furniture as he needed it and had the money to spend. Nothing actually went together, but somehow it all did. Of course, you know Sammy—he covered most everything with books so maybe that pulled it all together somehow. Anyway, Pamela didn't move in with Sammy and he never told me whether he thought his newly redecorated place was an improvement over the old look. And they continued to date. And then, one day—this was about six months later—Sammy announced he was going to retire and leave the city. And in less than a month, he had done just that. There was never even a hint that Pamela had planned on going with him. But they dated right up until the day he left."

"Did he ask her to? To come to the island?" Josie held her breath waiting for the answer to a question she had wondered about ever since hearing of Pamela Peel's existence.

"I don't know. I never asked. And Sammy never volunteered the information. But I wouldn't let that concern you, my dear. I've always thought that if Sammy had wanted to get rid of Pamela, moving to that island was an excellent way to do it."

"Why?"

"Josie, it's not exactly Southampton, you know."

"That's why we like it," Josie stated flatly.

"And that's why Pamela would have hated it. But you mustn't let me veer off track this way. I was beginning to tell you about Pamela Peel." Carol paused and Josie jumped in.

"Well, I know what she looked like—sort of."

"I wasn't thinking about that. I was thinking about you. Do you ever wear pink?"

"Sometimes. A very pale pink . . . with my red hair," Josie added, not explaining that the only pink article of clothing in her closet these days was a ragged sweatshirt Tyler had bought her years ago on a class trip to Great Adventure theme park. She rarely wore it in public since she felt it made her look like a gigantic blob of cotton candy.

"I have an idea. I'll be right back."

Their saleswoman dashed in as Carol dashed out, leaving Josie a bit breathless.

"I have the other things your mother—"

"She's not my mother," Josie protested. "She's a friend."

"Well, I brought the things she asked for and a few other ideas I had." She looked at Josie now standing in the middle of the small room in a bra and silk pants. "Are you sure a size eight . . ."

" . . . will never fit," Josie finished for her. "Size twelve," she said firmly. "And I don't suppose you carry anything in denim?"

"Why, we have lots of denim! Donna Karan did some wonderful things with it this season. And I think maybe Calvin . . . You said size twelve, yes?"

"Yes."

"Well, I'll be right back."

Carol and the saleswoman collided in the doorway. Josie took advantage of the few moments it took for the two women to regroup and collect the clothing that had fallen to the floor to hide a jacket she knew she would never wear and two more pairs of hip-hugging pants. The only people who should wear hip-huggers were those without hips. She put all three items in her discarded pile and turned to greet Carol.

"Look what I found, dear." Carol held out a shocking-pink tunic, orange silk slacks, a couple of white T-shirts, and some sort of long, turquoise, beaded scarf. "Try these on."

"I don't think—"

"I believe I was just going to tell you what I know of Pamela's background."

Josie reached for the clothing and prepared to listen.

"Pamela was always very secretive about her childhood. And I can't remember ever meeting any of her family in all the time she dated Sammy. But—"

"Isn't that a little odd?" Josie asked, holding the tunic up to her chest.

"Not really. I can't say that I know many of Sammy's friends' parents unless they just happened to live in the city and we happened to run across one another socially. So I don't think the lack of family means anything other than that she grew up someplace else.

"And put on that shirt," she ordered before continuing. "Anyway, dear Pamela was something of a snob and she used to drop comments about positively growing up on horseback, skiing in St. Moritz, the woes of private school dress codes. It was her way of letting us ordinary mortals understand that we were hobnobbing with the privileged. But, to tell the truth, I never believed that stuff."

Josie stuck her head through the top of her top, astonished. "You really didn't like her!"

"I admit I thought she was a snob. But don't tell Sammy I said so. You know I make it a rule to never interfere in his private life."

Josie knew nothing of the kind, but she kept her mouth shut. This revelation thrilled her.

"Anyway, Pamela may or may not have had a wealthy family. The truth is, it really doesn't matter. In New York City, it's what you can do that counts in most circles, not who your parents are. But Shepard Henderson's family was quite wealthy and he and Pamela probably used his family's connections to get their start in the decorating business. Henderson and Peel became well known almost immediately. And I can assure you that that sort of recognition—and publicity—is almost always gained through connections. I know she worked as a peon for one or two excellent firms before starting Henderson and Peel less than five years ago. One of their first jobs was for that awful Hollywood movie mogul—What was his name? Well, it doesn't matter now. What matters is that he was so famous that the living room Henderson and Peel designed was on the cover of *Architectural Digest*. And their names and faces were prominently displayed in the six-page article about his new home. There's been a long waiting list for their services ever since." Carol wrinkled her forehead and ordered Josie to turn around.

"The pants need hemming, but other than that, I think we've found our outfit." Josie looked down. In a room lined with mirrors, she had been so interested in what Carol was saying that she hadn't even bothered to check out her own reflection. Now she did. And for a moment, she forgot that there even was a woman named Pamela Peel. She looked wonderful—like someone else, of course—but wonderful.

"Good, huh?"

"Very good," Josie answered. "I can hardly believe it. I almost look like a New Yorker!"

"You look fabulous! And you didn't think I could do it, did you?"

"Well . . ."

"Don't answer that, dear. I don't want to damage our relationship and I certainly don't want you to lie. Now, the slacks come in taupe as well. So we'll get them and another shirt or two will be fine. Now, a coat . . ."

"Carol, I don't need a coat," Josie said firmly.

"But what if he suggests you come to his office? You don't want to ruin the image, do you? Besides, your parka has seen better days, you know."

Josie sighed. "Okay, a coat. But not on this floor. This is all designer clothing. I've had a chance to read the signs at the ends of the escalators. Saks does sell clothing without designer labels."

"I suppose we can look at those floors."

"We can and we will. Now tell me more about Pamela Peel and please show me what I'm supposed to do with this thing." She held out the long, beaded scarf.

"Oh, my dear, that dresses up the outfit for evening." Carol grabbed the fabric and started to drape it around Josie's shoulders. "You see, when you buy good clothing, it can be worn many different ways on many different occasions."

"That's exactly the way I feel about my Levi's jeans," Josie commented, staring at herself in the mirror. The scarf looked wonderful too, casually draped around her shoulders. She knew it would stay in place about five minutes, and then she would fidget with it for a while, and then, finally, take it off. Pamela Peel, she suspected, was the type of woman who could wear this sort of thing all day long and be found sipping cocktails in the evening with each and every bead still decoratively in place.

"Jeans are fine on the island, but this is New York. And we have to make a good impression tomorrow morning, remember."

Josie nodded. She wasn't terribly enthusiastic about Carol's plan, but she hadn't come up with any other and she had to help Sam.

"I was going to tell you about the last few times I've seen Pamela . . ."

"Since Sam left the city?"

"Yes. We did run into each other once in a while, of course. Usually I saw her and she didn't see me."

"What do you mean?"

"It's hard to explain. She was always polite. She didn't snub me, but she was cool. We exchanged greetings. I always suggested that we meet for lunch sometime. She agreed. And we didn't. And I knew we weren't going to when we talked about it. The whole performance was a polite formality. Or it was until two weeks ago."

"What happened then?"

"Well, we chatted a while. I told her that Sammy might be coming to town. She told me about the condo she was decorating for an anchorman. Then she pulled out her Palm Pilot and insisted on setting a date."

"You two had lunch recently?"

"No. The date she chose was today."

"Oh. Did she mention why she wanted to meet?"

"No. But she seemed to think it was important. She wanted to meet as soon as possible. But I was away and then she was busy." Carol shrugged. "It probably doesn't mean anything."

"It probably does. It's a connection. She wanted to see you. She was killed and her body found in Sam's apartment.

It really could be important. Did she give you any reason for wanting to meet?"

"Sort of. She said she . . . she wanted to hear more about how Sammy was doing. She said she'd been . . . that she had been missing him."

TWELVE

THE NEXT MORNING, Josie had kissed Sam good-bye, telling him that she was meeting his mother for another shopping expedition and then heading straight to the address Carol had given her.

Josie had worked on some fabulous homes, but nothing in her experience prepared her for Sissy Austin's East Side duplex. Her first impression was that it was big. On closer examination she changed that assessment to huge. Five floors hand laid in chestnut parquet, each floor having at least three large rooms, had been decorated by someone with no interest in austerity. The rooms were hung, draped, filled, and just plain crowded with overstuffed furniture, curtains, rugs, bows, beads, tassels, and swags in a rainbow of colors. Wood had been painted to look like paper; paper had been painted to look like wood. Plaster columns had been painted to look like marble. Marble columns had been covered with gilt. It wasn't Josie's taste, but she admitted that it was all very impressive.

But it had been decorated years ago, before Sissy got religion. Listening to Carol and Sissy chat as they walked Josie through the place, Josie couldn't be sure whether Sissy had begun to practice Buddhism, transcendental meditation, or something less well known, but the result of her conversion was a newfound need to live what she described as "a simple life." As far as Josie could tell, this simplicity involved dozens of brass bells, hundreds of crystals, artifacts from Tibet, and many, many yards of handwoven raw silk. Samples of these things were piled upon a French marquetry commode in the room Sissy had described as her library. There was a Mary Higgins Clark mystery open facedown on one of the room's three velvet-covered couches. It was the only book in evidence.

"I don't see how I'm going to do this," Josie muttered, a worried expression on her face. "Now, I tell Mr. Henderson . . ."

"Shepard or Shep, not Mr. Henderson," Carol corrected. "You are hiring him, remember."

"Okay. I tell Shep I'm interested in hiring Henderson and Peel to redo your entire place in a more, um—"

"On a more spiritual plane," Sissy explained. "Not feng shui—that's so 1990s. I'm thinking green plants, maybe even orchids or those little Japanese trees, perhaps some of those big statues of religious figures . . . you know the type of thing."

"It really doesn't matter what Josie asks for," Carol reminded them both. "It's not as though Henderson and Peel is going to get the job anyway. In fact, the vaguer you are, the better, Josie. Then Shep will have to spend time trying to figure out exactly what you're talking about. And that's what you need. You want to get some sort of impression of him as well as learn anything you can about Pamela and their relationship. You want him to spend as much time here as possible."

Josie glanced over at Sissy. She didn't know how Carol had explained their task, but Sissy seemed completely comfortable with an unknown woman taking over her home for the sole purpose of deceiving one of the most famous decorators in the city. "Are you sure you can't stay with me?" Josie asked Carol.

"I'm afraid not." Carol's response was brisk. "Shep just might recognize me. We met a few times back when Sammy and Pamela were dating. My presence just might blow your cover."

Josie smiled. "Blow your cover" was not a phrase she associated with Carol. "So I'll just introduce myself as Sissy and show him through the apartment. . . ."

"Exactly," Sissy jumped in. "I've let my staff go for the day so there won't be anyone around to tell him you're not who you claim to be."

"We should leave right away," Carol reminded them. "We don't want Shep to find us here. You'll be fine, Josie. How many times have you been interviewed by prospective clients considering hiring Island Contracting?"

"Lots, but in that situation, I'm the person trying to get the job, not the one doing the hiring," Josie pointed out.

"Think of this as role reversal and be as snobby as possible. Believe me, Shep Henderson will be surprised if you're anything else."

"Oh, and the most important thing to remember is money," Sissy said, getting up and moving toward the door.

"Money?"

"Yes, make sure he knows that you have it and intend to let him spend it. Nothing makes a decorator happier than spending lots and lots of other people's money."

The peal of the doorbell, a duplicate of the chimes of Big Ben, made further instructions impossible.

"We'll leave by the service entrance. You go greet Shep Henderson," Carol ordered.

And, in a flurry of mink coats, Carol and Sissy hurried off, leaving Josie alone and nervous. She took a deep breath, rearranged the turquoise-trimmed scarf around her shoulders, and walked toward the duplex's foyer.

Hidden within the duplex's baroque decorations lay a state-of-the-art security system, complete with cameras outside the building aimed at visitors standing on the brownstone doorstep. Josie checked the inside monitors, as she had been instructed, then opened the door to a man she assumed was Pamela Peel's partner.

"Mr. Henderson?" Realizing she had already failed to follow Carol's directions, Josie wiped the smile off her face and tried to look prosperous and in charge. "Please come in."

"You are Mrs. Austin?" he asked, entering the foyer.

Josie decided brevity was the best policy. "Yes. Why don't we talk in the library . . . or would you rather look around first?" she added. When being interviewed for a job on the island, Josie always liked to chat a bit to give the client a chance to get to know her and her company before they discussed the job itself. She wondered how Shep Henderson worked.

"Oh, that would be fine." He looked down at her without smiling. In fact, he didn't seem terribly interested in her or what she was claiming was her home.

It wasn't until they were seated that Josie suddenly realized she might be expected to offer coffee or tea. Having no idea where a coat closet might be located, she had been relieved when Shepard casually tossed his navy cashmere coat over the back of a sofa. "I . . . my staff is off today." She struggled to excuse her lack of hostess skills. "I could make us some coffee if you'd like." She crossed her fingers and hoped he refused. The kitchen she had been shown through had the best of everything including imported appliances. She had noticed a large Italian espresso machine, but she couldn't begin to imagine how it worked.

"Frankly, I'd rather have a drink."

"I . . . Oh . . ." Shep Henderson was staring over her shoulder and Josie, fingers crossed, turned around to discover an extensive bar that she hadn't noticed before. She jumped to her feet. "What would you like?" she asked, glancing around. Dozens of bottles were on display.

"A small brandy would be nice."

Josie walked toward the liquor—very slowly. A bottle of

brandy was easily found. But where were the glasses? And how could she explain having to look for them? Surely even people with servants occasionally prepared their own cocktails. She reached out and opened the doors of a nearby ormolu cabinet. Champagne glasses and large goblets appropriate for old burgundies were there, but no snifters. She grimaced and opened another door, thinking furiously. She could always explain her confusion as the result of a new maid putting things away, she had decided, when, much to her relief, she found dozens of snifters in two sizes and a pile of pale gold linen cocktail napkins as well. Feeling like the excellent hostess she was not, she turned back to Shep Henderson with a full glass and napkin in hand. "Here you are."

"Won't you join me?"

"It's a little early for me," Josie said, sitting back down.

"It's usually early for me too—very much too early." Shep Henderson ran a hand through his hair in a gesture reminiscent of a young James Stewart and then continued. "But these are difficult times. As I'm sure you've heard by now, my colleague has died. She was murdered. It was in all the papers this morning."

"Pamela Peel."

"Yes."

"I'm so sorry. It was good of you to keep your appointment under the circumstances."

"Everyone expects me to maintain Henderson and Peel's high standards despite this dreadful event. My parents . . . Pamela herself . . . I felt I had no choice but to go on," he ended rather abruptly. He raised his glass to his lips and drank.

Josie took the time to examine Shep Henderson while he sipped his brandy. He wore an elegant black suit with a sparkling white shirt and a pinstriped white-on-black tie. His shoes were polished. A heavy gold Rolex hung loosely from one thin wrist. A handsome man in his early forties, he wore his pale gold hair in a conservative cut. The more she looked, the more he reminded her of Jimmy Stewart. "You and Pamela Peel must have been very close," she said without thinking.

Fortunately, he didn't appear to find the comment odd. "We had been business partners for years. We worked together each and every day. We . . . we had to trust each other. And, of course, you know how rare that sort of relationship is in this city." He looked up at her.

"Of course." Josie paused and then plunged in. "Exactly how long had you known each other?"

"Oh, my. Forever. We met first in college years and years ago. But it wasn't until we had both moved to the city and were working for other decorators that we ran into each other again. Neither of us liked our situation. I was slaving for a man who took my ideas, presented them as his own, and then refused to allow me to work on anything original. Pamela was being used as a front person by one of the most irritating decorators in the business. He was using her looks and personality to charm potential clients into hiring him but not allowing her to contribute anything creative. We were both afraid that would go on for years. And we were both desperate to have our own design firm. I was positive we would make a good team and by joining forces we'd make a fortune." He smiled wistfully and ran his hands around his snifter.

"You were both ambitious," Josie prompted him.

"Yes, that goes with being young, of course. But Pamela and I were courageous as well. We decided to jump in with both feet—sink or swim we'd set up our own shop. We had ideas and connections. All we needed was money. You don't know how difficult it is to get a new business off the ground without cash coming in . . ."

"Or to stay in business," Josie jumped in, forgetting that she was supposed to be an upper-class lady of leisure.

Luckily, Shep Henderson didn't seem to find her response at all unusual. He sipped his drink and nodded vaguely. Josie wondered if this wasn't his first drink of the day. "But you two did find the money to start Henderson and Peel," Josie pointed out, hoping he would start talking again.

"Yes, my parents allowed me to cash in one of my trust funds and we started our company." He looked up at Josie with an appealing expression on his face. "We have been very, very successful. Heaven knows what will happen now." He shook his now empty glass and Josie remembered her duty as hostess.

"Would you like another?" she asked, getting up.

"Yes, thank you."

Josie poured more brandy, glad to have her back to him. She ran her own business, she had met potential clients many times; she had never acted like this. On the other hand, she remembered that after Noel Roberts, the founder of her company had died, she'd felt disoriented, frightened, and in a panic over Island Contracting's future. She poured the golden liquid into his glass and glanced over her shoulder at Shep Henderson. He had gotten up and was looking closely at the oil painting over the mantel. Oh, Lord, what if he made a comment that required her to know the name of the artist? She took a deep breath and spoke up. "Interesting, isn't it?"

"If you like minor impressionists." His tone said that he didn't.

"Here's your brandy," Josie said.

He looked at the glass she offered with a frown. "Perhaps we should look around your place. I can't spend all morning here drinking."

"Yes, of course," she agreed, surprised by his response. "Why don't we start upstairs," she suggested, trying to take charge.

"Fine. And you can tell me what you're thinking of . . ."

"Oh, um . . ." For a moment Josie couldn't figure out what he meant. Then she realized that his back was straighter, his eyes brighter, and he had taken a small leather-covered notebook from his breast pocket. Shepard Henderson was back on the job. "I'm thinking simplicity," Josie explained. "I'm looking for a more spiritual environment." She could tell from the puzzled expression on his face that Sissy's words meant as little to him as they had to her. "I want to use things like these . . ." She pointed to the artifacts Sissy had left on the commode. "I'm thinking green plants, orchids . . . um, raw silk . . ."

"Perhaps we should start upstairs as you suggested."

"Excellent idea." Now she just had to hope that she could find her way around.

Half an hour later, she showed Shep Henderson to the door. "Good-bye, Mr. Henderson," she said, not worrying about whether or not she was addressing him properly.

His response was equally abrupt. "Good-bye." He didn't suggest that she call him. She closed the door behind him and leaned against it with a sigh. She'd blown it. She had learned nothing. And there was no way Shep Henderson would see her again.

No decorator wanted a client who couldn't distinguish the door to her closet from the door of her bathroom.

THIRTEEN

"I BLEW IT."

"Josie, dear—"

"Carol, it was a good idea, but I couldn't pull it off. He never loosened up. He didn't tell me anything useful. He probably thought I was weird. Hell, of course he thought I was weird. How many women don't know the way around their own apartment?"

"You did the best you could," Betty reminded her. Carol and Josie had joined Betty for lunch in the lobby lounge of The Four Seasons Hotel. JJ's baby-sitter being previously engaged, the young man was enjoying the first ladies' lunch of his short life. Carol hadn't allowed the child to leave her lap since their arrival. Now she was dangling a silver teaspoon in front of him, much to the baby's delight. Josie was nursing a white wine spritzer, a drink she would normally have avoided, but somehow it seemed appropriate in this large formal space. She leaned back in the comfortable leather chair and sighed. "I had one chance and I blew it."

Betty put down her menu and smiled at her baby before turning her attention to Josie. "You do know one thing."

"What?"

"He was drinking early in the morning. Surely that's interesting."

Josie shrugged. "I don't see why. Maybe he always drinks in the morning. Maybe he's an alcoholic."

"And maybe he's devastated by Pamela Peel's death. Maybe he's worried about the future of Henderson and Peel. Maybe Pamela was the brains behind the business and he's convinced he can't carry on without her."

"Nice theory," Josie said, "but what does it prove? Henderson and Peel is a successful business. He'll find another partner and go on. A company that has a waiting list of clients can't be in serious financial trouble. Unless things are really different in New York City."

"Probably not in this particular case," Betty agreed with her friend.

The reappearance of their waitress ended Josie's speculation. After a rather extended discussion of the menu and the ingredients in various offerings, the young woman headed back to the kitchen with their order and, with a sigh, all three women reached out for the bread basket.

"I usually don't . . . ," Carol began, choosing a baguette.

"It's been a long morning," Josie muttered, picking up a whole-wheat roll spiky with raisins and walnuts.

Betty laughed and took one of each. "Nothing like nursing to keep your weight down," she said, adding a large pat of butter to the pile of bread on her small plate.

They munched quietly, each involved in her thoughts. Josie looked around the large space at the other diners. Tourists, businessmen, tired shoppers, everyone seemed to be occupied with the serious business of eating and drinking. One young woman stood out; thin, with unkempt hair, and dressed in a more artistic manner than the other guests, she sat alone at a small round table devouring a huge, bloody steak.

JJ closed his eyes and began to doze, eyelids fluttering in what all three women agreed was a charming manner. But the appearance of their waitress with plates of lobster salad, crab cakes, and grilled shrimp returned them all to the subject at hand.

"So what do we do now?" Josie asked, picking up her lobster-filled baguette and taking a large bite.

Betty smiled at the waitress, who was waving well-manicured fingertips at her now awake son, then returned her attention to the topic. "What about finding Pamela's friends and—"

"Carol and I don't think her friends would talk with us," Josie interrupted. "After all, why would they? And how are we going to explain our interest?"

"I suppose you're right. Not many people are comfortable discussing the lives of people they hardly know with strangers." Betty stopped speaking and reached over to take her son's sock out of his mouth and replace it on his foot. She removed a big plastic ring with bright colored wooden keys hanging on it from her purse and offered it to the child. He frowned and returned his attention to the empty spoon Carol had offered him. Betty shrugged and picked up her fork.

"My dears, it's not one's friends who know our secrets. It's the people who take care of us who know the truth about our lives." Carol stopped speaking and placed a dab of tartar sauce in the exact center of her crab cake.

"You mean doctors?" Josie asked, mystified.

"Perhaps one's plastic surgeon or psychiatrist. But I was thinking of the more intimate caregivers—one's hairdresser, manicurist, masseuse, nutritionist . . . you know."

Josie didn't, but Betty jumped right on Carol's bandwagon.

"Then maybe we should go back to Elizabeth Arden," she said.

Josie was astounded. "Betty, Sam may be arrested for murder. What difference does it make how we look?"

"We're not going to work on our appearance. We're going to get information. We're going to talk to the people who worked on Pamela Peel's looks."

"Brilliant!" Carol cried out, beaming. "Betty, you're brilliant! We'll spread out all over the city. We'll find her hairdressers, manicurists, masseuses, personal trainers, nutritionists . . ."

"You are kidding" was Josie's response.

"Why not? There are three of us. Well, four if you count JJ. We should be able to interview a dozen people easily."

"That's not what I'm talking about," Josie protested. "I just can't believe that Pamela would go to so many people. No wonder she looked so great all the time."

"Josie dear . . . ," Carol began.

"How do you know that?" Betty asked directly. "How do you know how she looked? I thought you told me you'd never met her. And you can't judge by a cover story in a magazine. They probably brought in makeup artists and professional photographers."

"You're right, we never met. Well, not officially, but, well . . ." Josie glanced over at Carol before continuing. She hated for Carol to hear this, but . . . "Sam has all these photo albums on the shelf in his closet. I was going through them last night after we got home. I mean, I told him I was going to look through them and he didn't seem to care. He was busy . . . on the phone with someone." She hoped she didn't look as embarrassed as she felt.

Carol reached over and placed a hand on Josie's sleeve. "Oh, my dear, this trip is really not working out as anyone planned, is it?" she asked, a sad expression on her face.

Josie took a deep breath and decided not to whine. "No, but the important thing is keeping Sam out of jail."

"Good for you!" Carol perked right up. "We must focus. There's nothing we can't do if we put our minds to it." She reached down and picked up her spacious green suede handbag and rummaged around in it. "I don't know why I can never find a pencil or paper . . ."

Their waitress, ever attentive, reappeared holding a small

bowl of creamy rice pudding. "I told the chef there was a baby out here and she sent this out. She says her son lived on it for his first year."

"How wonderful!" Betty beamed. "Thank you!"

"Can I get anything else for you?"

"I don't suppose you could dig up a pencil and some paper?"

"Oh, that's easy. I'll be right back!"

Betty picked up a spoon and dipped the tip of it into the pudding and took a taste. "Delicious," she said and offered a few grains of rice to her son.

"I thought we were going to focus on keeping Sam out of jail," Josie reminded them.

"We are. Just as soon as we have something to write with and on. I like to start out with a list," Carol explained. "My second husband was in advertising and he was always talking about brainstorming. I think, this once, we just might take his advice."

"What are we brainstorming about?"

"We need a list of the professionals Pamela went to see regularly over the years—hairdressers and the like. And then we need to figure out exactly who these people are. And then we need to go see them."

"And what makes you think we'll be more successful than I was with Shep Henderson this morning?" Josie asked ruefully.

"Oh, but it won't be like this morning," Carol protested. "These people will know that we're interested in learning who killed Pamela Peel. We won't have to pretend to be someone else."

"What?"

Their waitress appeared with three little pads of paper imprinted with the name of the hotel and three white pencils similarly embossed and Carol repeated her suggestion. "We need to make a list of all the people we're talking about—

hairdressers and the like—and then we need to make appointments to see them!"

"But—," Josie started.

"Fantastic!" Betty interrupted.

"But how will we find them?" Josie asked so loudly that everyone in the room glanced in their direction.

"Find who, dear?" Carol asked, putting down her fork and directing all her attention at Josie.

"Find these people—the people who took care of Pamela Peel. It's not as though we have her address book to go through."

"An address book—or her Palm Pilot would be a big help," Betty agreed.

"Oh, we'll find them easily enough," Carol said blithely. "We have to find only one or two and they will lead us to others. If we're lucky, we should be finished in less than forty-eight hours."

"Of course," Betty agreed. "That's why I mentioned Elizabeth Arden. When we were there yesterday, the woman who does my hair—"

"And does it wonderfully, dear. I was going to tell you how much I love the new style," Carol said.

"I miss having long hair, but, with JJ, it's just so much easier to have short hair," Betty said, momentarily diverted.

"Someone was going to explain how we're going to find these people," Josie reminded her easily distracted companions.

"And we really need to make that list, remember," Carol said.

"Okay, list first," Betty said, passing out the pads and pencils to the women and offering her son the crust of a whole-wheat roll, which he gladly accepted, using it to poke himself in the eye a few times before finding his mouth.

"Hairdressers. Colorist. Manicurist. Personal trainer . . ."

"How do you know she had a personal trainer?" Betty asked.

"Ha! I was talking about losing weight once—you know how you do—and Pamela suggested that I might be better off adding some muscle instead of trying to lose fat. And she offered the name of her trainer."

"Then you have a name."

"Heavens no. This was years ago. And I never even considered going to a personal trainer so I didn't bother to remember the name. But I do know that she had one," Carol explained. "And," she added a bit too loudly, "I do believe I lost some of that weight."

"I sure could use the name of a good personal trainer," Betty said. "Maybe someone who would come to the apartment while JJ naps . . ."

"So you have a perfect excuse to interview Pamela's trainer," Carol said.

"If we find him," Josie reminded them.

"Yes, if we find him," Carol said, ripping a sheet of paper off the pad and handing it to Betty. "I have another name, not that you need it, but I understand that this woman is the best in the business. And I've known her mother for years. So drop my name and she'll take you on as a new client."

Betty blushed. "Thank you. This is wonderful," she added, putting the paper in her purse.

"Can we possibly get back to the business at hand?" Josie asked, not bothering to hide her sarcasm.

"Of course," Carol said as though she had never even considered anything else. "Masseuse. Everyone who hires a personal trainer has a masseuse. And I'm sure she had facials. It's possible that she had a lot of these things done at the same salon."

"Oh, that's what I was saying before. She used to go to Elizabeth Arden. Remember, Josie?"

"Sure, but—"

"It's just possible that she had everything done there—

hair, fingernails, toenails, facials, whatever—and when her hairdresser left and she followed her . . ."

"Or him," Carol put in.

"Or him," Betty agreed. "Anyway, it's possible that we only have to find where her hairdresser went after leaving Elizabeth Arden to discover all these other people we're talking about."

"So what are we going to do? We just had our hair done yesterday," Josie reminded Betty. "And I assume we can't just call on the phone and ask a lot of questions about clients."

"No, but—"

"But I think I could use a haircut and maybe a new color." Carol spoke up.

Josie smiled. She had always thought Carol's hair a bit outrageous, but . . .

"And I know Josie could use a manicure, pedicure, and definitely a facial."

"I—," Josie began her protest.

"Pamela Peel used to swear by weekly facials," Carol added, clinching her argument.

FOURTEEN

JOSIE FELT MORE confident the second time she walked through the famous red door into Elizabeth Arden. Her hair was styled. She was wearing a fashionable outfit bought less than twenty-four hours ago at Saks Fifth Avenue. She knew which button to press in the elevator. . . .

Well, she realized, at least this time, she knew which button to press if she wanted the hair salon, but she and Carol were going to part there and then Josie would have to find her way to the woman who was scheduled to give her her first facial.

Betty had set up an appointment for Carol to see her hairdresser and, as Carol was expected to be busy for well over an hour, Josie had been scheduled for a facial, a manicure, and a pedicure. Of course, Josie reminded herself, the point wasn't beautification, but information. Carol was convinced that all they were required to do was bring up Pamela Peel's name for the information to flow. Josie hoped so. She had insisted on spending some time while they shared two amazingly rich desserts making a list of questions. That list was tucked in her purse, ready for her to consult.

"Now where are we going to meet when we're done?" Josie asked as Carol was whisked off to her appointment.

"Don't worry, dear, I'll find you." Carol waved over her shoulder as she disappeared down the dark hallway toward the dressing rooms.

"I'm scheduled to have a facial, but I'm not sure where to go," Josie told the elegant young man behind the circular desk that dominated the floor.

"Check in with the receptionist on the fourth floor," he said. "Someone up there will help you."

"Thanks."

"No problem. Enjoy."

The elevator doors opened to reveal three middle-aged women wearing brown robes and bright red plastic thongs; they were all giggling like schoolgirls. "So I'm thinking red highlights," one was saying as Josie passed by.

"Oh, you'll look wonderful . . ."

The doors closed, ending Josie's eavesdropping, and she pulled the list from her purse for a last-minute review. Carol believed that the most important thing to discover was whom Pamela was dating now. If nothing else, she thought that information would provide an alternative suspect. Betty and Josie had agreed, but, in fact, Josie was more inclined to look for motives. Josie felt that motive would lead them to other suspects. But she hadn't bothered to argue the point. She would be thrilled to get any information at all. Both Carol and Betty had assured her that just bringing up the name of a famous person would elicit information. Josie couldn't imagine that being true.

The elevator doors opened and Josie found herself on yet another bustling floor. She headed straight for the large desk where an elderly woman was stocking up on cleansers and creams. The total of her bill made Josie blanch, but the woman passed over her American Express card without hesitation. "After all," she said to the saleswoman, "you can't take it with you."

Josie moved up to the counter as the woman left, staggering under the weight of the three bags she carried. "Hi, I'm Josie Pigeon and I have an appointment for a facial at two . . ."

"Pigeon? Yes, you're on with Marguerite. Have you been here before?"

"Well, I had my hair cut just the other day, but I've never been on this floor before," Josie answered, a bit disappointed that she hadn't managed to give the impression that Elizabeth Arden was her natural habitat.

"The dressing rooms are back that way, and I see here that you're also on the schedule for a manicure and a pedicure. If you tell the woman who runs the cloakroom that, she'll take care of you."

"Fine." Josie did as she had been told and, fifteen minutes later, she reemerged robed and with her own red plastic thongs. She was offered tea, coffee, or water and, after refusing all, she sat down to wait. She chose the only seat available, between two exceptionally well-groomed young women who were, she discovered, discussing Pamela Peel's murder.

"It's hard to believe she was found murdered like that. I mean, it's just not the way you think about Pamela Peel. You know, she was always at the big society functions. And she dated famous men—that star of that musical on Broadway last fall."

"That's right! Bob something or other, right?"

"Yes. It just goes to show, doesn't it? No one is safe. Not even the rich and famous. Nothing can protect you."

"You're right. I'm thinking of taking a self-defense course."

Josie was wondering how she could return the conversation to Pamela Peel when a heavyset blond woman in a white nurse's uniform called out her name.

"I'm Josie Pigeon," she identified herself.

"I'm Marguerite. If you'll just come this way."

Josie followed Marguerite down a long hallway, stenciled with sayings purportedly made by the late Elizabeth Arden herself, into a small room with a window looking out onto

Fifth Avenue. The chair in the middle of the room looked suspiciously like one found in a dentist's office. A counter to the right was covered with pots, potions, and strange pieces of equipment. Josie took a deep breath; it smelled wonderful.

"You can put your purse over there and sit down and put your feet up. Relax. This is your time for yourself."

Josie did as she was told and found her thongs being slipped off. Then delicious scented cream was rubbed into her feet and hands, and large electric pads were slipped over both.

"Wonderful." Josie sighed.

"Is this your first facial?" Marguerite asked, pulling Josie's hair back from her forehead and wrapping it in a small white towel.

Josie suspected Marguerite knew the answer to that one. "Yes. My skin's not in very good shape. I work outdoors. In the sun and all," she added.

"You have lovely fair skin," Marguerite lied, reaching out and grabbing a large glob of pale green cream from a nearby tub and beginning to smear it all over Josie's face.

"Thank you," Josie said. A small drop of cream slipped into her mouth. It tasted as good as it smelled. "A woman I know recommended you. She said you gave facials to a friend of hers. I don't remember her name. The name of the friend, that is." Josie took a deep breath and threw her card on the table. "The woman who recommended you is Pamela Peel."

"The decorator."

Josie wondered if she had imagined a change in Marguerite's touch at the mention of Pamela Peel. "Yes."

"She was killed just a few days ago." Marguerite had turned her back on Josie and was removing a white terrycloth towel from a steaming bowl.

"Yes. It's so sad," Josie added, feeling she had to say something more.

"Yes. She had lovely skin."

"Oh, so you knew her."

"Not really . . . I'm going to put this on your face for a few minutes. We need to get to the bottom of those pores. You just close your eyes and relax."

Josie had no choice but to obey Marguerite's directions as she wrapped a warm cloth around her face, leaving her able to breathe, but neither see nor speak. It was disconcerting. She could hear Marguerite walking about, moving things on the counter. But she had no real idea what was going on.

"I'm going to leave you alone for a moment or two. If you need anything, just call out. Yes?"

Josie heard the door closing before she could agree or disagree. Oh well, this was her chance to devise a new plan. To figure out another way to mention Pamela Peel. Maybe she would get a better response this time. She could have heard more about Pamela Peel by hanging around the waiting area. . . . Her eyes were closed, her hands and feet were warm, gorgeous cream was sinking into her skin. She hadn't been sleeping well since coming to the city. And she'd eaten such a big lunch . . .

Ten minutes later, Marguerite returned to find Josie snoring gently.

"Did you enjoy your nap?"

"I . . . I didn't mean to fall asleep."

"Many people do. Especially in the winter. You come in cold and tired. I wrap you up and warm you up. Of course you fall asleep. Now let's just see what we have here. This will be a little cold. And perhaps it will sting just a bit."

Cotton balls soaked in some sort of astringent were used to wipe every last trace of cream from Josie's face. Then a different cream was layered on and massaged in. Determined to stay awake, Josie moved right to the point. "How did you hear about Pamela's death?" she asked.

"Like everyone else, I read about it in the *New York Post*."

"Really?"

"Yes. It is all over the *Post*. The police, they think her old boyfriend did it, you know."

"Why do they think that?"

"She was found in his apartment. In fact," Marguerite leaned down, possibly to examine Josie's pores, possibly to impart some significant information. "She was found by his new girlfriend. Probably his much richer and younger girlfriend. You know how some men can be."

Josie took a deep breath. "Does the paper say anything like that? About the girlfriend being younger and richer?"

"No, but I am reading between the lines. You wouldn't believe the stories I hear working here."

"I'm sure. But maybe . . ."

"And Pamela Peel wasn't a young woman, you know. I heard that she was thinking seriously about a face-lift."

"Do you think that's necessary? I mean, if she took care of her skin, got regular facials and all . . ." Josie looked up at the unlined face leaning over her. "You have perfect skin."

"I have taken care of it. And I have excellent genes. I do not go to plastic surgeon. In Russia, we do not go to doctors unless we have serious problem."

"You're Russian?"

"I have lived here for over forty years. My training was in Russia. In Russia, beauty culture is very important. At least when I was a girl this was true. Now . . ." She shrugged. "Now who knows?"

"So you're one of the internationally trained aestheticians. I read about them in the elevator," Josie said.

"Yes, there are many of us here at Elizabeth Arden."

"You were talking about Pamela Peel," Josie reminded Marguerite.

"Yes. She used to come here."

"To see you?"

"No, I never saw her although I have been here for almost twenty years. See, I have a room with window."

"Yes, it's nice." Not so much for the client whose eyes were closed while lying in the chair as for the person working, but Josie didn't say that. "You know the people who worked on Pamela?" Josie prodded.

"Yes."

Josie took a deep breath and decided it was time to tell the truth . . . at least a bit of it. "I'm the woman the paper wrote about."

"You're which woman?"

"The younger and richer new girlfriend—not that I'm richer. I'm not rich at all, and . . ." She took a breath and threw in her trump card. "I found her. I found the body," she added when Marguerite didn't respond.

"You . . . oh, my goodness. I can't believe it. You poor thing. No wonder your pores are in such terrible shape. Stress is so bad for the skin."

"Yes. But you can see why I want to find out more about her . . . about Pamela Peel. My . . . my friend hasn't told me much about her and . . ." Josie just stopped talking, having no idea what to add.

But apparently she had said enough to cause Marguerite to open up. "Pamela Peel was not liked by everyone here, that much I can tell you. And I only tell you this because she no longer comes here. I have a rule. I do not talk about clients no matter how famous."

"Why wasn't she liked?"

Marguerite squinted at Josie's nose before answering. "She tipped badly. She tipped very, very badly. And she always wanted something extra. That is not a combination that will make you popular around here."

"What do you mean?"

"Look, you come in here, you sit down and I do what I do. I am a good facialist and I always do it well. I take pride in what I do. But sometimes there are clients who try to squeeze a bit extra. They ask questions about other services, about more expensive treatments. And, when I answer, they ask for demonstration. Just a little demonstration. They act as though they will come for more expensive treatment next time. What can I do? I spend as little time as possible trying to show them what can be done. But if I act like I'm in a hurry, they don't tip me. And many times they don't come back for any treatment. And then I end up late for next client and that client gets mad. This is not good for Elizabeth Arden Salon and Spa and not good for me."

"I guess not! And Pamela did this?"

"That is what I was told. You are going to have manicure and pedicure after me?"

"Yes, how did you know?"

"You're not wearing your shoes, so I know there are more treatments coming. Who is going to do it?"

"I'm not sure."

"I find out. Maybe I can get you someone who knew Pamela more than I do."

"That would be wonderful." Josie only had one problem now: Considering the extra service, how much should she tip Marguerite?

FIFTEEN

PEDICURES AND MANICURES were given back down on the second floor so Josie took a moment to see if she could find out how Carol's research was going. She found her sitting in front of a mirror, dozens of little pieces of foil covering her head, a big smile appearing on her face when she spied Josie.

"Josie, dear, your skin looks wonderful. Come a bit closer so these old eyes can get a better look. You won't believe what I've learned!" she added in a whisper as Josie did as she was told.

"What?"

"I know where Pamela Peel went after she left here!"

"Where she went . . . you mean where she went to get her hair cut?" Josie asked, catching on.

"Exactly! And you won't believe what else."

"What?"

"I think it might be time to wash out your hair."

A very young man with very gray hair had joined them. He held a towel in one hand and a comb in the other.

"This is Arturo. My colorist," Carol explained.

"We're right in the middle of a very complex color process," Arturo added. "Timing is very important."

"Then I'll go find the woman who's going to do my feet and hands," Josie said, heading toward the back of the room.

"What sort of pedicure are you having, dear?" Arturo asked in a shrill voice.

"I . . . just the regular kind, I guess."

"Oh, treat yourself. We have the most wonderful nail treatments."

"Do, Josie, dear," Carol urged. "Arturo and I are going to be quite a while."

Josie smiled weakly and continued on her way. She had been in the city long enough to begin to feel naked without polish on her fingernails, but a pedicure? In the middle of winter?

"Are you Josie?" A heavyset woman with long red hair appeared by her side.

"Yes. You're Anna?"

"Yes. My place is right over there. What color polish do you want?"

They had stopped beside a glass case where dozens of bottles of nail enamel were displayed.

"I . . . I have no idea."

"Do you want the same color on your fingers as on your toes?"

Josie knew it would be easier to make one decision instead of two. "The same please."

"Light or dark?" Anna picked up a tiny bottle of pale pink polish.

"That color's perfect," Josie said, relieved to have the decision made for her. She followed Anna's directions, sat down in a comfortable seat, and looked in the mirror. She was beginning to understand why the large place was full; not only did she look considerably better than she had looked before walking through that famous red door, but she was beginning to feel very relaxed. And under these circumstances, that was quite an accomplishment.

"Pedicure first?" Anna asked, gently picking up Josie's

feet, sliding off her thongs, and guiding her feet into a large bowl of warm, sudsy water.

"Sounds good." Josie wiggled her toes. There were small round things in the water.

Anna pulled a towel-covered footstool closer, removed one of Josie's feet from the water, picked up a large, white plastic file and began to scrape at the callus on Josie's heel.

"Have you worked here long?" Josie asked. Anna was decades younger than Marguerite.

"Almost five years. I sometimes think it's almost time to leave."

"Would you go to another salon?"

"I'd like to own my own place." Anna laughed. "Most of us would like to own their own place—except for the people who already had their own places. They seem glad to be here working for someone else."

"Yes, they're smarter," said the elegant black woman sitting at the next nail station, filing her own perfectly oval nails.

"Trish had her own salon," Anna explained, looking up at Josie.

"I own my own company," Josie said. "I know how difficult it can be."

"I don't know what sort of company you own, but it's got to be better than owning your own salon," Trish said.

"Why?" Josie asked. She was interested and she also knew that letting someone bitch about his or her life was an excellent way to bond. And once they bonded, she would change the topic to Pamela Peel.

"Lord, where do I start? The real problem with being an employer is the employees," Trish began, answering her own question before either Josie or Anna could offer a suggestion. "I had four girls working for me. And they were all good workers. I made sure of that. At the first sign of laziness, I fired them. I set a standard, had high expectations, and hired talented people. After six months, I was making money and I had enough loyal clients to think that would continue forever."

"And it didn't?"

"Ha! One of my girls' sisters opened a salon and so she left. A quarter of my business went with her. I ran that business with a twenty percent profit margin. Suddenly losing a quarter of my profits was a disaster."

"I don't understand."

"You see, when a beautician leaves a salon, she takes some—sometimes almost all—of her clients with her."

Josie thought of Pamela Peel. "What about when someone leaves here?"

"Oh, this place is so big and well known that beauticians come and go all the time. Most of the time clients go with someone they like."

"And sometimes they come back and find someone else they like here," Anna added.

"Why?"

"Well, you know how it is. Every place is different. Clients come here because they like their previous service and they like the place, our ambiance. They don't necessarily like the place where their beautician ends up."

Josie nodded, trying to act like she'd been in lots and lots of beauty salons in her life.

Anna had picked up a pair of nail clippers and was flicking pieces of toenails onto a towel lying on the floor. "What sort of business do you own?"

"I'm a contractor."

"Really? Your company remodels apartments and all that?" Trish asked.

"Yes. Although we usually work on single-family homes."

"Wow, there aren't many of them in the city. Do you work outside of Manhattan? In Brooklyn Heights?"

"I work in a resort area . . . at the shore," Josie explained.

"Cool," Anna said.

"Too bad you don't work here," Trish said, putting down her nail file and standing up. "We could use someone to figure out what's wrong with the water pipes. Oh, I've gotta go. My very late client goes ballistic if she has to wait five minutes for me."

Josie resisted becoming involved in Elizabeth Arden's plumbing problems and peered down at her feet as Anna replaced one foot in the water and pulled out the other. "Oh, it's bleeding . . ."

"No, no. That's just a rose petal," Anna explained, removing the deep red oval from Josie's big toe.

Josie leaned over and realized that there were many petals floating in the water. "And what are the little round things in the bottom of the bowl?"

"Small disks of glass. I don't know why we put them in the water for pedicures and manicures, but we do."

"Oh. Actually, they feel good."

"That's the point . . . the flower petals are more for looks, I think." Anna glanced over her shoulder and saw that Trish had vanished. "Marguerite told me that you're interested in Pamela Peel."

"Yes. When did you talk to her?"

"She found me in the employees' lounge before I came out onto the floor. Everyone back there is talking about the murder, but she said you actually know some of the people involved and that you found the body."

"Yes, I found her. But I've never met her."

"She was coming here when I started working." Anna frowned. Josie didn't know whether it was the memory of Pamela Peel or her flat little toe, which was causing the distress. She waited, hoping for an explanation.

"Pamela Peel almost got me fired," Anna continued, still frowning. "I was glad when she left here."

"What happened?"

"It was partly my fault. I know that now. But I was young and new and so happy to be working in such a nice place."

"What happened?" Josie repeated the question.

"Well, I wasn't assigned to her right away. But I was so thrilled to see someone famous."

"You knew about her then?" Josie asked, amazed by just how famous a decorator could be.

"I did not know who she was, I mean she wasn't like a movie actor, but she was pointed out to me by someone else. And I was warned that she was very particular, that she wanted everything done exactly the way she wanted. So I was very worried when I was told that she was in a hurry and wanted a pedicure while she was having her nails done. I knew my job depended on her liking me."

"And she didn't?"

"No, we got along just fine. She was nice. I was nervous, of course, and the very first thing I did was spill a pan of water on the floor next to her. She laughed and told me not to worry about it. And I gave her a pedicure—an excellent pedicure. And she appreciated it so much that she asked for me the next time she made an appointment. I was thrilled. So thrilled that I ignored the fact that she hadn't tipped me that first time. Of course, I wasn't so thrilled when she didn't tip me the next time either. But she always said she was going to bring me more clients and I knew that was the most important thing. So I tried not to mind."

"But you did."

"A bit. But she came back week after week, which was important."

"Did she talk about herself, her life?"

"Oh yes, she was always talking about the parties she was going to and the famous people's homes she was decorating. But she never talked about personal things like some women do."

"You mean who she was dating."

"Not really. She talked about who she dated—but more like trophies, not like many clients who worry about men, about themselves. You know we hear many, many things from clients. They tell us their fears, hopes, dreams, and about their affairs. But not Pamela Peel, she does not let down her hair . . . her guard . . . and let anyone get into her life. And then, one Friday she not show up for her appointment and I hear that KiKi—her hairdresser—has gone to . . . to another place and Pamela Peel has gone with her. Right before the holidays too."

"What difference would that make?"

"Tips. Regular clients give good Christmas tips." Anna shrugged. "I'm being foolish. There was no way I would have gotten a tip from her. I have had clients like her since then. They always seem to be away—on a cruise or in the Caribbean or someplace wonderful—when it is time for the big tip. Oh well."

Josie's feet were done, each toe pink with polish and warm cream. Anna turned her attention to Josie's hands.

Josie was silent for a moment. All she seemed to be learning was that Pamela had been self-absorbed, well groomed, and cheap. Josie couldn't imagine how any of these things might have led to her murder.

"When Pamela Peel was coming here, she wasn't so famous. And no matter what she said, I didn't think she was so rich as she was always trying to be."

"What do you mean?"

Anna took the time to examine Josie's cuticles before she responded. "You must understand. There are many different types of rich people. They do not fall into one group. They are all different. Some are warm and wonderful and generous. Some are not so nice. Some are smart. Some stupid. You know what I'm trying to say."

"I think so."

"But all rich people are rich. They may not want to part with their money, but they have certain expectations."

"I'm not following you," Josie admitted.

"Pamela Peel did not strike me as rich. She was not comfortable with her money."

"You mean she was cheap," Josie said.

"No, just because a client has money doesn't mean she— or he—wants to give it away. But rich people do not have to worry about what things cost. If they want something, they can buy it. That is not the same as throwing money away. It's just that they have the . . . the resources to have and to do what they want."

"And you got the impression that things weren't like that for Pamela," Josie guessed.

Anna sighed. "Do you want me to trim this cuticle?"

Josie looked down at her hand. "Whatever you think. So you don't think Pamela was as rich as she claimed to be."

"What I think is that money was too important to her."

"Because she was careful with it?"

"No, because she loved showing off what she had bought. I thought it might be why she was such a good decorator. She lived for the display of wealth."

Josie frowned. That didn't sound at all like a description of Sam's place. "You said she almost got you fired," she reminded Anna.

"Yes, after she left."

"What? How did she do that?"

Anna put down her nail file and clippers and looked at Josie. "You must understand. She never complained about me when she was here. Never. Not to me. Not to anyone."

"But after she left . . ."

"Stories came back to us that she was telling other clients at this new place that I had caused an infection, that I did not sterilize my tools."

Josie looked down at the metal clippers now lying on a towel by her hands.

"I always keep my things clean. Everyone here knows how important that is. No one has ever gotten an infection or a fungus or anything from a manicure or pedicure I gave. Never!"

"Who told you about this?"

"My clients stopped coming to see me. I was puzzled and worried, of course. But then a woman whose nails I'd been doing for years asked me how clean my equipment was, and told me why she was worried. She had heard from a friend, a friend who followed Pamela Peel to the new salon, that I had caused Pamela Peel to almost lose a nail. I was very, very upset."

Josie frowned. She didn't know how to ask her next question without sounding like she doubted Anna's story. But she had to ask. "Why would Pamela Peel tell lies about your work?"

"That's just it. I have no idea. Except for the lack of tips, I never got the feeling that she was unhappy with my work. She came to see me week after week. She told her friends about me. She always said she liked my work." Anna shook her head and shook the bottle of nail polish at the same time. "I have no idea why she would lie about me. Unless, of course, she was trying to make an excuse for not tipping."

Trish returned with her client and Anna stopped talking.

SIXTEEN

C AROL'S HAIR LOOKED weird. There were four, maybe five, different shades of blond and red layered one upon the other. What might have been interesting and chic on a younger woman was just plain bizarre on the head of a woman well past sixty. Or so Josie thought, glancing at her as they walked up Fifth Avenue together.

"Awful, isn't it?" Carol said, grabbing the collar of her mink coat and pulling it up around her head. "I had a terrible time convincing Arturo to do it. The poor man must think I have the worst taste of anyone in the city."

"Then why did you ever have it done?"

"So we can check out this new place where Pamela Peel went. I'll call up, complain about the horrible job done at Elizabeth Arden, and beg for an appointment. Corrective coloring is very expensive. I'll bet they start to drool before I finish. I just hope my hair doesn't fall out before we find Pamela's killer."

Josie, who knew just how much Carol cared about her appearance, smiled. For Carol, this was one of those big sacrifices that mothers make for their children—even after those children had grown up. "But, what about me? I think my hair looks okay and . . ."

"You're going to find a nutritionist. You need to go on a diet."

125

"Carol . . . Oh, you mean I'm going to go to Pamela's nutritionist."

"Yes, if we can find him. I have an address and phone number, but they may not be current. Anyway, you should eat a lot for dinner tonight. Tomorrow you may be living on baby lettuces and lemon juice."

Josie had no intention of going on any diet, but that wasn't the issue now. "Anna, the woman who did my nails, had nothing good to say about Pamela Peel. Among other things, she didn't tip."

"Really? I wouldn't have thought she was cheap . . . Maybe she just didn't rely on the good opinion of the people who worked for her. . . . Josie, that's it! That's the next place we look!"

"Where?"

"Pamela hired workers, workers like you and the women you hire. We should find them and talk to them. They might have some very interesting insights, don't you think?"

"I suppose it's possible. Do you think one of them might have killed her?"

Carol frowned. "I have no idea. I just wish we could find out who she was dating before she died."

"Or maybe more about her family. Carol, is it possible that we've been going about all this in the wrong way? Shepard Henderson didn't tell us anything, and, so far, we haven't heard anything significant from the spa."

"Let's give this spa thing one more day. I can't believe any woman would spend hours, days even, having her hair and nails done and getting facials and massages—and not give away some of the personal details about her life." A man walking what looked to Josie to be at least a dozen dogs passed by, and Carol paused to smile at a little Yorkie struggling to keep up with the retrievers, Dalmatians, and collies in the group. Then she turned her attention back to Josie.

"You know, I was wondering if we might ask Betty for some help."

"I don't know when she has a sitter."

"I was hoping she could do some phone work for us."

"Phone work?" Josie repeated the words as she followed Carol around the corner. A blast of icy wind nearly took her breath away as it blew grit into her eyes. "What sort of phone work?" she asked when she was able to speak again.

"If we can convince Betty to call a lot of contractors, as though she's having some work done in her apartment, and ask for references from Peel and Henderson—or some such story—she might be able to discover the names of some of the workers—carpenters and, you know, other people like that—who worked for Peel and Henderson. And then we could figure out a way to ask them questions about Pamela."

Josie, who hoped that anyone who worked for her—"carpenters and, you know, other people like that"—wouldn't talk about her behind her back, especially if she had just died, didn't answer.

"We have to find out who killed her before Sammy is arrested for something he didn't do," Carol reminded her.

"Of course. I was just . . . just thinking that maybe we should find out where Pamela lived and talk to her neighbors. That's what I'd do if we were back home. Of course, I don't know how we'd find out where she lives."

"That's not a problem. I know where she lives. But, you know, Josie dear, things aren't quite the same here as they are on your island."

"What do you mean?"

"Well, dear, you can't just go knocking on doors and asking questions. You can't even get to most people's front doors."

Josie thought about Sam's doorman and nodded. A half dozen little girls, dressed in light blue uniforms as well as an assortment of boots, parkas, and hats raced down the sidewalk giggling despite the weight of massive packs on their narrow shoulders. They were followed by two stern-looking nannies who seemed to be paying absolutely no attention to their charges as they chatted in a language Josie didn't recognize. "Where did she live?" Josie asked.

"A few blocks from here." Carol pulled back her suede glove and checked her Cartier watch. "We have the time to walk by there, if you're curious."

"Yes, I am."

"Then we can cross over on Sixty-seventh. And you can tell me everything you learned from Anna on the way."

Josie did as Carol asked, although there was little to tell. But their walk, as Carol had said, wasn't long and in a few minutes they were standing on Park Avenue in front of a large prewar apartment house. "This is it. Pamela lived on the fifth floor. She had a one-bedroom place, but there's lots of space in these old buildings. She used the maid's suite for an at-home office."

"Maid's suite?"

"It sounds more impressive than it is. A small bedroom, a tiny sitting area, and bath behind the kitchen. There's usually only one minuscule window that looks out on an airshaft. Almost no one uses them for servants anymore, but the space is invaluable for nurseries, home offices, and the like. I would have adored one when Sammy was growing up. You can't imagine how his toys and clutter used to absolutely fill our apartment. There were a few years there when you couldn't cross the Orientals in your bare feet for fear of stepping on one of those horrid little green plastic soldiers. Dreadful!"

"Tyler and I had the same sort of problem with G.I. Joe action figures," Josie said. Although, of course, she had never owned an Oriental carpet in her life. "I don't suppose you know anyone else in this building?" she asked.

"No, sorry. I have a friend who lives up a block. . . ."

"Well, then you could ask her. It's likely that she might know someone who lives just around the corner."

Carol chuckled. "Josie, dear, you know nothing at all about New York City."

"No, I guess not."

"We should get going. Sammy will be at my place in less than fifteen minutes and I need to stop at the bakery on the way."

"I thought we were just going to have cocktails at your place and then go on to a nearby restaurant."

"We were, but I was thinking that perhaps we could stay home this evening. Sammy might even be convinced to chat about his life with Pamela if we can get him to relax."

"Why do you think that's more likely to happen at home in your apartment? Carol, you don't want anyone to see your new hairdo!"

"Well, dear, you may not know your neighbors in the city, but, believe me, all you have to do is appear in public looking terrible for everyone you've met in the past ten years to show up."

Carol Birnbaum lived on one of the top floors of a high-rise apartment house built during the building boom of the late eighties. She and Josie had stopped at a fabulous bakery on the way and Josie carried a shopping bag filled with a selection of bread and rolls, each one purported to be "Sammy's favorite," as they walked into the apartment. The foyer opened onto the living room and they could look out the wall of windows to a fabulous view of downtown New York City. The women paused for a moment to enjoy the sight, and then Carol reached out and switched on the lights.

"The kitchen is to your right," Carol said.

But Josie wasn't listening. She walked slowly into the living room, looking around. "Carol, this is gorgeous."

And it was. The walls were painted a soft apricot. Two

couches, upholstered in rich gold silk, had deeper jewel-toned silk pillows tossed on them. A jade green mantel surrounded a fireplace on the wall across from the windows. Large glass lamps stood on enameled end tables. And gold sconces with cream-colored candles shared the wall space with golden frames around large, colorful, modern watercolors. A big Samarkand carpet pulled all the elements together and walking across its cushioning nap was a pleasure after the hard sidewalks and streets outside.

"Thank you." Carol was hanging her fur in the closet next to the front door so Josie couldn't see her face, but she sounded rather strange.

"Carol! Henderson and Peel decorated this place, didn't they?" Josie asked, suddenly understanding Carol's uncharacteristic reticence.

"Yes. Well, Pamela did. Yes." Carol sighed. "If only I'd gone with another decorating firm." She sighed again. "Come into the kitchen. I'll get out some munchies, pour some wine, and tell you all about it."

The kitchen was as marvelous as the living room. The cabinets were black cherry, the countertops pink granite, the tile and paint on the walls a deep eggplant. The combination was unusual, but it worked. Josie made a mental note to remember this the next time Island Contracting was hired to remodel a kitchen. Three stools, their seats covered with plum silk, were tucked underneath the counter. Josie pulled one out, perched on it, and waited for Carol to explain.

"You may know that Sammy has dated a lot of women," she started.

"Of course." She didn't like it, but she knew it.

Carol sighed. "But no one for very long. His girlfriend in college joined the Peace Corps the week they graduated. There was a woman in law school who I thought he might be serious about, but then she accepted a position with a law firm in San Francisco and he came back to New York.

Here . . . well, playing the field is easy for a good-looking young professional in the city. There are thousands of single women looking for straight, successful men. Sammy just couldn't seem to settle on one. And then he came over to see me one evening after a long day in court and met Pamela Peel."

"Love at first sight?" Josie asked, hoping the answer was no.

"Yes."

Oh well. "You must have been pleased," Josie said, hoping she didn't sound as shaky as she felt.

"I was thrilled. Pamela was exactly what I had been hoping for for Sammy—gorgeous, successful, intelligent, ready to settle down and have children—Do you think Sammy would like olives or artichokes marinated in herbs?"

"I . . ." Josie was too surprised by the change of topic to make an intelligent comment.

"We'll have both," Carol continued without waiting for an answer to her question. She emptied two plastic pint containers on a large black pottery platter and surrounded the resulting mounds with disks cut from a long baguette. "Sammy's not eating enough to keep an ant alive."

"Do you think he's upset that Pamela's dead?" Josie asked.

Carol's head was in her refrigerator and she either didn't hear or didn't choose to answer Josie's question. "There!" She reappeared with a large chunk of cheese. "This is Spanish. I can't remember its name . . . starts with an M. Sammy will love it. What were you saying, dear?"

"I . . . nothing. You were telling me about Pamela and Sam's relationship," she reminded her.

"Well, now that I think of it, there's not all that much to tell. They started dating, went everywhere together. They went on vacation together. Even rented a summer place out on the island . . . Long Island," she explained in case Josie hadn't picked up on the reference. "They did everything together except make plans for the future."

"You mean they didn't become engaged to be married," Josie said quietly.

"Exactly. I never understood it. Even after she decorated his place, they said nothing publicly about the future. And then, suddenly, Sammy announced he was going to change careers. And a few months later he was gone and a photo of Pamela Peel on the arm of a very rich venture capitalist was on the society page of the Sunday *New York Times*."

"You said . . . When you were talking about the night Sam took you and Pamela to the Rainbow Room, I got the impression that he wanted the three of you to be close," Josie said.

"Close." Carol stood in the middle of the kitchen, a bottle of Cabernet in one hand, a corkscrew in the other, as though mulling over the question. "We did a lot of things together. I couldn't say I was close to Pamela. She . . . she never really let me share her life." She put the wine on the counter and looked up at Josie with a smile. "She was nothing like you, dear. You've been so sweet and let me into your life. You know how I feel about you and Tyler. . . ."

Just when Carol might have gone on and given Josie a hint concerning what she thought her own future with Sam might be, a buzzer interrupted them. Carol's face broke into a wide smile and Josie realized, for the first time, just how anxiously she had been awaiting her son's appearance.

As Carol hurried off to open the door for Sam, Josie sat and reminded herself that finding the identity of the person who had killed Pamela was the important thing. Once there was no longer any danger that Sam would be arrested, she would worry about whether or not she had met him on the rebound and if they had a future together.

"Good God, Mother. What the hell did you do to your hair?"

Sam had arrived. Josie slid off the stool and went to greet him.

"I know. Dreadful, isn't it? First thing tomorrow morning, I'm going to look for someone to undo the damage." Carol followed her son into the kitchen, smiling happily. "We were thinking of takeout here tonight instead of going to a restaurant."

"Whatever you want to do," Sam answered. "If you want to go out, you could wear some sort of hat, couldn't you?"

"I suppose, but there's sushi, Chinese, Thai, Italian, Greek, and a good deli all less than a block away. Why don't we just make a phone call or two and have dinner delivered?"

"Whatever you want," Sam repeated, walking over and kissing the top of Josie's head. "Did you have a good day?" he asked.

Josie leaned against him and allowed herself to be warmed by his concern. "Yes. I may just become addicted to this life of leisure."

"Is that a bottle of California Cabernet I see?" Sam asked, releasing Josie without acknowledging her comment.

"We were waiting for you to open it," Carol said.

"Well, wait no longer," Sam said, picking up the bottle and corkscrew and getting to work.

Carol was busy fussing with their appetizers and Josie sat back and watched mother and son. They worked together well, moving around the small space without getting in each other's way and she was soon sipping wine and selecting olives with her newly pink fingernails. "How was your day?" she asked Sam.

"Not bad. Oh, I met Jon for lunch and he gave me a message from Betty to you. She asked that you give her a call."

"Why don't you do that now, dear? You could use the phone next to my bed—if you want some privacy," Carol added rather pointedly.

"That's a good idea." Josie picked up her wine goblet and stood up. "Where. . . ?"

"Right through the living room," Carol answered the unasked question.

Carol's bedroom was small and almost filled by her king-size bed. There was a phone sitting on the brass nightstand and Josie put her glass down carefully, picked up the receiver, and dialed Betty's phone number. Betty answered almost immediately. Josie heard JJ crying in the background.

"Poor little guy has lots of gas tonight," Betty explained. "But Jon's with him. Which is just fine. He probably won't be able to hear what I'm telling you over his son's wailing."

"Listen, Betty, I was going to call and I want to ask you a question before Sam comes in the room. Could you possibly make a few—well, maybe more than a few—phone calls tomorrow. It's to help Sam," she added.

"No problem. Just tell me who you want me to call and why."

"We're looking for people—contracting companies—that worked for Henderson and Peel. Carol thought that perhaps people who worked for Pamela could tell us something more about her. And I sure hope she's right. We haven't learned much except that she was a lousy tipper."

"Even in New York, I don't think that particular habit could get you killed," Betty said. "But, listen, I'd be happy to do it. I'm looking for someone to refinish the floors in our place. There are some tiny splinters popping up in the hall-way and I don't want JJ to get hurt when he starts to crawl. I'll call all the major upscale contractors, mention Henderson and Peel and see what I can find out. Is that what you're looking for?"

"Perfect!" Josie picked up her wineglass and sipped. "Now tell me why you wanted me to call you."

Five minutes later, Carol entered her bedroom and discovered Josie kneeling on the floor. "What are you doing?"

"I . . . I spilled my wine. I'm trying to make sure it doesn't stain your rug." She was rubbing the carpet with a pink towel that she had pulled off the rack in the bathroom.

"Why don't I call Sammy to bring us a sponge and . . ."

"Don't do that!" Josie insisted, grabbing Carol's arm and pulling her down to the floor. "I talked to Betty. She says . . ." Josie took a deep breath and finished the sentence. "She says that Jon told her that Sam refused to tell the police if he's seen Pamela Peel since he returned to the city."

SEVENTEEN

THEY DECIDED NOT to tell Sam what Betty had told Josie. As Carol said, "After all, Sam's a smart man, if he wants to tell us, he will. If he doesn't want to tell us or talk about it, we can't force him to. And, if we don't tell him we know, we won't have to tell him what we're going to do."

"What are we going to do?" Josie whispered, following Carol back into the living room.

"We're going to try to get him to talk about Pamela. . . . No, you shouldn't be the one to do it," she added. "This is a job for an interfering mother. I'll do it!"

Sam was stretched out on the sofa, glass in hand, when they reentered the living room. "How about Thai for dinner?" he suggested. "Is King of Siam still in business, Mother?"

"New owners. New name—something about a rainbow. Still wonderful, wonderful food," she answered, sitting down on the other sofa and examining a tiny Lalique bowl sitting on her coffee table as though she'd never seen it before.

"Mother, are you okay?" Sam asked.

"Just a bit tired. Getting a really bad dye job takes it out of someone my age, you know. Josie, dear, there are a number of menus in the drawer underneath the wall phone in the kitchen. Would you mind getting them for us?"

"Sure!"

Josie had no trouble locating the drawer, which was

136

stuffed with menus of many shapes and sizes. She laid them out on the counter and, finding three that appeared to feature Thai food, she returned to the living room with them in hand. Neither Sam nor his mother appeared to have moved. Josie handed Carol the menus and sat down.

"What do you want?" Carol asked.

"I don't know anything at all about Thai food," Josie said. "Is it like Chinese?"

"No." Sam sat up and held out his hand to his mother. "Why don't you let me order? I know the type of thing Josie likes. I'll pick out a selection of dishes and we can share."

"Wonderful! Just don't forget how much I like Pad Thai," Carol added, beaming at her clever son.

"Fine." Sam stood up and headed toward the kitchen phone. "Would you like another glass of wine while I'm here?" he called over his shoulder.

"I'd love one," Josie said.

"And have one yourself," his mother suggested. "Remember you're in the city now. It's not as though you have to drive home tonight."

Sam didn't answer and Josie heard him dialing the phone. When the restaurant picked up and he seemed to be involved in a rather long conversation about the relative hotness of various dishes, Carol leaned over to her. "Let's wait until he's had another glass or two of wine and then I'm going to flat out ask him about Pamela Peel."

"Okay, but I don't see . . ."

"Here's your wine, Josie." Sam put the glass down on the coffee table in front of her. "Now why don't you tell me what you and Mother have been whispering about ever since I arrived?"

Josie glanced over at Carol, panicked. "We . . ."

"We'll tell you in our own good time," Carol said. "Women like to have their little secrets, you know."

If this type of coyness was as unlike his mother as it was

Josie, Sam didn't seem to feel the need to protest. "Fine." He picked up his glass and drank it down. "Perhaps I should open another bottle."

Carol applauded his suggestion. "Excellent idea!"

"When are we going to pick up dinner?" Josie asked.

"It will be delivered to the desk in the lobby and they'll call us to come down and pick it up," Carol explained. "It won't take any time at all. The restaurant is just around the corner and everything is either stir-fried or steamed."

"Good. I'm starving," Josie added, feeling someone should say something.

Sam pushed the plate of olives and artichokes in her direction. "I left the cheese in the kitchen. I'll get it and the wine."

"Josie and I had an interesting day, you know," Carol stated.

"Well, your hair did. I can see that. What did you do?" he asked Josie.

"I had a facial and a manicure—and a pedicure," Josie explained, kicking off her shoes and wagging her fingers and toes at him.

"Oh, very nice, I guess."

"You guess?" his mother repeated his words.

"Carol . . ." Josie wanted to tell her to be quiet. This conversation could only upset her.

"Josie did all that to look better for you," Carol continued, ignoring Josie.

Sam looked from one woman to the other. "Josie knows she doesn't have to do that. At least not for me. I love her the way she is."

Josie felt tears welling up and bit her lips. This was the Sam Richardson she loved. This was the Sam Richardson she had been missing ever since Pamela Peel's body appeared in his apartment. She smiled at him, but remained silent.

"But I can't tell you how glad I am that you didn't go to

the same hairdresser as Mother did." He winked at her and got down to the business of refilling their glasses.

Josie picked up hers and sipped, taking a moment to admire her nails before getting up and walking to the window. "You have a fabulous view," she said, looking down at the southern tip of Manhattan.

"That was one of the reasons I bought this place," Carol said, standing up and joining her. "Of course the view has changed a lot since I moved in, but I still love it."

Josie took a deep breath and turned back to Sam. "Carol said that Pamela Peel decorated this place as well as yours."

He looked around and agreed. "That's true. I've always thought this place was much more successful than mine."

No one in the room was going to disagree with that. "This place is beautiful," Josie said sincerely. She turned to Carol. "What did you ask for?"

"What do you mean?"

"Well, did you say that you wanted something formal or elegant or whatever . . . or did you leave all the decisions up to Henderson and Peel?"

"I left all the decisions up to Pamela. In this case, it was just Peel. I don't remember seeing Shepard Henderson during the entire project. Too bad too," Carol added a bit wistfully. "I've always thought he was something of a hunk."

"Good-looking, yes, but a hunk . . . ," Josie began and then realized that Sam didn't—and shouldn't—know that she and Shepard Henderson had met.

Carol seemed to realize the same thing at the same time. She got up quickly and hurried to the wall intercom to call down to the doorman and ask if their dinner had arrived. "Sammy, will you go down and pick it up now?" she asked. "It will take less time that way and Josie and I really are hungry."

"Of course." He jumped to his feet.

Neither Carol nor Josie said anything until the door

slammed behind him. Then, "Do you think he realized what I just said?" Josie asked.

"I have no idea. We'll just have to hope that he didn't, or that if he did, he forgets it before he comes back up here. I thought everything was going so well. When you brought up Pamela's work here, I was a bit doubtful, but it was perfect. Sam couldn't possibly have known you were interested in anything other than my apartment."

"But what am I going to say if he asks how I know what Shepard Henderson looks like? Oh, I've got it! I'll just explain that I saw photographs of him in Sam's albums."

"Brilliant! But if he doesn't ask, don't mention Shep Henderson again."

"Oh, believe me, I won't!" Josie paused before continuing. "How do you think Sam looks?"

"Tired and unhappy. He'd usually spend the evening teasing me about my new hairdo. And most of them haven't been nearly as odd as this one!" Carol added, frowning.

"But he'll be just fine once we discover who killed Pamela Peel," Josie said, wishing it was the truth. It was possible that Sam was upset by Pamela's death. "Don't you think?" she added when Carol didn't respond.

"I hope so. I certainly hope so." Carol sighed and then seemed to gather herself together. "Where shall we eat? In here or the kitchen?"

"Whatever you think."

"We'll eat here. I'll just go get placemats and plates. You clear off the coffee table, dear. And maybe get the candles off the mantel and put them in the middle. Perhaps they will cheer us up a bit."

By the time Sam returned, a large bag full of sweet-smelling food in hand, there were three places set up around a trio of lit candles. Fresh (and in Sam's case, full) glasses of wine sat by straw placemats and black enameled chopsticks, and fine linen napkins surrounded large white china plates.

"Sit down and have more wine, Sammy. Josie and I will take the food out to the kitchen and put it on platters."

"This is great, Mother, but why not make things easier and just pass around the cardboard containers?"

"That's a good idea," Josie said, realizing that Carol was looking very tired.

"If you really think so."

"The Pad Thai, a double order, is on top," Sam said, starting to remove a half dozen cartons from the bag and lay them all out. "Josie, the drawer to the left of the sink is full of silverware. Grab a bunch of big spoons, and maybe a bottle of water and some glasses. We're going to be thirsty after eating all this."

"I can—"

"Yes, you can, Mother, but so can Josie."

"I can and I will," Josie said, hurrying back to the kitchen and doing as Sam had asked. When she returned to the living room, spoons in hand, Carol was already digging into a carton of spring rolls.

"Hmm. Looks good."

"Delicious," Sam agreed. He spooned a pile of thin noodles and shrimp onto his plate then passed the carton on to his mother.

They all served themselves and began to eat with Sam pausing only to explain an unfamiliar ingredient or to warn the women about an unusually spicy dish. But after the first pangs of hunger had been assuaged, Sam spoke up. "I don't remember," he began slowly. "How did Pamela come to decorate this place, Mother?"

"Everyone I know was either hiring or trying to hire Henderson and Peel. How could I have considered anyone else?"

"But I don't remember you having a decorator for your other apartments."

"Well, maybe not a decorator as such, but there was this lovely man in the furniture department at Bloomingdale's who was such a big help with the place I had before this. Back when you were living at home, I didn't have enough money to spend on decorations, much less pay for a decorator."

Josie stopped shoveling food into her mouth long enough to ask a question. "How does a decorator get paid?"

"Well, it depends," Carol answered. "When I worked with a decorator employed by a store, they were paid by the store. I mean, I didn't pay anything extra for their services."

"But did they make a commission on what you bought or were they just paid a salary?" Josie asked.

"I have no idea." Carol examined a huge shrimp before popping it in her mouth and chewing thoughtfully. "I did sometimes feel that I was being steered toward the most expensive items though. And at Bloomingdale's that can run to a whole lot of money."

"Peel and Henderson worked on an hourly and cost-plus basis," Sam spoke up. "And on some of their larger projects they insisted on a retainer up front."

"How did all that work?" Josie asked. She wasn't surprised at Sam's knowledge. She had been asking him to check out Island Contracting's contracts for the past few years.

"They had a flat hourly rate—about two hundred dollars per when I left the city, but I suspect it's more now—for planning the job, travel to stores and galleries, time spent with the client, stuff like that. They also got wholesale prices on furniture, accessories, even artwork, and they added a standard markup before billing the client. They added twenty percent to the bills of subcontractors as well." He looked up from his food and over at Josie. "Sound like a lot to you?"

Josie grinned. "It does."

"But a decorator is a lot like a contractor," Sam explained.

"You get money up front when you start a job, right? Usually a third of the final payment."

"Yes, but I need that money to pay for supplies. It sounds like the retainer is just to keep the decorator working on your project. And if I ever tried to charge an hourly fee for time spent traveling back and forth to the lumberyard, or meetings with clients, I'd be laughed right out of a job. It sounds to me like being a decorator is pretty cushy."

Sam leaned back, lifted his arms over his head and stretched. "You might have trouble finding decorators to agree with you."

"Why?"

"It's a different type of work than you do," Sam replied. "It depends more on the whim of the employer, for one thing."

"What do you mean?" Carol asked.

Sam answered her question with a question. "How many times did you change your mind about fabric for the curtains in your bedroom?"

"I'm not sure. Maybe three or four . . . possibly more, I guess." His mother frowned. "Did Pamela complain about me?"

"No, she just mentioned it. As I recall, she said you were better than most clients. She used to tell stories of clients who had entire bathrooms ripped out because they didn't like the floor tiles. Or . . . I remember she told me about a woman who had two dozen pillows made up in different upholstery fabrics because she couldn't decide which she wanted to use."

"What did she do with the pillows in the fabric she rejected?" Carol asked.

"She gave them away to a thrift store and took a substantial tax deduction. I remember Pamela telling me that the woman wanted a receipt from Henderson and Peel so she could take a tax deduction. A receipt for twice the amount she had actually spent."

"Did they give it to her?" Carol asked.

Sam shrugged. "I don't know. Probably. Pamela knew that I didn't want to hear about anything illegal. I have my law license to protect, after all."

"I've had difficult clients who want to make changes," Josie said.

"Yes, but your clients know what you're going to do— pretty much—when you start a job, right? You have blueprints of the job. And they know they have a certain amount to spend on materials. And if they go over that amount when they pick out appliances or whatever, they have to pay extra, right?"

"Sure. What else?"

"What else is that clients frequently try to get decorators to get discounts for them. Pamela always said that a good decorator can save a client money, but more than a few of her clients wanted discounts that were unreasonable. And, in this city, a firm's reputation is its future. High-profile clients can be pretty demanding and they do tend to get what they want. I always suspected that some of Henderson and Peel's less prominent clients were charged a bit more to compensate for the lower fees charged to the rich and famous."

"Really?" Carol looked around her apartment as though wondering for what, if anything, she had been overcharged.

"Island Contracting would never treat clients like that!"

"I seem to remember a family who got a great discount on the addition at the back of their bungalow just a few years ago."

"I . . . oh, I remember. But that was different. The Giambrettis are some of the last fishermen on the island. They really couldn't afford to build anything, but they were expecting triplets at the time. I just gave them a discount and took a loss on the project. I didn't—I wouldn't ever—add to a rich person's bill to make up for it."

"But you could give the Giambrettis a break because you had done a few big jobs for wealthy summer people in the same year," Sam reminded her.

"I suppose." Josie wasn't at all willing to put herself and her company in the same corner as someone who would give a financial break to those who need it the least. "But my reputation, Island Contracting's reputation, doesn't depend on working for a few wealthy or prominent people."

"Really? Weren't you enthusiastic about remodeling the Point House because you thought the job was going to be covered in *Architectural Digest*? Don't I remember you telling me that?"

Josie couldn't do anything but admit the truth of that. Of course Hurricane Agatha had destroyed the Point House and probably Island Contracting's only chance for fame.

"Things are different in the city, Josie dear. There are so many decorating firms, so much more competition than on the island. Henderson and Peel were always in danger of becoming one of the lesser firms and no longer being offered the best jobs."

"And that would have killed Pamela if someone hadn't already done it," Sam said and then added, "but let's stop talking about Pamela, or Henderson and Peel, or decorators, or murder. Let's just enjoy the food and the company and the evening."

Carol and Josie exchanged meaningful looks; so much for their well-laid plans!

EIGHTEEN

A MAZINGLY ENOUGH, THAT night turned out to be a lot like the nights Josie had imagined when Sam first suggested she accompany him to New York City. Slightly drunk and certainly more than well fed, they had left Carol's apartment with their arms around each other and strolled slowly back to Sam's place. The city had been enchanting: lights glowing in the crisp, cold air. Everyone seemed to be well dressed and everyone appeared to be hurrying off to have fun.

They walked down Park Avenue, peeking in windows. Restaurants—tables covered with glasses, silver, linen, and flowers—were full of people, leaning toward one another over plates of food, all talking at once.

They walked a block over to Madison Avenue and window-shopped, making jokes about the expensive, desirable, and not so desirable objects on display. They talked and laughed, relaxed as though they didn't have a care in the world. When Sam suggested they stop in at a little café for a nightcap, Josie readily agreed, not wanting to pass up an opportunity to be part of the New York nightlife she had always heard so much about.

Sam asked that they be seated near the window so Josie could look out at the crowd passing.

"It's marvelous," Josie said after they had ordered, at their waiter's suggestion, two Big Apple martinis.

"Having a good time?" Sam asked.

"You know it!"

"This is what I wanted our time here to be like," Sam said, a bit wistful.

Josie reached across the tiny table and took his hand. "It isn't your fault that Pamela Peel was murdered."

"No, but I do keep wondering why she was in my apartment. Except for Mom and a few friends, I don't have any real contact with the city anymore. Jon keeps asking who hates me so much that they wanted to connect Pamela's murder to my life, and the only answer I have is that I don't know," he ended sadly.

Josie had an inspired idea. "Sam, maybe this had nothing to do with you. Maybe it has to do with selling your apartment. Maybe the body was placed there to be found by someone looking around. Maybe someone doesn't want that apartment to be sold."

Sam looked skeptical.

"Sam, it is an idea, right?"

"I suppose, but—"

"So let's think it through. You told me last Christmas that you were going to sell your condo, right?"

"Yes."

"Is that when you decided to do it?"

"Pretty much then. I'd thought about it once in a while since leaving the city. There is a certain amount of annoying paperwork that goes with being a landlord. But I had a great tenant who kept the place up and who paid enough rent to cover all the monthly fees and taxes. Real estate prices in this part of town are only going to go up. Keeping the place made financial sense. And, to begin with, it made emotional sense as well."

Their waiter returned with two huge martini glasses topped with shimmering, thin, sugared apple slices. Josie waited until he'd left to ask another question. "What do you mean, 'emotional sense'?"

Sam smiled across the table at her. "Josie, the first few days I was on the island, I came close to turning around and running back to New York."

"Why?"

"Well, in the first place, almost every single person I knew had told me I was doing the wrong thing. Two of the men I worked closely with for years had spent what seemed like every lunch hour for the last month I was here telling me that I was acting like an idiot, that my move was just the result of an exaggerated case of male menopause and I shouldn't make spur-of-the-moment decisions that could change my life forever. I suppose that may be part of the reason I rented my place out instead of putting it on the market right away. There was a part of me that doubted my decision."

"Sam, you weren't running off to Tahiti to paint naked women. You were moving less than two hundred miles away and buying an established business, a business you knew a lot about."

"But I was giving up my career. And I admit it: I was burned out, not just professionally but personally. I no longer enjoyed living here. But there were days when I thought that my friends might be right, that I was just another male becoming involved in a flurry of activity to try to forget that I was getting old.

"I arrived on the island on a day in early spring when icy rain was falling and the winds were high. I went to check out the store I'd bought and discovered that the roof leaked. Rain had poured right down onto shelves full of expensive imported liquors. My house, which had seemed perfect when I'd bought it less than a month before, looked bleak and inhospitable. I didn't know anyone on the island. If I hadn't been so exhausted, and so worried about the strange clanking sound my car had started making sometime around exit fifty-nine on the parkway, I think I would have turned around and come right back."

"I'm glad you didn't," Josie said quietly.

"I'm glad I didn't too. But, until the day that you came into my store looking for a phone, I had doubts. Serious doubts." He picked the candied apple slice off the side of his glass and popped it in his mouth. "Anyway, I told myself that I was keeping the condo as an investment, but for a while there it was also my fall-back position. But then my tenant was transferred overseas sometime around Thanksgiving and, after thinking about it for a few weeks, I decided to sell." He looked up at Josie and smiled. "My future's on an island a bit smaller than Manhattan."

Josie sipped her drink. It was slightly sweet and very strong. But she didn't need it; she was feeling wonderful.

"But I don't see how selling or not selling my apartment could possibly have anything to do with Pamela's murder," Sam continued, and her elation vanished.

"What if a potential buyer had opened that window seat?" Josie asked. "Don't you think that would have stopped the sale?"

"But, Josie, it didn't get that far. And it wouldn't have. No apartment goes on the market without all sorts of inspections. Someone would have found the body before a potential buyer did."

"So why was the body there?"

"Josie, you know why. It was placed there to implicate me in her murder." He leaned across the table and stared at her. "What else?"

"I don't know," Josie admitted.

"There can't be any other reason," Sam insisted, sounding angry.

Josie bit her bottom lip. They had been having such a nice time and it was unlike Sam to respond in this manner. "How

many people knew you were going to be selling your place?
The man who was renting it from you?"

"No, he told me he was leaving the place vacant. But he
never asked if I had any plans for it. He's been in Singapore
since the first week in December. I think we can assume he
is out of the picture."

"Did your Realtor list it anyplace?"

"Not yet. I wanted to come clean everything out before
she even looked through it. I didn't think I'd left anything of
value here, but I wanted to check before it was officially put
on the market."

"Why did you leave those photo albums in the closet? I
would have thought that you would have had to clean everything out before you left."

"I did. They weren't there when I left. That closet was
empty."

"Then where were they?"

"You know, I think I may have left them in the window
seat."

"Where I found Pamela?"

"Exactly."

"You know," she said slowly, "it's a perfect place to hide a
body. It's almost as though someone built it for that reason."

Sam chuckled. "I used to keep records, case files and the
like, in it. Before the place was redecorated, I had four old
oak file cabinets in the living room. Pamela hated them. Said
they made the place look like an office in a trashy noir detective film. The window seat was built so I'd have a place to
store paperwork. Anyway, I put a lot of my personal things,
records and so on, in my storage locker in the basement when
I rented out the place. But I didn't want to leave photos down
there. It's supposed to be dry and all, but photographs deteri-
orate so easily. I brought most of them along with me to the
island. But I think I left some of them, the most recent albums, in the window seat."

Josie picked up her glass and peered at the remaining golden liquid. She realized the import of what Sam had just said. He had brought many of his photo albums to the island with him, but not the ones he had most recently filled. Not the ones with photographs of Pamela Peel.

"You had your hair cut, didn't you?" Sam asked, changing the subject.

"Yes. Do you like it?"

"Sure. You know I always like the way you look."

"Speaking of looks, did you really like what Pamela did in your apartment? It's so different from your place at home," she added.

"Well, it's not me, that's for sure. But, Josie, you know me. I don't pay a whole lot of attention to things that don't matter to me. And the way that apartment was decorated was one of those things. I chose it because of the location, the building, and because I could afford to buy it. And, when I lived there, I furnished it pretty much the way I've furnished my house. I bought things when I needed them. I sure don't buy anything I think is ugly. But when I buy furniture, I care how functional it is—whether it fits my spaces, whether it will do what I need it to do."

"I guess that's not the way Pamela liked things," Josie said. She was a bit hesitant. This was the closest they had come to actually talking about Pamela.

"I don't think many decorators furnish a place the way I do. Even the ones that claim to be interested mainly in functionality want to buy all new functional things. And, remember, my apartment wasn't exactly like the house you know. My house now is nice because I can afford nice things. When I was starting out, I bought mostly junk because that was what I could afford. And, to tell the truth, once I live with something for a while, I don't really see it. What I replaced, I replaced because it fell apart, not because it was ugly or in bad taste. But all that changed when I started seeing Pamela. I'm afraid she took my apartment as a personal affront. And I could see what she meant. After all, every time anyone came over, they commented on the fact that the hand of a talented and well-known designer had rather obviously not been at work in my home."

"So she got tired of hearing those comments?" It was something Josie understood. Sam was not only furnishing his house in the dunes, but also remodeling it. And he didn't always ask for her expertise.

"Yes. And then she gave me the decorating job as a Christmas present."

"That's what your mother said. She also said that Pamela announced the present at a party . . . in front of all your guests."

"Yes, so, of course, I couldn't refuse."

"Sounds a little manipulative," Josie responded without thinking.

"Oh, I think she was just trying to be generous. It was really very sweet of her."

Josie wasn't about to change her first opinion, but she wasn't going to speak up again. "So you liked the way it turned out?"

For the first time, Sam hesitated before answering. "Not particularly. I did hate the whole decorating process. To tell the truth, after Pamela had tried to drag me to furniture showrooms two weekends in a row, I protested and refused to go. So Pamela did what she wanted without any input from me. Well, not a lot of input. I did tell her that I needed to have files somewhere in the place and a few other things. I really have no one to blame for how depressing that place turned out but myself. Every time Pamela asked me a question, I told her to go ahead and make the decision herself. She was the professional, after all. Now, of course, thanks to you, I know that I placed a real burden on her."

"What do you mean? Thanks to me?"

"Josie, you're always complaining about clients who can't, or won't, make up their minds. I put Pamela in that exact same position and then I was critical of the decisions I forced her to make."

"So you don't like the way she decorated your place?" Josie asked again.

"Not really. But it's not as though I lived there for very long. I probably would have made some changes if I hadn't retired and moved away."

"I always feel uncomfortable when a client doesn't like my work. And I would think it would be even more difficult if the work I was doing was for someone I knew," Josie said, thinking she was being subtle.

"Like the deck you designed for my house?" Sam asked, a twinkle in his deep blue eyes.

Josie laughed. "Yeah, like that. And one day you're going to discover that my design is superior to the one you came up with."

"Can I get you another drink?" Their waiter materialized by the side of the table.

Sam raised his eyebrows at Josie.

"I'll have one if you will." She wasn't really interested in more alcohol, but she didn't want this evening to end.

"We'll have two more. And perhaps something small to munch on."

"We have a bar menu." The waiter pulled a stiff cardboard rectangle from his pocket and offered it to them with a smile.

"What do you think?" Sam asked Josie, their heads together as they read through the list.

Everything looked wonderful. "Whatever."

"We'll have the Venetian tower," Sam announced.

"What's that?" she asked when their waiter had gone off to the kitchen.

"A fancy name for all sorts of little Italian munchies. They bring it out on a three-tier plate, hence the tower. They also have a Japanese selection called Tokyo Rose Tower. Or Mexican—Bandito Tower. I don't know who names these things," he added.

She smiled at him.

"Josie, you're more interested in Pamela than in my apartment, aren't you?"

"I . . . I'm worried that you're going to . . . to get involved in her murder. Oh, hell, Sam. I'm afraid you're going to be arrested."

"I wish I could tell you there's no possibility that will happen."

"You mean . . . ?" It was too horrible for Josie to even say out loud.

"I don't know what's going to happen, Josie. I am getting special attention. After all, I worked with the police in this city for decades. And there was no physical evidence to connect me with the murder, no DNA or fingerprints. But she was found in my apartment. And we weren't getting along well right before I left New York. . . ."

"Sam, that was years ago. You haven't seen her in years!" She glanced across the table at Sam. "You haven't, have you?"

"I saw her the first morning I was in town. The day before you arrived. Probably forty-eight hours before she was killed, as it turned out."

NINETEEN

THEY TALKED ALL night.

At first, Josie, feeling betrayed by Sam's admission that he had visited an old flame as soon as he found himself within range of her heat, had been less than her usual receptive self. Sam had already told her that he was coming to the city a day early to make sure that his place was ready for them. He'd mentioned getting in a few groceries, coffee beans and the like. He had not mentioned getting together with Pamela Peel. But Sam had explained that he had run into Pamela in the local deli when he was doing exactly what he had told Josie he was going to do.

"She was as surprised to see me as I was to see her," Sam said. "She suggested we go back to my place for a cup of coffee. I didn't see any reason to refuse."

Josie had noted that apparently he had seen a good reason not to tell her about this meeting, but she didn't comment on it.

"We chatted for a bit, catching up on our lives . . ."

Did you tell her about me? Josie was afraid she had spoken her thought aloud.

". . . then she said she was meeting someone about a new Henderson and Peel project and she left."

It wasn't until later, telling Betty about the evening, that Josie realized that Sam had not told her what exactly he and Pamela had "chatted" about.

"But it was a wonderful evening. We talked more and walked more and went back to Sam's place . . . Well, it was wonderful," Josie concluded.

"And now back to reality?" Betty suggested.

Josie groaned. "Yeah, I guess." She swiveled in her seat and looked around. "I wonder what's holding up Carol?" The three women were meeting in the local corner coffee shop to plan their day —and their investigation. Seated in one of the six booths that lined the wall across from the lunch counter, Josie and Betty were an oasis of calm in the midst of early morning mayhem. A line of customers wound through the room and out the open door, ordering and picking up bags of takeout. Everyone was talking loudly. The four men cooking behind the counter had given up trying to communicate in anything other than shouts. Newspapers were open and the air was filled with the scent of grease, which an ineffective, but loud, exhaust fan failed to eliminate.

"Every time someone's late it doesn't mean that there's a crisis," Betty said gently. "Jon says he will call the second he knows anything. Sam may be the only suspect the police are looking at, but they'll want physical evidence tying him to Pamela before they make an arrest. Jon seemed sure of that."

"What sort of physical evidence?"

"I don't know. DNA, I guess. And things like that," Betty added vaguely. She picked up her heavy white mug of coffee and sipped the bitter brew. "Sorry, he may have told me, but I was up most of the night with JJ and I don't remember exactly what he said."

"You gave him my cell phone number though."

"Yes. And he promised to call you the second he heard anything."

"Bad or good."

"Good or bad" was Betty's reply.

"I can't bear thinking about Sam being arrested," Josie

said. "This isn't like we're back home on the island where we know the police and there's only a few cells behind the community center. If Sam were arrested in New York City . . . well, who knows what would happen to him."

"Which is why we have to keep that from happening," Carol Birnbaum said, plopping a huge orange suede tote bag down on the bench beside Josie and sliding in next to Betty. "I've been up half the night making lists. Josie, dear, there's a copy of the Manhattan Yellow Pages in the bottom of my bag. If you'll just get it out for us and turn to the pages I've marked . . . Oh, I'd like tea with skim milk and artificial sweetener and a bran muffin buttered and toasted . . . one with blueberries, if you have it." She interrupted her directions long enough to place her order as a harried waitress passed by, her arms full of platters of eggs and pancakes.

"Good luck," Josie said. "We had to ask three times for coffee and who knows where our food order went." She looked around the disorganized place and shook her head. "What's in the Yellow Pages?"

"Hairdressers, spas, manicurists. I wanted to be prepared if we decide we need alternative sources." Her order was placed in front of her. "Thank you. Perhaps you might check on my friends' orders?" she suggested to the waitress.

"Yeah. I'll find 'em."

"How does she do that?" Josie asked Betty, who shrugged and picked up the heavy book, flipping to the pages marked with bright pink Post-its. "Do we actually need all these names?"

"I should hope not. But it never hurts to be prepared. Besides, we don't need to worry about that. There's a list in there. Read it and tell me what you think."

Josie did as she was directed, easily finding the sheet of writing paper embossed with a small gold fan and the words

"Oriental Mandarin, Hong Kong." She read it quickly and passed it on to Betty.

"Motive. Opportunity. Access," Betty read. "I've read enough mystery novels to understand the first two, but access?"

"That's the key!" Carol said, becoming excited. "Sammy lives in a building with a doorman. No one could have gotten into that apartment without being carefully scrutinized."

"I don't know about that," Betty said. "We have a doorman on duty twenty-four hours a day too, but I know for a fact that one of those men actually helped some friends of his break into one of the penthouses last month. He was arrested."

"How long had he worked there?" Carol asked.

"Just a few months."

"Well, see, you're in a new building. But Mentelle Park is old and established. Harold and the other men have been there for years. They can be trusted. So access is the key here. Who had a key to Sammy's place and who could have gotten into the building. Such a simple thing."

"I'm not so sure . . . ," Josie began.

"I know, but Betty can find out. A gorgeous young mother begging to be allowed to be let into a friend's apartment where she left her baby's favorite toy . . . well, can Harold resist that?"

Betty put down the list. "You want me to see if I can gain admittance to Sam's place?"

"Exactly. And, if you can't get in, we'll know that the murderer is—must be—another resident." Carol finished her point and sipped her coffee.

Josie frowned. She didn't agree, but as long as Betty was willing, what did they have to lose? The waitress put a large oval plate in front of her. Half of it was covered with a Greek omelet, bursting with feta cheese, onions, and spinach. Crispy hash browns were piled on the other half. Josie smiled and picked up her fork.

"What is Sammy doing today?" Carol asked, and Josie lost her appetite.

"Errands," Josie answered, glancing at Betty through lowered eyelids. They both knew that Sam was with Jon, working on a possible defense for a case that had not even begun officially.

"Poor dear," Carol lamented. "He's much better at paperwork than I am of course. But selling your condo is so much work. I'm sure he'll be glad when it's done."

"I'm sure he will be too." Josie decided to eat. Betty was almost halfway through her waffle and was beginning to attack a small mound of bacon. Carol's next words convinced her that she was making the right decision.

"Now, while Betty is busy at Mentelle Park Apartments, Josie and I are going to head downtown. We have appointments at the New Age Way."

Betty looked up from her food. "The what?"

"I think it's some sort of spa-gymnasium-school-hippie sort of place. I've seen the name on flyers around town and in *Time Out New York*. They teach classes about getting in touch with your inner frog."

Josie looked up from her plate. "Carol, that can't be right."

"Well, some silliness. That may have been a typo. Anyway, Pamela's nutritionist and her personal trainer both work there. So I set up some appointments for Josie . . ."

"Some appointments for me? What are you going to be doing?"

"Getting rid of this horrible hair color, I hope. I'm going to try Pamela's colorist. You never know about these downtown places though. I may just turn up at dinner tonight with a purple 'do."

Betty laughed. "You may, you know."

Josie was less interested in Carol's hair than in what she was supposed to do during time spent with a nutritionist and personal trainer.

"You'll be fine, dear. Just make it up as you go."

"Remember, Josie, you're not there to go on a diet or change your body. You're there to find out about Pamela Peel."

Josie looked down at the plate she had just emptied in record time. "Good thing. I think I already flunked the diet part."

Downtown was nearly as different from midtown as Manhattan was different from Josie's island. The first thing Josie noticed was that the sky seemed lower and the streets were narrower. Josie peered out the taxi's windows as they made their way down Broadway.

"It is different down here," Carol said, noticing her interest. "Midtown is Ferragamos, Manolo Blahnik, and jewels from Harry Winston. Downtown is Doc Martens, Birkenstocks, and tattoos." She looked over at Josie in her new Saks Fifth Avenue outfit and smiled. "I don't think either of us is properly dressed."

But Josie, watching out the window, realized that the people walking on the street were looking more and more like people she normally hung out with. Of course, there had been people wearing blue jeans in Sam's neighborhood, but those jeans had been freshly washed and pressed and, in some cases had hung around designer's showrooms long enough to have fancy names embroidered upon them. Here jeans were patched or ripped; some were even dirty. Hair was longer here and, in many cases, less kempt. There were fewer minks, many sheepskins, and lots and lots of down-filled puffy nylon. Their cab made a turn and Josie recognized the arch at Washington Square.

"Isn't this SoHo?" she asked.

"This is the Village. We still have a few more blocks to go."

Their driver shouted as a group of college students jay-walked in front of them, causing him to stamp on his brakes and curse in a language that, possibly fortunately, neither woman understood. As the streets became even narrower, and certainly more crowded, he pressed harder on the accelerator and Josie felt nothing but relief when they finally arrived at their destination.

To enter New Age Way, they had to pass through doors emblazoned with Yin Yang symbols, leading Josie to expect a monastic, contemplative interior. A waterfall perhaps, and certainly one of those Zen gardens composed of a minimum of plants and a maximum of raked sand. Instead the first thing to greet visitors to New Age Way was a wall so covered with posters, notices, and announcements that it was impossible to see if a cork bulletin board or the like lay beneath. A few people, mostly at an age when one has turned one's hairdo into a statement of identity, were flipping through the notices. Even more were standing around chatting. Cold air rushed through the door as people came and went. The place, as Carol whispered in her ear, was jumping.

A beat-up old desk stood in one corner of the lobby and a young man looked up at them. He had string-embellished dreadlocks hanging down his back and the tattoos on his hands disappeared into the sleeves of his thick wool pullover. His earlobes were pierced as well as studded. And he had a warm, welcoming smile. "Can I help you, ladies?"

"She has an appointment," Carol announced.

"Well, I have two appointments," Josie corrected her.

"I'm here to just look around," Carol admitted. "I'm thinking of coming here for . . ." Her eye alighted on a poster advertising a new series of high colonics. "A massage of some sort," she ended, sounding a bit faint.

"Excellent idea. We have Swedish, deep muscle, craniosacral, reiki, and Shiatsu. My girlfriend does the Shiatsu and I can recommend it highly," he pronounced, his smile getting even brighter. He turned to Josie. "And your appointments are for . . . ?"

"She's seeing Carollynn and Dawn this morning," Carol answered.

"Oh, going to take control of your physical self, are you?"

"I'm thinking about it," Josie lied grimly.

"That's the first step, isn't it? Intent is a powerful thing. You'll want to go to the end of the hallway and turn left when you reach the wall. Carollynn is the first door on your right. When you're done with her, she'll direct you to Dawn's lair."

"Thank you." Josie turned to Carol. "Where will we meet when I'm done here?"

"There's an excellent restaurant across the street," Dreadlocks suggested.

"Perfect. I'll see you there. Enjoy your morning, dear. And good luck." Carol moved toward the door, wrapping her mink around her and running smack into a teenager wearing a T-shirt proclaiming FUR IS MURDER. Carol smiled weakly and rushed out into the street.

"Right down that hallway?" Josie asked, pointing behind her.

"That's the one!"

Josie had no trouble finding the nutritionist's door. A large quilted rainbow hung outside, her name embroidered across the yellow stripe. A cardboard pocket had been attached below it and printed recipes spilled out onto the floor. Josie picked one up.

Seaweed Soup, she read. And that was all she read; she crumpled the paper and stuffed it in her coat pocket. She was just getting rid of the evidence when the office door opened and a pale, thin woman with stringy hair stood before her. "You must be Josie Pigeon. I'm Carollynn. Come in. Let's get started on changing your life."

TWENTY

"**C**HOOSE YOUR SEAT."

Carollynn—she apparently didn't feel the need to add a last name to the mix—pointed to three butterfly chairs set in a circle in the middle of the room. Josie picked the red one and sat down, immediately wishing she had removed her coat first as it bunched up around her. Carollynn chose the yellow chair and lowered herself into it slowly.

"I always think it's interesting what color first-time clients select," Carollynn announced, a serious expression on her face. "Red can signify many things. Dominance. Sexuality. Anger. Which is it for you?"

"Anger," Josie answered immediately. She hated being treated like a child. Then she looked more closely at her new teacher. "Didn't I see you yesterday? I was eating lunch with some friends in the lobby of the Four Seasons Hotel . . ."

"Why would I be at a hotel? I live in the city."

"No, this was in the lounge there. It's a place to eat . . ."

"I told you, I wasn't there. Now perhaps we should talk about you rather than about me. Why are you so angry?"

Josie, preoccupied with the thought that Carollynn's doppelgänger had been at the restaurant with her yesterday, was surprised by the question. "Angry? Oh, you mean the color of the chair." Then she had a great idea. "A good friend of mine was murdered recently. I . . . I'm angry at the person who did it."

Carollynn leaned forward and placed her hands on Josie's knees. "How hideous! Of course you are."

"I think you may have known her," Josie continued. "Her name is . . . her name was Pamela Peel."

"Pamela . . . Pamela's dead? She was . . . you did say murdered, didn't you?"

Bingo! "Yes," Josie replied as sedately as she could manage. "It was in all the papers and on television too," she added.

Carollynn sighed deeply. "I've been trying to purge all negative thoughts from my mind for a month. I find it an impossible task if I am exposed to the relentless negativity of the news media. I haven't read a paper or watched television in weeks. What happened? Why do they think she was murdered? How was it done? Where did it happen? Has anyone been arrested?"

"She was strangled. It couldn't have been an accident. And she was found in . . ." Josie paused. Just how much did Carollynn need to know? "Found in an apartment she had decorated for . . . for a client."

Carollynn nodded slowly. "She would have liked that. Not being strangled of course—such a violent way to die. But Pamela would have liked spending her last few hours here on earth in a place of beauty that she herself created."

Josie couldn't imagine anyone describing Sam's apartment as a place of beauty, but she wasn't here to argue. "I can't believe someone would have killed her. Pamela was . . . well, she wasn't someone you would expect to end up murdered." That, she realized, was something you could say about pretty much everyone. On the other hand . . .

"Oh, I don't know about that. Pamela was a . . ." Carollynn paused and Josie expected that the next words out of her mouth would be either Pisces or Gemini or another astrological sign. "She was a little self-centered. I can see how she

could have passed through this world making enemies . . .
almost without knowing she was doing it."

"Really?"

"She wasn't terribly popular with everyone here, I can tell
you that."

"To be honest, this doesn't seem like her sort of place. I
mean, I always thought of Pamela as being more uptown,"
Josie added, hoping she was making sense.

"Yeah, I know what you mean. When she first came here,
I thought she was slumming. Rich lady with big career
comes down to little hole-in-the-wall place to get a cheap
manicure. Only she had wandered into the wrong place because we don't do manicures. You can have your hands hen-
naed though." She nodded at a poster on her office wall. It
displayed a photograph of hands reaching out to each other.
All of them feminine. All of them covered with ornate de-
signs in some sort of blood red ink. It didn't look like something Pamela would have had done.

"But she came to you for nutritional advice, I thought. I
mean, I seem to remember that someone told me she saw
you for that reason."

"She was recommended to see me. She came here because Dawn came here to work. And Dawn recommended
that she change her diet and come see me."

"Did . . . was she easy to work with? I mean, changing
your diet can be very difficult."

"Changing your diet is changing your life. Changing your
life is changing the world."

That seemed a bit extreme, but Josie reminded herself
that she wasn't here to argue. "Yes, of course. But was
Pamela interested in changing her life?"

"Pamela was interested in Pamela. She took my advice
when she thought it would make her thinner or give her more
energy. When I explained that what we eat has global im-
pact, she was completely uninterested. She wanted to be

thin." Carollynn shrugged. "Anyone can be thin. I helped eliminate fat from her diet and gave her a few herbal supplements. She lost nine pounds. Big deal."

To Josie it was a very big deal and she had to remind herself that she was here for information, not for a diet. "It sounds as though you didn't like her."

"Let's just say she was not my type of person, but I don't let my opinions affect my work. I'm a professional."

"No, of course not. But I can't help wondering who would have killed Pamela. I wouldn't think a decorator had lots of enemies."

"Oh, I don't know about that. In this city people are nuts when it comes to their apartments. That's why Pamela was so rich. People pay big money for someone to give them a lifestyle."

"What do you mean?"

"Well, say you're a rich Wall Street type. You have a lot of money, but not much personal life. You grew up in Jersey or the Midwest somewhere and you certainly don't want your place to reveal that particular aspect of your life to the world. You're too young and too busy to shop for things that mean something to you. So you think you'll hire a decorator. But which decorator? There are some that specialize in fancy-pantsy faux English stuff—you know, lots of chintz, pillows, and bunches of little china pug dogs. And there are designers who are known for their modern stuff. But Henderson and Peel is known not for what they do, but for whom they do it."

"I still don't understand."

"They work for rich people. Pamela Peel used to say they would do anything as long at they were well paid for doing it. Used to think it sounded a little like whoring myself. Not that I ever would have said that to her. Even as a joke. You know Pamela. She had a rotten temper."

"Yes." Josie did remember that Sam had said he and

Pamela had fought. Sam had always been remarkably easy-going. Pamela must have been the catalyst to their fights because it was impossible for Josie to imagine Sam flaring up without good reason. Then, because she had to say something, "Do you think that might have had anything to do with her murder?"

"Good question. It's really interesting that she was murdered, isn't it? I wonder if it was, like, someone she was dating. The last time I saw her, she said something about an old flame beginning to rekindle."

"She said what?" The question came out as a squeal.

Carollynn seemed shocked by Josie's outburst. "She said something about an old flame beginning to rekindle." She repeated her statement, and then she squinted her eyes and leaned closer to Josie. "Why? Does that mean something to you?"

"Not really . . . I just . . . um, was thinking about who she used to date. You know, the men she's mentioned to me in the past." Josie hoped Carollynn took the hint.

"Yeah, interesting thought. There was that politician. But he went back to his wife, right?"

"That's what I heard," Josie lied. "And how about . . . ," she started, praying that Carollynn enjoyed playing fill in the blank.

"The psychiatrist! God, I always thought he was nuts. But he did take her to Paris for the weekend. And Pamela claimed that he was dying to marry her—as soon as he dumped his wife."

Josie nodded. So Pamela had dated married men. Didn't that mean the wives might be logical suspects? This woman was a gold mine; if only she kept talking. "I guess his wife is probably thrilled now that Pamela is dead."

Carollynn shrugged. "Maybe. Maybe not. I heard that she was having an affair herself. Apparently she and the doc were early proponents of what used to be called an open marriage."

"Oh. I guess Pamela didn't know that."

"Maybe. But you know Pamela. She always believed she could get men to do anything for her."

"Do you think she could?"

"You know, I think that thinking you can is what's important. Men really seem to buy into that sort of confidence. I mean, Pamela was interesting looking, had a pretty nice figure when she stuck to her diet and exercise regime. But she wasn't a great beauty now really, was she?"

Josie remembered just in time that she was supposed to know Pamela Peel and she nodded her head vigorously. Unfortunately, the reference to diet jogged Carollynn's recollection of why Josie claimed to have made this appointment in the first place.

"But we have less than half an hour left of your appointment. The very first thing I need is a list of every food you ate at your last meal."

"Oh, that's easy. A Greek omelet and coffee. Oh, and orange juice. And hash browns."

"No. Not what was written on the menu. A list of foods. Now, what was in that omelet?"

Josie answered her question as well as she could.

"I don't suppose you know what sort of oil was used to fry it in?"

"I have no idea. It was done on a grill in a little corner coffee shop."

Carollynn shuddered. "Animal fat. It was probably fried in animal fat. You may not be aware of the recent studies that connect eating animal fat with loss of brain tissue."

"Oh, and I had bacon too," Josie added, realizing she had just condemned herself in the eyes of this woman.

Carollynn stood up and grabbed a book off the shelf behind her desk. "I see we have a lot of work before us. Why don't you take this home and read it and make another appointment for next week? Perhaps you could work on changing your diet along the lines the author suggests for a day or two before your appointment."

Josie struggled out of the butterfly chair and grabbed the book. If she wasn't going to learn any more about Pamela, she might as well leave. She sure didn't want to have to start listing what she had eaten yesterday—if she had enough brain tissue left to remember.

"You know who might have killed Pamela?" Carollynn said suddenly. "That lawyer. The one she was so hot for a few years ago. I think he left New York and moved to Montauk or something."

"Sounds like he's out of the picture," Josie said, hoping she sounded more confident than she felt.

"Yes, but he might have come back recently. Pamela had gone off her diet during the holidays—so many people do— but a few weeks ago she came back here for a guided fast. She said she had a reason to lose as much weight as possible as quickly as possible. That frequently means a man. And I know she was almost hysterically in love with that lawyer . . . what was his name?"

Josie pretended not to know. "Was it something like Peter? Ah, Peter . . ." She didn't continue. The only thing she could think of was Peter Rabbit.

"No, it was Sam . . . Sam Richardson. I'm sure that was it. Sam Richardson. You know something? I'd call the police about it if I had any faith that they would listen to me. I offered my services to the local precinct and they completely ignored it."

"You thought the precinct needed a dietitian?"

"Oh, no. I'm a psychic. You know, I'm getting the impression that maybe you didn't know Pamela as well as I thought . . ."

Josie didn't hang around to hear more. She grabbed her purse and hurried out the door, leaving the diet book behind.

The second floor of the New Age Way had been divided into a number of large studios. Drumming echoed up and down the hallway. Through an open doorway, she saw a class in Tai Chi going through its paces and she stopped to admire the slow, graceful movements.

A woman in a purple leotard with a green shawl wound around her shoulders was leaning against the doorjamb watching as well. "I've always wanted to try that," Josie said.

"You should. There are beginner level classes here Tuesday night."

"I . . . I'm strong rather than graceful," Josie said.

"So branch out. Give your body a chance to express itself in a different manner."

Josie grinned. "You don't happen to be Dawn, do you?"

"Yes, and I assume you're Josie."

"Yes."

"My studio is right down there. Would you like a cup of herbal tea or something to munch on? I think we have some sesame cookies—home baked—I can offer you."

"Sounds good!"

"Excellent. Then we'll stop in the kitchen. I sometimes find that clients who have been to see Carollynn before coming to me discover they're extra hungry."

Josie grinned. "All that talk about food."

"The woman's a fanatic. What can I tell you? And she's not the only one around here, which is why I can't offer you anything with caffeine."

"Herb tea would be just fine," Josie said as they entered a small kitchen.

"I usually junk it up with lots of honey," Dawn explained, pulling two mugs off hooks hanging on the wall.

"You're in great shape," Josie said enviously.

"I teach step classes, aerobics, yoga, and kickboxing for six hours a day, five days a week. My problem is keeping the weight on, not taking it off," Dawn explained, picking up a handful of cookies.

"I'm jealous," Josie admitted.

"Don't be. Someday I'll quit all this. I'll go back to school and get my degree and get fat, fat, fat. And I won't be less happy than I am now. I've been doing this sort of thing for almost three years and the only thing I've learned is that thin people aren't likely to be a whole lot happier than fat people." She looked at Josie. "But people who are in good physical shape are happier. And you look like you work out."

"I don't, but I'm a contractor. I build houses. That takes a lot of muscle," Josie explained.

"So why did you set up an appointment with me?"

Josie took a deep breath and decided to tell the truth. "I'm looking for information about Pamela Peel. She was murdered, you know."

"I know. I read about it in the paper."

"I was told that she came here to work out with you."

"Yes . . . Why is a contractor interested in Pamela Peel? Did she stiff you?"

"Uh, no. I'm . . . um, I know the man whose apartment her body was found in."

"Did he kill her?"

"Of course not!"

"Then you're investigating her murder? Like in a mystery novel?"

"I've done it before," Josie stated flatly.

"Good for you. Let's head into my studio. It's more private there."

"You're going to help me?"

"I don't know what I can tell you that might help. But I'll

do anything I can. It's not that I'm so hot on justice. It's just that you've got your work cut out for you."

"What do you mean?"

"There must be so many suspects. Pamela could be very irritating."

TWENTY-ONE

D AWN'S STUDIO WAS lined with mirrors on one wall. The opposing wall was covered with six arched windows. The resulting reflection was stunning.

"Gorgeous, isn't it?" Dawn said. "I love working here."

"It's a wonderful studio," Josie agreed.

"It is, but it's the clients I like best. This place attracts people who want to change their lives. I don't buy into all the spiritual stuff that's taught here, but the people who are interested in that type of thing don't believe the way to all happiness is in whittling an inch off your hips."

"Was Pamela interested in spiritual stuff?" Josie asked.

"Pamela wasn't interested in anything but Pamela," Dawn answered, repeating Carollynn's earlier statement. "She stalked down the halls, with her arms wrapped around her as though she was afraid of catching something from the walls—or the other students. I was rather surprised that she came here to be honest."

"But you had worked with her before."

"Oh, yes. I was her personal trainer for almost a year."

"I don't know what a personal trainer is exactly. Did she come to your studio for . . . sort of private lessons?"

"I went to her apartment and worked with her there."

"Really? Do a lot of people have personal trainers?"

"Yes. It's a business that sprang up in the late eighties when there was lots of money around. I quit college in the

173

middle of my sophomore year and came to New York to be a star. Star of what I wasn't sure, but I was determined. I ended up being an aerobics instructor at a big midtown athletic club like lots of determined but untalented and untrained young women."

"Did you like it?"

"It was okay. Those places are all alike. Tons of new members sign up in January and February. Most drop out in March. And by December the numbers working out are just about the club's optimum capacity. Then New Year's Eve rolls around and it all starts again."

"So you left."

Dawn nodded. "After three years of it, I'd had enough. And I was qualified to move on. So I found a job with a company that provides personal trainers and started going out to work in rich people's homes."

"Only rich people?"

"Mostly rich people. Not because it costs so terribly much to hire a personal trainer, but because you have to have lots of extra room in your apartment to spread out. In New York, extra rooms are as rare as spreading chestnut trees. Besides, the company I worked for was located on the Upper East Side, in the eighties. Lots of money up that way."

"When did Pamela hire you?"

"Actually, she didn't. Her partner at Henderson and Peel did. Shepard Henderson."

"Weird."

"Not really. He gave her two months of twice-a-week sessions for her birthday. She had hurt her back sliding off a ladder or something and he thought a personal trainer might help. I went to her home twice a week before work. And then, when her gift certificate ran out, she started paying herself."

"So you helped her back?" Josie had had more than a few back problems.

"To tell you the truth, I don't remember much about her back. Maybe it was feeling better by the time I started working with her. But I do remember how thrilled she was to lose an inch and a half around her waist. She did it in record time. Say whatever you will against her, Pamela Peel was a very hard worker."

But Josie wasn't interested in Pamela Peel's work ethic at the moment. "What was her apartment like?"

"Fabulous. Really, really fabulous. It was a big, prewar two bedroom right around the corner from the office. She had converted one of the bedrooms into a combination walk-in closet and exercise space. The entire thing was bigger than my place, including my kitchen and bathroom. And she had the most incredible bathroom, simple but expensive. Watery aqua walls, white and gray marble floors. Jacuzzi, a walk-in shower that half a dozen people could fit in, two big windows. There were always lots of candles around. My guess is that it was a very romantic, and sexy, spot."

Josie didn't reply immediately. She was thinking of her tiny closet and her bathroom, which, while fairly large, was old, ugly, and worn. No one, she was sure, would ever describe her bathroom as a "sexy spot." For the first time, she found herself wondering if Sam had missed not just Pamela's good looks, education, money, talent, or sophistication but also her lifestyle. But she had reserved only half an hour of Dawn's time; she didn't want to waste it. "Sounds very modern. How was the rest of the place decorated? In what style?"

"God, I don't know. It was just gorgeous. Not modern exactly. The main colors were black, taupe, white, and this creamy off-white. The furniture was big, upholstered, and mainly made out of some sort of dark woods. There weren't a lot of accessories and nothing at all ditzy or feminine. Even the bedroom was elegant, but somewhat neutral. I'm not explaining at all well. It's just that it was perfect in an impersonal sort of way. Like the bedspread—it was made from heavy, natural raw silk, and the stitching was geometric rather than curvy. The artwork was modern, abstract." Dawn stopped talking and smiled. "I liked it a lot. And it looked a lot like Pamela—expensive, well dressed, and . . . well, sort of impersonal. She was not," Dawn concluded, "the sort of woman who had little notes and photos attached to her refrigerator."

Josie grinned. "Sure doesn't sound like my place."

"Mine either."

"And it doesn't sound like the place where she was photographed for *New York* magazine," Josie added.

"It wasn't. I always wondered why she moved."

"She did?"

"Yes . . . oh, I'm sorry. I thought you knew. She moved a few years ago. Around the same time I decided I was tired of going to people's homes and started working here."

"Did you ask her why?"

"Yes. And she just told me it was time to make a change. Pamela was not one to answer questions. She talked about herself when she wanted to, and, when she did, she chose the subject. Other than that, employees—and I'm sure she put me in that class and looked down on me for belonging to it—were not allowed into her life."

"Is it that way with most of your clients?"

"Oh, no! Of course, when I was working in people's homes, I knew a bit about them. If not their actual income, how much credit they were allowed to accumulate to get their big mortgages. But most people I work with tell me all sorts of things about their lives."

"Men as well as women?"

"Yes. But the women are more interesting. They tell me about their hopes and dreams. Whether they're married or who they're seeing if they're not. They talk about their kids, their vacations, their jobs—you know the type of thing. The men talk more about their work and careers than the personal stuff. It's a cliché, but it's true."

"And did Pamela tell you about her personal life? Who she dated and all?"

"Sometimes. Mainly she talked about her work. She didn't name-drop. In fact, she made a big deal out of not name-dropping. Said over and over that her clients demanded confidentiality."

"As though she was a priest or a psychiatrist."

"Yeah, but I think she was trying to make the point that they were important and famous people. And that she was famous and important because she worked for them." Dawn laughed. "And I suppose you could say that if she was famous and important because she worked for famous and important people, I was famous and important because I worked for her. Not that she would ever suggest such a thing. Pamela was not the most generous person when it came to sharing the credit."

"Or her money," Josie muttered, remembering the comments about Pamela's tipping practices at Elizabeth Arden.

Dawn caught on immediately. "Yeah, she was a lousy tipper. But some people are. What can you do?"

"Did she talk about the men in her life?"

"Some. She talked about her partner once in a while. I could never tell if she liked him or not. She didn't exactly complain about him, but she implied that he didn't pull his own weight in the partnership."

"What do you mean?"

"Well, she'd talk about having to rush off to an appointment that she really wished Shep would have taken. Or she would mention that he didn't bring as many clients into the firm as she did. I think that one really galled her."

"Because she mentioned it more than once?"

"That and the fact that Shep was the one with the society background."

"Really?"

"Oh, yeah. The Hendersons were big deals in New York society back when there really was society."

"Really?"

"Yeah. I still see their photos in the society pages. Listening to Pamela, I got the impression, more than once, that their partnership had a lot to do with his family."

"I don't know what you mean."

"He was the connection, maybe the initial connection, to the people Pamela wanted to work for."

"That's interesting. So she used him."

"Or maybe he used her. Maybe he had all the connections and she had all the talent."

"I suppose that's possible," Josie admitted slowly.

"How did you come to so dislike a woman you have never even met?"

"She dated the man I'm in love with. Before I dated him. Before I even met him," Josie answered.

"You're jealous."

"Yeah, I guess so. She was everything I'm not. And I've wondered about her for years. I almost didn't come on this trip because I didn't want to meet her. On the other hand, sometimes I think I came here because I didn't want Sam to see her when I wasn't along."

"Sam is your significant other?"

"Yes."

"And he doesn't live in the city anymore."

"Nope. He left almost three years ago. That's when I met him. When he left the city."

"Did he plan on coming back?"

"No. Definitely not."

"Are you sure?"

Josie thought for a moment, surprised by the question. "Yes, I'm sure. He has a house and a business now. He came back to the city in order to put his condo on the market, not to reestablish contact with anyone here."

"He's rich." It was a statement, not a question.

"Sam? No. He has more money than I do, but he's not rich."

"Then you don't have to worry about him . . . well, maybe you do have to worry about him. He might be interested in Pamela, but she couldn't have been seriously interested in him."

"Why not?"

"Because Pamela Peel was only interested in marrying a rich man."

"You're kidding!"

"Nope. She made no bones about it. She said she had expensive tastes and she wanted someone who could indulge them."

Josie frowned. "Didn't she make a lot of money?"

Dawn laughed. "She spent a lot of money. She didn't wear shoes; she wore Manolo Blahniks or Pradas. She didn't buy suits; she bought Armanis. She didn't want a mink; she wanted a Fendi fur. And you should have heard her when she talked about decorating. She hung modern art on her walls because it was less expensive than the Monets and Manets that she coveted. Let me tell you, unless your boyfriend has lots of bucks, he was just a passing fancy in Pamela Peel's life."

"They dated for over two years."

"The lawyer, right?"

"Yes, Sam was a prosecuting attorney before he left the city." Josie leaned closer to Dawn. "Did she talk about him to you?"

Dawn frowned and looked at the floor.

"Please, I really need to know. Sam . . . the police may think he killed her. He didn't, of course, but . . . well, anything you know might help him."

Dawn didn't speak for a moment. "I don't have real conversations with clients. At least not with clients like Pamela. I listen to what she says, but I don't ask . . . well, I don't ask anything you could call a piercing question. Mostly I 'uh huh' and 'yes' and 'you're right.' Clients like Pamela really only want affirmation. Not intrusion into their lives, certainly nothing like advice or criticism."

"But she did talk to you about him!"

"Yes, she did."

"What did she say?"

Dawn hesitated. "You're sure he wasn't rich when he was living in the city?"

"I'm not sure, but I don't think so. Please tell me what you know."

"Well, either he was rich and you don't know about it, or she was sincerely in love with him because that's what she used to say. That your Sam was her chance to get everything she wanted out of life."

TWENTY-TWO

I T WAS THE last thing in the world Josie Pigeon wanted to hear. And now she was going to have to ask for the details. She sipped her herb tea, reminded herself that Pamela's feelings for Sam might not have been reciprocated by him, took a deep breath and said, "Tell me about it."

"I can tell you only what she told me—and only what I remember."

"That's fine. Just do the best you can do."

"She wasn't dating him when I began working with her. I remember her telling me about the first time she met him."

"Go ahead," Josie urged, feeling this was going to be painful.

"It was at his mother's apartment," Dawn said.

"She told me about that," Josie said. She took a breath and asked another question. "Was it love at first sight?"

Dawn shrugged. "Who knows? I figured he was just a rich, single, society lawyer—a catch and Pamela was beginning to get old enough to be looking for a catch."

"I guess. Go on. When did they next meet? Did Sam ask her out?"

"I don't think so," Dawn answered slowly. "I think they had some mutual acquaintances and they were both invited to a dinner party."

"That's a coincidence!"

"Oh, it wasn't a coincidence. One of them must have set

181

it up. I just don't remember which one, if I ever knew. Anyway, I don't remember the details, but Pamela, who was always obsessed with her appearance, became something of a fanatic at that point. She doubled her workout schedule and lost a few pounds. And, of course, bought an entire new wardrobe. How that woman could spend money . . ." She looked at Josie. "Maybe Sam gives the impression of being rich?"

"How would he do that?"

"Wear Armani suits. Drive a Porsche. Stuff like that."

"I'm not sure I'd recognize an Armani. Besides, he's more chinos and docksiders. And he drives an MGB. It's older than my truck."

"Restored?"

"Yes," Josie answered.

"Where did he go to school?"

"Yale."

"Are you absolutely sure he doesn't come from old money? He sure sounds like it."

Josie opened her mouth and then closed it. She had no idea what Sam was worth. He never worried about money. He bought what he wanted and didn't buy more. It wasn't his style to show off. She thought about his mother. Carol had always spent lots of money, but Josie had been under the impression that that cash was accumulated during one of her marriages. That Sam might be wealthy was an idea she had never considered, but it was possible. And that meant that Pamela's interest in him might have been only monetary. For some reason, Josie found the thought comforting.

"Pamela was real fond of quoting that old cliché about it being just as easy to fall in love with a rich man as a poor one. I assumed that she had managed to."

"Maybe. Did she talk about their relationship much?"

"She didn't talk so much as brag. I heard all about the expensive restaurants they ate at, the islands in the Caribbean where they went to sunbathe. It wasn't all that interesting, to tell the truth. Pamela seemed to find status in eating in the right restaurant when all anyone has to do is call, make reservations, and pay the bill. It's not like she was seated at the best table at Elaine's."

"I don't know what you're talking about," Josie admitted.

"Name-dropping. Pamela approached her life as she approached her wardrobe—everything had to have a designer name attached for her to be interested in it. She chose where she ate and where she vacationed in the same way. If it was well known or famous she went there. Sometimes I thought that the only reason she went anyplace was so she could brag about it afterward."

"That doesn't sound like Sam," Josie muttered.

"Is your Sam the type of guy who is always trying to impress people?"

"No, just the opposite. He's . . . he's genuine. Like he knows a whole lot about wine. It was his hobby and now it's his business, but he never makes a big deal about it. He just buys the best and drinks it, without any fuss or ostentation." And, she realized, as though he had been doing it all his life. Was Dawn right? Was it possible that Sam had been brought up in a wealthy family? Did he have family money? Is that what had attracted Pamela Peel to him?

"Well, maybe it was true love. Maybe Pamela Peel fell for him because of who he was as opposed to what he had."

"Do you think that's possible?" Josie asked.

Dawn took a moment to consider the question. "I suppose. She was ambitious, of course. But we're not talking about a gold digger here, you know. Pamela Peel worked hard and had a lot of talent. She was at least half the reason Henderson and Peel was so successful. New York City is a place a lot of people come to with a dream. I know I did. But I wasn't good enough or a hard enough worker. Pamela Peel was both. I admired her professionally."

"And personally?"

"She used people. But Sam Richardson may not be in that category. She may have sincerely cared about him."

That didn't make Josie feel better. "Were you surprised when she followed you here? I mean, couldn't she have just hired another personal trainer to come to her house?"

"You know, I thought that was exactly what she would do. Not only was she the only client I had who followed me here, but she was the most unlikely. And I did explain that there were other options. The company I was working for then sure didn't want to lose clients. And, to be honest, I was looking for a new type of client when I changed jobs. But, what can you do? I'm not in the position of picking my clients, unlike Henderson and Peel."

Josie thought for a moment. "Do you know why they broke up? I mean, did she talk about it?"

Dawn frowned. "I remember knowing that something was wrong." She paused and continued slowly. "There were little things. She complained a lot more and about different things. Pamela was a woman who was bragging when she complained. You know the type of thing. 'Oh, I just hate that man. He keeps buying me expensive presents, blah, blah, blah, blah.' Much of the time I just turn off my mind and stop listening. But suddenly she was complaining about decisions that were nothing to brag about. Like Sam had refused to spend the weekend with her at Gurney's out in Montauk. It's a spa, right on the water, gorgeous. He wanted to go to a car show somewhere in the middle of Pennsylvania." Dawn chuckled. "I cannot imagine Pamela at a car show and then she said that they were going to be staying at the local Holiday Inn. No way she was going to do that. I think she took off for Montauk by herself. And in a huff."

"You think they were breaking up then?"

"Well, yes and no. She decorated his apartment—it was a gift. A very generous gift. I remember her talking about having two large sofas covered in suede. The cheapest workman she found charged over four thousand dollars per couch. And there was something about a fireplace mantel. The marble was imported from India, taken to Italy to be formed and then flown over here from Italy so it could be installed in time. I couldn't believe it. The cost was incredible and she wanted everything to be perfect. Well, I guess that's why she's so well known. Have you seen the apartment?"

"Yes, I'm staying there now."

"And?"

"And what?"

"Is it gorgeous?"

"No. It's hideous. And I'm not the only person who thinks so. My friend saw it and agreed with me."

"I suppose the only person who matters is the client."

"I can't imagine Sam liking it," Josie protested. "I mean, he owns a house now and he's decorated it himself. And it's as different from that apartment as can be. It's warm and inviting. He likes fifties retro stuff more than I do, but it has color and light and charm. His apartment looks like a dead elephant."

"A very expensive dead elephant," Dawn reminded her.

"Yes, but it's not like Sam!"

"Maybe it's what she wanted him to be like rather than what he was," Dawn suggested.

"I suppose." Josie shrugged. "What do I know about it? I build things. Someone else decorates them. But, you know, I can't help thinking that it's a little odd that she decorated his apartment and then, less than six months later, he decides to retire, leave New York City and move to the shore."

"Sounds like he's an impulsive guy."

"But he's not. He felt that he had done all he could do working for the city, that he wanted to change careers while he was still young enough to enjoy what he was doing. He had always wanted to live near the water. I mean, I always got the impression that he had thought about the change for years and years."

"But you're not sure about that."

"No. That's part of the problem with all this. I never really thought about any of those things. Sam's past had always stayed in the past. I mean, I've met friends of his from the city. And his mother visits from time to time. But I never thought much about what caused him to change his whole life. It was done before I met him."

"Did you realize a woman was involved?"

"Sam's dated lots of women. And he's talked about them from time to time," Josie explained, not adding that she had not enjoyed hearing about any of it.

"Pamela Peel?"

"I think I always knew Pamela Peel was special," Josie answered slowly. "I knew that they dated for quite a while. And I knew that she was the last woman in his life before he left New York. I thought his mother liked her and compared me to her, but now that I'm here, it turns out that she couldn't stand her."

"And what about Sam? Had you judged their relationship correctly?"

"I don't know," Josie admitted. "The more I learn about her, the less I understand."

"Yeah, I know how you feel. I'm taking an Italian course at the New School," Dawn explained, recognizing the surprised expression on Josie's face. "I knew a bit of Italian for two or three weeks. But now that I have a larger vocabulary and know some grammar, the classes are getting harder and I find myself recognizing fewer and fewer words and stumbling around more than ever. My teacher," she added, "says it will get better in time. That you have to work your way through the confusion."

"Yeah, I guess. I just hope the wrong person isn't arrested before my confusion goes away."

"You know, I may be able to help you more."

"Anything you can tell me . . ."

"This isn't me. It's a friend of mine. She's a personal trainer too, but she went back to school and became a licensed physical therapist. She works out of Mount Sinai's Rusk Clinic, mainly with people who have had strokes. She's a medical worker and isn't supposed to talk about her patients. But . . ."

"But?" Josie repeated, wondering what was coming.

"But Sterling Henderson, Shep's father, was one of her patients. She worked with him during the time he was a patient there and then he hired her privately to see him in his home for a few months. He was not an easy patient. Having a stroke doesn't always improve patients' personalities. And he had spent his entire life telling people what to do. Having people tell him what to do was more than a little difficult. But my friend, Gayle, is a fabulous therapist and she became good friends with Mrs. Henderson. Such good friends that Mrs. Henderson introduced her to Shep. She apparently hoped they would get together. They didn't, but Gayle became something of a friend of the family. She and Mrs. Henderson have lunch together occasionally."

"Could I talk to her? Maybe she knows something . . . ," Josie said.

"Gayle won't talk about patients to strangers. I'm sure of that. But maybe she could figure out a way for you to meet Mrs. Henderson. She must know a lot about Pamela Peel."

"That would be sensational!"

"Look, it's a long shot. Gayle may just flat out refuse . . ."

"But you'll call her and talk to her. You'll explain . . . won't you?"

"I will. Where can I get in touch with you?"

"I'll give you Sam's phone number. And my cell phone number. And my friend, Betty, she has a new baby and she's home a lot of the time and she'll make sure I get a message."

Josie pulled a poster from the wall and began to write on its reverse side. "And . . ."

"That's fine. I'll get hold of Gayle and ask if she thinks there's any way she can get you in to meet Mrs. Henderson. I'll call you."

"Right away."

"Yes, right away." Dawn glanced down at the Swatch on her wrist. "It's time for my next client. You pay downstairs."

"Oh . . ." Josie grabbed her purse and stood up. "I . . ." Hell, she had told this woman all sorts of intimate things about her life; why be embarrassed about this. "I don't know whether or not I tip you," she blurted out.

"This is the New York City rule: when in doubt tip and tip well. But not me, not here, not now. I'm glad to help. I told you. I came here to help people lead better lives. Keeping your boyfriend out of jail sounds like it falls under that heading."

TWENTY-THREE

JOSIE WAS WRITING notes about what Dawn had told her at the little café across the street from New Age Way when Carol joined her.

"You . . . you look wonderful!"

"I feel wonderful! There is nothing like finding a new hairdresser who charges less than half of what I'm paying uptown! I should have come down here years ago!" She pulled out a chair and sat down beside Josie. "I have lots and lots of things to tell you, but I'm starving. Where is our waiter?"

"The menu is on that blackboard on the wall and you order for yourself at the counter."

"Okay, just let me look for a second . . . what is all this stuff?" Carol looked at the selections offered.

"Macrobiotic. Vegan . . . ," Josie read.

"Rice and roots!" Carol said dismissively.

"There are some salads."

"With tofu!" Carol sighed loudly. "Oh well, what are you having?"

"I thought a number three and coffee."

"Do you think that number three looks less disgusting than the number five?"

"I really don't think it matters, Carol!" Josie answered, trying to keep the irritation from her voice. Everything looked equally awful, but they had to eat and compare notes.

She didn't want to waste more time looking for a suitable place.

"I'll place our orders," Carol announced, getting to her feet and heading to the counter.

Josie looked down at the page before her. There were several possibilities there—especially that of meeting Shep Henderson's parents. Certainly they would know a lot about Pamela Peel. Of course, she couldn't even begin to imagine why they would share their knowledge with her.

"So what did you learn?" Carol asked, sitting back down. "I heard some very interesting things—one in particular," she added, not allowing Josie to answer her question. "Pamela Peel didn't want to marry Sammy!"

"Really?"

"That's what KiKi said. I couldn't believe it, of course."

"Why not?"

"I . . . well, I . . ." Carol looked across the table at Josie and didn't finish her thought.

"You can't imagine any woman not wanting to marry Sam. It's true, isn't it?" she said when Carol didn't reply.

"He's good-looking, smart, well-educated, kind . . ."

"Nice to stray cats, drives a cool car," Josie added, now smiling broadly. "I know just what you mean. And I'm sure I'll feel the same way about Tyler when he's older," she added. "But we're not talking in general here. We're talking about Pamela. Did Sam ever say anything to you about wanting to marry Pamela Peel?"

"Well . . . he . . ."

Josie recognized the problem. "Carol, don't worry about my feelings. I have them, of course, but that's not what's important now. I need to know how Sam felt about Pamela."

"He . . . I think he told me that she was the one. You know, the woman he was going to marry."

"You think he told you?"

"Josie, dear, I've been going over this in my mind and,

while I'm positive he felt that way about her at one time, I can't remember exactly when he would have told me that Pamela was going to be my daughter-in-law. Or if he even said so in just those words."

Josie realized it was entirely possible that they were moving into the area of wishful thinking on Carol's part—interesting in a personally painful way, but not particularly productive. "Was KiKi sure that Pamela didn't want to marry Sammy?"

"Oh, my dear, that was the only way she could explain something Pamela did that didn't make sense. Something that didn't make sense to me either."

Josie was completely mystified. "What?"

"She knew he would hate the way she decorated his apartment!"

Josie had been anticipating anything but this. "You're kidding. How did she know that?"

"Pamela told her so! Pamela always wore her hair short. Just a pert little cap that suited her so well, and she knew it. But that summer she had started wearing it even shorter than usual and she had to have it trimmed and highlighted every four weeks, so she saw KiKi a lot. KiKi claims Pamela was in her chair at the salon when she came up with the idea of redecorating Sammy's apartment."

"What did she say? I think I'll redecorate my boyfriend's apartment and make it as ugly as possible?"

"No. After all, this was a few years ago. And, remember, these women hear a whole lot of stories. And . . ."

"I'll take it all with a grain of salt," Josie said impatiently. "Just tell me."

"She said that Pamela was complaining that she wanted to entertain potential clients in Sammy's apartment, but that it was just an embarrassment that he hadn't let her redecorate it. And then she had the idea of redecorating it as a gift—and announcing it publicly so he couldn't refuse."

"Well, not without looking like an ungrateful cad," Josie agreed, thinking how incredibly manipulative Pamela's plan sounded. Although she knew Pamela would have needed to manipulate Sam to accomplish her own goal. Sam had built a hideous deck on the front of his little house in the dunes. Josie had taken the fact that he didn't consult her or ask for suggestions while the work was in progress as a personal and professional insult. From the moment it was finished, she had hoped it would fall down. Fortunately, Hurricane Agatha had dropped a tree on it last summer. Sam and she had designed the new deck together and Island Contracting would be building it as soon as they could put the pilings in the ground. "Why didn't Sam design the apartment with Pamela?"

"I know the answer to that one. After all, I was there when she announced the gift. She explained that the design would be a surprise." Carol paused. "I think she said something about the project being a breakthrough for Henderson and Peel—or a change of direction. Something like that. I remember thinking that it was foolish to do something different when you're so successful. But, of course, I probably was wrong about that."

"Why?"

"You have to stay ahead of the game. Fashion designers, interior designers, all those creative professions—they either follow or lead. And the big ones lead. And leading means changing. It's the only way to stay one step ahead of the herd." She smiled at Josie. "You don't have to be around New York long to realize that. And I suppose that may be why it never occurred to me that Pamela would ask for Sammy's input. If I thought anything was odd about it, I thought it was strange that she didn't try to talk him into moving into a place where they could both live and decorate that for him. But we've talked about this, dear. What I want to tell you is what she told KiKi. See, at first, KiKi assumed that it was just a nice gift. But then, listening to Pamela describe her work for a few weeks, she realized that it was a really odd job and that not only was Pamela not interested in what Sammy would want, but she didn't care at all that the apartment wouldn't suit him. She thought minimalism would be the next wave in decorating and so that's what she did."

"But she had that window seat built so that Sam would have someplace to keep all his paperwork. So she did account for his needs, at least some of them," Josie said.

"That's a good point," Carol said slowly, considering the suggestion.

"Did KiKi explain why Pamela did this to Sam's place?"

"Well, she thought that it was a selfish gesture, not a mean one. She got the impression that Pamela wanted to do something different from what Henderson and Peel usually did and couldn't find a client who would allow it. By doing something Sammy didn't know about, she could do what she wanted. And then, of course, she probably thought she'd get a lot of publicity about the place in the *Times* and all and she'd move Henderson and Peel a step ahead of the competition."

"Oh." Josie said nothing else.

"I believe those two big platters on the counter are ours," Carol stated flatly.

Josie jumped up. "I'll get them."

Two large, heavy pottery platters were indeed waiting for them. Josie picked up one in each hand. Each had a pile of dun-colored rice in its middle flanked by various steamed vegetables and grains that Josie couldn't identify. She placed them on the table she and Carol shared. "I have no idea which is which."

Carol peered down at the plates, an unenthusiastic expression on her face. "I don't think it can matter much, do you?"

"Probably not, but I'm hungry." Josie sat down, picked up her fork, and plunged it into her pile of vegetables.

"Is there any salt?" Carol asked, looking around at the other tables.

"You don't need it. It's really spicy," Josie said as she chewed. "And it's not bad."

Carol picked up her fork and followed Josie's example. Soon the women were eating so enthusiastically that they didn't notice Dawn's approach.

"Oh, this is nice. I'm glad I ran into you."

Josie introduced Dawn and Carol to each other and suggested that Dawn might like to join them.

"I'd love to, but I'm meeting someone for lunch. But I have some good news for you. My appointment after you canceled at the last minute, so I took the time to call my friend, the one who knows . . ." Dawn suddenly stopped speaking and let her eyes wander over to Carol. She lifted one eyebrow in a quizzical manner.

"Carol knows all about this." Josie answered Dawn's unasked question.

"Great! My timing was perfect. Gayle was on her way out the door to attend a big charity event down on the pier."

"But she gave you the information?" Josie asked.

"To be honest, she was concerned about giving you any information without meeting you."

"But time . . ."

"I told her you were anxious and she suggested that you meet her at the Spotlight Sale."

"What a wonderful idea! I love going to those sales!" Carol spoke up.

"Do you have time?"

"I need to make some calls." Josie looked at Carol. "I should call Betty and Sam."

"We'll call in the cab on the way there. Oh, I never knew

detective work could be so much fun! Or fattening," she added, looking down at her almost empty plate.

"One of the little-known facts of life is that a person can gain weight on a macrobiotic diet. It's all those carbs," Dawn explained. "Oh, there's my friend, I have to go."

"But how will I recognize Gayle?" Josie asked.

"She's about fifty, is in great shape, has short gray hair and she'll be looking at evening dresses. Size six or eight," Dawn said, moving away from them.

"Oh, wait," Josie cried. "I have a question . . . a quick question."

"What?"

"It's about Carollynn." Josie hesitated before continuing. "I was wondering . . . Is she honest? I mean, does she tell the truth?"

"Carollynn? I wouldn't trust her, no. Now I've really got to run."

Carol stood up. "And we'd better get going."

"Yes, of course." Josie followed her lead and a few minutes later they were in a taxi heading back uptown. "What is the Spotlight Sale?" Josie asked, scrounging around in her new purse for her cell phone. "Oh, look!" she yelled before giving Carol an opportunity to answer. "There's Tyler! And Tony! And that girl named Toni too. In that white limo there . . . Oh they're turning! Damn! I wish we could have talked to them."

"What a lucky young man to be chauffeured around the city in a luxury car. I'm sure he's having the time of his life," Carol said, moving her coat away from a spot of something sticky on the seat's worn upholstery. "Now, about the Spotlight Sale . . . it's famous. It's one of the oldest charities in the city. It's organized by the most wealthy women, many of whom belong to what used to be New York society. It's a real honor to be asked to be on their organizing committee."

Josie stopped dialing. "I thought you said it was a sale."

"It is."

"Of what?"

"Clothing. Fabulous, fabulous clothing. Designer things."

"Where does it come from?"

"Oh, it's donated. It's all used, of course. You won't believe it!"

Josie already couldn't. That Carol would be this excited
about a sale of used clothing. It just didn't fit her image of
Sam's mother. But she didn't have time to think more about
it. Sam, finally, had answered his phone.

"Sam? Josie. Any news? Oh, well, that's good, isn't it?"
She listened a bit more and then, after explaining where they
were heading, she said good-bye, hung up, and turned to
Carol. "Sam's busy. The Realtor is at his place and they're
going over various options. But he says that he hasn't heard
from anyone official."

"From the police department?"

"Exactly. He hasn't heard from them and neither has
Jon—he called. And I told him . . . Well, you heard what I
told him."

"We'll call back after we're done at the sale," Carol said.

Josie was busy dialing Betty's number. She answered almost immediately. And her answer to Josie's question was
short. "No way!"

"Betty could not convince Harold to open the door to
Sam's place for her," Josie reported to Carol.

But Carol just nodded, leaned forward, and peered out the
windshield.

The cab they were in was flying up the one-way street,
dodging buses, cars, trucks, other taxis, and pedestrians. The
radio was blaring music played on instruments Josie didn't
recognize, accompanying a singer crooning in a language
she couldn't understand. Nothing was going as she had expected or hoped. But she realized she was seeing an incredible city in an incredible way. Now all she had to do was

convince someone she had never met to introduce her to someone who had no reason to want to talk to her.

The cab swerved. A young man on a bicycle, a huge bulging pack on his back, yelled out a familiar curse in a language she knew well. The driver lowered the window to raise one finger in the air and freezing cold air swarmed into the car. Carol pulled her coat closer to her neck and Josie took a deep breath. It didn't matter how many dead ends there were. She had no choice. She had to succeed. Sam's life depended on it.

TWENTY-FOUR

IT WAS THE largest enclosed space Josie had ever seen. From where she stood, waiting by the door as Carol paid their entrance fees, it looked as though two or three old-time ocean liners could have been dry-docked inside this building. But now, instead of ships, racks of clothing filled the right side of the space. Tables of folded scarves, sweaters, T-shirts, hats, purses, and shoes marched down the middle of the pier. Tents had been set up to serve as dressing rooms. Shoppers waited in long lines, clothing piled high in tired arms, to pay for their purchases, and at the far back, long racks of glittering full-length dresses were guarded by stern-looking helpers as customers were exhorted to look, but look carefully. Josie and Carol knew exactly where they were going. They marched through the crowd toward those formal dresses.

"Oh, is that a Hermès bag?"

Josie grabbed Carol's arm and prevented her from straying. "We'll look at it later."

"If it's real, it won't be there later. See, that woman just picked it up."

"Carol, a woman with short gray hair just walked into one of those tents!" Josie said, spinning around. "Maybe I should follow her."

"And I'll go back to the evening gowns," Carol said.

But Josie knew Carol wouldn't easily abandon an opportunity to acquire a rare bargain and she grabbed her arm, preventing her from leaving. "No, you go see if the woman in the dressing room is named Gayle. I'll go look in the racks."

"Gayle who?"

"You know, I don't know her last name, but, remember, she's here to try on evening gowns."

"Josie, when you go out to buy a new pair of jeans, don't you sometimes end up looking at T-shirts?"

Josie got the point immediately. "You think we might find Gayle anywhere in this place."

"Unless she's a truly amazing woman, it's definitely a possibility. But I will head right back to the evening gowns if I don't find her in there," Carol explained, peeling off in the direction of the dressing area.

Josie continued on, astounded by the activity around her. Hundreds of shoppers were pawing through the goods. Even more walked slowly up and down the temporary aisles, looking for the correct size or most valuable designer label. She recognized many of the names she had become familiar with on her journey into Saks with Carol a few days earlier.

Josie had been patronizing thrift shops for over a decade. Tyler had worn clothes from a secondhand children's store when he was growing up. Even her couch had done some time in the local Salvation Army store. But she had never seen anything like this. A lot of the clothing looked new. Two sweaters she just happened to pick up as she passed still had tags hanging from their sleeves. Barney's New York tags!

But she wasn't here to shop and the evening gown section put any thoughts of that out of her mind. She had never worn an evening gown in her life and couldn't imagine a need for one in the foreseeable future. Besides, this type of fancy-schmancy thing didn't appeal to her. Not at all, she reminded herself, reaching out and fingering a skirt fashioned from layers of multicolored organza. Suddenly, Josie remembered being five or six years old and running around the house tripping over an old gown of her mother's, a crinoline slip tied on her head. She had been pretending to be a bride on her wedding day, one of her favorite grown-up fantasies. How little she had known what the future had in store for her she thought, reluctantly dropping the skirt.

"Beautiful, isn't it? That particular dress was donated by a very famous actress." The middle-aged woman who had approached Josie picked up the manila tag tied to the hanger on which the dress hung. The name printed there confirmed the woman's claim.

"Were these all worn by famous people?" Josie asked, looking down the long rows of dresses.

"No, and, of course, some of the women, some very prominent women, who donated some gorgeous items preferred to remain anonymous so we cannot guarantee the provenance of each and every gown. But I could show you something that I'm told belonged to Anne Bancroft . . ."

"I think I'll just wander around by myself. If that's okay with you."

"We encourage you to look. The larger sizes are toward the rear of the room."

Josie realized the gown she was admiring was a size four. "I'm shopping for a friend as well as myself," she lied.

"Oh . . . well . . . I hope you find something for you both. Dressing rooms are to the left. Cash registers to the right. And we take all major credit cards. And some of the women who pay by check make a donation to our cause as well. We are tax deductible, you know."

"Yes, thank you very much." Josie moved away, looking for Gayle as she skimmed through the gowns. A lot of women had gray hair, she thought, and almost instantly realized it wasn't true. Very few women here had allowed themselves to go gray. Feeling a bit more confident, she resumed her search for Gayle.

And found a woman who fit Dawn's description of her looking through the size eight gowns. She took a deep breath and asked, "Are you Gayle?"

"Yes. Josie Pigeon?" Gayle asked without looking away from the dresses.

"Yes."

"I only have an hour to find something to wear to my idiot cousin's formal wedding, so we're going to have to talk while I shop."

"Of course. I . . . I don't know where to begin."

"You could tell me if you think I'll look like a green bean in this thing." Gayle held a jade gown up in front of her.

"Well, I like green . . ."

"But not this dress. Well, you're honest and tactful. That's good. Now let's put this back and find three or four things for me to try on. We'll chat while I'm dressing. I'm a size eight and hate sequins or beading. And I don't like this particular cousin and don't want to spend a whole lot to see her get married to her trophy fiancé. The only good thing to be said for him is that he went to Princeton and didn't flunk out. But, if you knew my cousin, you'd know that for her, he is a real catch. Now let's get busy." Without waiting for a response, she began flipping through the dresses.

Taking a moment to regain her bearings, Josie joined her. Within ten minutes Gayle had four dresses slung over her arm and Josie had, rather tentatively, chosen four more.

"Let's go. The dressing tent over there seems to be the least crowded."

Working hard to prevent the dresses from dragging on the floor and to keep up with Gayle, Josie trotted after her. She liked this blunt woman; she only hoped she could convince her to feel the same way about her. But how was she going to impress her in a small dressing room?

It wasn't size that was going to be the problem, she realized, as she followed Gayle into the large tent. There were no small dressing rooms. Everyone was trying on clothing in the large open area. Josie had never seen so many matching bras and panties in her life. A dozen full-length mirrors on the far side of the tent were almost invisible through the crowd gathered in front of them peering at their reflections.

"You hold. I'll dress," Gayle suggested.

Josie grabbed the dresses eagerly. "Fine. Ah . . ." She didn't know how to begin.

"You want to tell me why I should introduce you to the Hendersons," Gayle reminded her.

"Yes. I'm trying to figure out who killed Pamela Peel. She was Shepard Henderson's partner. In Henderson and Peel," Josie added. Gayle was pulling her sweater over her head and didn't answer immediately.

"You think Mr. or Mrs. Henderson did it?" she asked when she was free.

"I . . . oh, of course not!"

"Are you so sure they didn't?"

Josie realized what Gayle was saying. "Why? Would they have? Did they hate her?"

"They couldn't stand her. On the other hand, they are probably too civilized to actually kill someone."

"Do you think Shepard Henderson knows how they feel?"

"Actually, I doubt if they shared their thoughts on that subject with their son. The Hendersons are a close family in some ways but not in others. As Mrs. Henderson would say, 'We don't intrude on each other's lives.' They certainly wouldn't criticize the professional opinion of their only beloved son."

"Really? Doesn't sound like my family," Josie commented, trying to help Gayle close the zipper on the gown she was wearing without dropping anything.

"Mine either. Unfortunately. And I'll have to run a gauntlet of questions and suggestions at this damn wedding next week. Mainly concerning my status as a single woman."

"I know exactly what you mean," Josie said, frowning.

Gayle turned and smiled at her. "Okay. We've bonded. Tell me, why do you think one of the Hendersons killed Pamela Peel?"

"Oh, I don't. I mean, I'd be happy if one of them did. Because I'm looking for suspects, not because I have anything against them. The man I'm involved with is the main, maybe the only, suspect at the present time," she explained.

"Dawn told me. How about the black one?" Gayle handed Josie the green gown and reached out for another.

"Oh, okay." Josie handed Gayle a silk sheath. "Anyway, I wanted to talk to the Hendersons because I wanted to hear what they thought of Pamela. I was hoping to learn more about her."

"You're hoping to discover that she was dating a homicidal maniac."

"Exactly."

"Can't quite imagine her doing anything like that, at least not from what I've heard about her."

"Have you heard much?"

"Oh, tons. Most of it completely biased, you understand, but, yes, while Sterling Henderson was a patient of mine, he talked about her endlessly."

"Why?"

"He and Mrs. Henderson thought she was after their son and, in turn, their money. What do you think?"

"Well, just because you're involved with someone doesn't mean you end up with any of their parents' money."

"No, I mean about this dress." Gayle was wearing a long black column of silk topped with a short jacket.

"It's a little . . . uh, severe, isn't it?" Josie asked.

"Too nunlike?"

"Just a bit. Or more like you're in mourning. You don't want to give that impression, do you?"

"Oh no! I want everyone to think I'm happy, happy, happy."

"Try the red," Josie suggested, untangling the sleeves of two different gowns and passing a red number over to Gayle. "So, are you telling me that Pamela and Shep Henderson were romantically involved?"

"That's a good question. . . . Oh . . ."

"Wait . . . Let me . . ."

It took a few minutes for Josie to figure out how a hook and eye had become wound up in Gayle's hair, then a few more minutes for both women to realize that this size eight was more like a size six. "Too bad. The color is terrific."

"Alas. Well, let's try the silver. Brocade isn't usually my thing, but I'm desperate. Now where were we?"

"You were going to tell me whether or not Pamela and Shep were dating."

"Not dating. No. Well, not that I know of. According to Mr. Henderson, his wife was obsessed with the possibility that they might get together."

"Why?"

"I have no idea. I do know that Mrs. Henderson desperately wanted her son to marry the daughter of one of her friends. And I do know that she didn't want him to marry Pamela Peel. But why she thought that might happen is beyond me."

"But something must have happened in their professional life for her to even consider the possibility."

"Oh, not that I know of. This was years ago. They were just forming Henderson and Peel."

"Really? Do you know how his parents reacted to that?"

"I sure do." Gayle paused, took a deep breath, and zipped up the silver dress. "This much I can tell you. Shep Henderson was supposed to follow his father to Harvard or, if he really wanted to prove his independence, to attend Yale. Instead he chose to go to Brown." She grinned at the expression on Josie's face. "Okay, it's not running off to join the foreign legion or a cult, but, remember this is a very conservative family. And then, instead of investment banking, the field that had made his parents very, very wealthy, he decided to become an interior decorator. They were horrified."

"Were they concerned about his . . . lifestyle?"

"I know what you're thinking. Mrs. Henderson insisted that her son was not gay and, although I'm sure that in many cases the mother is the last to know, Shep apparently provided her with proof."

"Proof?"

"They paid for abortions for more than one of his girlfriends when he was young. At least that's what Mr. Henderson told me. 'Damn fool kid,' he called him, but I think he was proud of him in a way."

"How male."

"Very. Anyway, although he decorated rich people's homes instead of investing their money, his parents always seemed proud of him. They were constantly talking about him and they never said anything negative."

"But that didn't hold true for Pamela Peel."

"No, they said a lot against her." Gayle stopped speaking and drifted over to the mirrors. Josie followed, clothes in hand.

"Perhaps you don't want all these items?" The woman who had rushed over to them had a stern look on her face.

"No, we don't want this . . . or this . . . or this." Josie handed over the rejects and then hurried off to find Gayle.

"What do you think?"

"You look beautiful. I love the silver with your hair color."

"Okay. Sold. I'll just pay for this and we can get going."

"Where to?" Josie asked, confused.

"To see Mrs. Henderson. Where else?"

TWENTY-FIVE

CAROL REFUSED TO accompany Josie on her visit to Mrs. Henderson. "You'll be fine without me and I have another lead that I'd like to follow up," she had answered when asked. Josie suspected that it was another shopping opportunity that was tempting Carol, so she hurried on alone only to find that Gayle had made her purchase and was anxious to be on the way.

"How are you going to explain my presence?" Josie asked as they got into one of the cabs that had just unloaded a group of women at the entrance to the pier. Snowflakes were beginning to fall as the taxi drove onto the Henry Hudson Parkway.

"I already did," Gayle answered after announcing their destination to the driver.

"When?"

"I called her right after Dawn called me."

"You were going to introduce us without meeting me?"

"Yes. In the first place, I trust Dawn's judgment and she felt that helping you was worthwhile. And, of course, I did need someone to help me hang on to dresses while I tried on others. Put something down in that place and it's lost," Gayle admitted.

"So where are we going?"

"To the Hendersons' home. They live on the East Side."

"What did you tell her about me?"

"Just that you were looking into Pamela Peel's murder."

"And that I wanted to ask her some questions?"

"No, she said right away that she would like to speak with you."

"Really? Did she tell you why?"

"No, but she will. This family is very up-front. When the worst thing that's happened to you is that your son chose the wrong career to be successful in, there's little reason not to be," she added.

"I guess."

The sky, visible between the tall buildings, was ominously dark and Josie wondered if this was the beginning of a full-scale snowstorm.

"Gonna be ten inches by tomorrow morning," their driver said. "I'm going home as soon as you're dropped off."

"But don't people need cabs in bad weather as much, or more, than in good weather?" Josie asked.

"They need cabs. But not my cab." He hit the accelerator and Josie and Gayle were thrown against the backseat, ending their conversation.

"I haven't heard a weather forecast since I arrived in the city," Josie said, looking out the window.

"There was something about a storm moving in from Canada on the *Today* show this morning," Gayle said. "To tell you the truth, I wasn't paying much attention. I don't worry about these things a whole lot. You know those guys on TV. They're forever making a big deal out of storm systems that turn out to be absolutely nothing."

"I hope you're right," Josie said as the cab swerved over to a curb and flung her against the door.

"This is it, ladies. This is as far as I go in this snow."

"I guess we get out here," Gayle said, paying the driver the amount on the meter and no more. Either in retaliation for the loss of his tip or because he was in such a hurry to get away, their driver took off in a spin of wheels causing filthy water and slush to run up their legs and soak the hems of their coats.

"Damn! First he doesn't take us the whole way and now this. I don't suppose you got his license number?"

"No, I never even thought to look."

"Oh well, let's get going. We don't want to be late and now we have three blocks to walk," Gayle informed her, striding across the street.

Josie followed, deciding that she was too wet to worry about more water. The flakes were becoming larger and the sky seemed darker. They hurried down 75th Street, past small specialty shops, dry cleaners, doors with brass plaques identifying the services available within. Josie noticed that some of the town houses had only one mailbox and wondered briefly about the people who could afford such a large chunk of New York real estate. When they stopped, Josie realized they were at the river.

"The Hudson?"

"Wrong direction. That's the East River. You'll have a great view of it from the Hendersons' place. Come on."

Shep Henderson's parents' duplex had river views from every window, Renoirs and van Goghs on the walls, antique Oriental carpets on inlaid marble floors, and staff to open the doors for guests. Josie found herself working hard not to find it all incredibly intimidating. The maid led them into a sitting room and explained that she would inform Mrs. Henderson of their arrival. Gayle and Josie headed straight for the large bay window.

"Incredible, isn't it?" Gayle asked.

"The view, the apartment, or the uniformed staff?"

"All of it, I suppose."

"Then I agree with you."

"The snow seems to be coming down more quickly, doesn't it?"

If Josie had had more experience of the upper classes, she

would have recognized the accent and tenor of a fine prep school education in Mrs. Henderson's voice.

"Yes, it does," Gayle agreed, turning around with a smile on her face, a smile that faded when she saw Shep's mother.

Josie turned. The woman standing in the doorway of the room had gray hair sweeping across her high forehead before coming to an end in a shoulder-length pageboy. There were faint lines around her eyes and lips; otherwise her skin was unmarked. Her eyes were the same pale blue as her son's. And she was dressed entirely in black. Even without knowing the situation, Josie would have recognized formal mourning attire.

"Good afternoon, Gayle, it's nice to see you again. And you must be Josie Pigeon."

"Yes, I am. Thank you for seeing me," Josie added as Mrs. Henderson drifted into the room.

"I'm glad to do anything I can to help. Please sit down. My maid will be here with coffee and tea. Unless you would like something stronger?" She waved toward a dark chestnut bar standing in the corner. Dozens of gleaming decanters stood upon its mirrored surface.

"No, I think we're just fine," Gayle answered.

"Yes, fine," Josie echoed.

"Then why don't we sit down? I'll light a fire." She reached out and turned a switch above the travertine marble mantel and flames leapt up between pristine birch logs. "So much easier and less messy than a real fire. But I do miss the crackle and the divine scent."

"Uh, yes." Josie sat awkwardly in an embroidered wing chair facing the chintz love seat where Mrs. Henderson perched ramrod straight, not allowing her back to rest against the piles of needlepoint pillows arranged behind her.

"It was nice of you to see us on such short notice," Gayle began.

"Such a sad occasion," Mrs. Henderson said. "I haven't heard when the funeral is to be, have you?"

"Well, the police have to release the body first," Josie explained. She had been unprepared for Mrs. Henderson's reaction. She seemed far more upset by Pamela's death than her son had been.

"Oh, yes, of course. I hadn't thought of that. We're not . . . well, to be frank, we're not accustomed to being involved in these hideous police matters."

"No one is," Gayle said.

Josie decided this was no time to disagree. She merely nodded and remained silent about the murder investigations in her own not so distant past.

"Of course, the entire family is devastated. Such a dreadful loss. She was so young, so vibrant, so warm, and so talented. We all loved her."

Josie wondered if they were all speaking about the same person. Apparently Gayle had the same question—only she asked it. "This is Pamela Peel we're talking about, yes?"

"Yes, dear, dear Pamela. We had our differences, of course."

Josie resisted the urge to ask for more information and Mrs. Henderson continued uninterrupted.

"You see, Sterling and I didn't totally agree with our son's choice of career. We were hoping he would grow into his father's position at Henderson Investments. Shepard always was so good at money and numbers. But dear Shepard had other plans. I fear we blamed Pamela Peel for a while there. We simply could not understand why Shep would rather pick out furniture instead of stock for our friends. But, of course, we came around to his way of thinking in time. My husband and I are rather set in our ways, I'm afraid. But we understand that the younger generation must go their own way. Are you a mother, my dear?"

Josie realized the question was being addressed to her.

"I . . . yes. My son is seventeen. He's a student at . . ." Josie mentioned the prep school Tyler attended and was pleased to see Mrs. Henderson's eyebrows raise a bit and the expression on her face soften. Josie didn't add that his tuition and expenses were paid by a small legacy from an old friend, supplemented by a scholarship for his expenses.

"Then you understand what I mean."

Josie nodded. She did understand now that Tyler seemed determined to become a movie producer. She had always imagined him surrounded by computers, not starlets. But this was no time for a philosophical discussion. "You blamed Pamela Peel for the fact that your son became a decorator?" she asked.

"I'm afraid we did, yes. Of course that was Shep's fault."

Josie was mystified. "Why?"

"Oh, Shep has always said that without Pamela Peel as his partner, he would have been forced to work with another, less talented, decorator. He would have hated that. And his father and I always believed that he would have preferred to go to Wharton or Harvard Business School rather than work as a gofer for some no-name decorator on the Upper West Side."

"How did they happen to become business partners?" Josie asked, realizing that this woman, at least, blamed Pamela Peel for Shepard's decision to become a decorator.

"Oh, she came after him. Women are always coming after Shep. Well, why not? He's good-looking, talented, educated. . . ." She took a breath and continued. "And wealthy, of course." She had turned slightly and was staring at the evenly burning flames in the fireplace.

"Do you happen to know if your son's money was used to finance Henderson and Peel?" Josie asked. She knew the answer to this question, but she wondered if it was possible that Shepard Henderson had kept his parents in the dark when it came to his financial situation.

For the first time, Mrs. Henderson paused before answering. "I was brought up not to discuss money in public. You understand."

Actually, Josie did. But, although her own parents would agree with Mrs. Henderson's statement, she had spent the last eighteen years discussing money with everyone—her small family, her friends, her crews, her landlady, the people for whom she worked. She repeated the question. "So you think that your son's money was needed to begin Henderson and Peel."

"I am quite sure of it. Pamela was talented. Even I will admit that. But, to be quite honest, she certainly did not have the resources at her command that my son had—and has."

"Mrs. Henderson, if your son's money was used to create Henderson and Peel—"

"And I believe it was," Shep's mother interrupted, making her point again.

"Then why is he so worried about the future of the company now that Pamela is dead? I mean, doesn't he own most of the company?"

"Who do you think will use a company whose background is stained by an unsolved murder? My friends are not any more accustomed to this sort of thing than I am, I can assure you. Some people who don't know what happened may hire Shepard. And he may be sought out by people who are dreadful enough to want to be near any sort of notoriety." She shuddered. "But in time an unsolved murder will seriously damage if not destroy Henderson and Peel."

Josie leaned forward. "I want this murder solved too," she admitted. "And anything you can tell me about Pamela Peel . . ." She left the sentence unfinished. Something had passed across Mrs. Henderson's face. Was it fear? "They say the victim is always the key," she ended, fearful that anything she could add would prevent this woman from continuing.

"But that's just it. I cannot imagine why anyone would

want to kill Pamela. My son and I were just talking about this over cocktails last night. He feels, as I do, that Pamela was the victim of a random killing. There are so many of them in this city, I'm afraid. It is possible that the person who killed her moved out of the dark wasteland of the slums, murdered, and then moved right back out of our lives."

"But she was found in . . . ," Gayle began.

"In an apartment Henderson and Peel had decorated," Josie jumped in before Gayle had an opportunity to mention Sam's name.

"Sheer coincidence. She must have been there for some reason; the murderer was there for some other reason. They met. And . . . and tragedy." Mrs. Henderson lowered her eyes.

Josie was suddenly reminded of something her mother used to say when she was growing up: "Just because you say it doesn't make it true." She wanted to repeat this phrase right now. But she knew it would only stop Mrs. Henderson from talking. "That could have happened, but do you know why Pamela would have been in that particular place at that particular time? I mean, I understood that Henderson and Peel decorated it years and years ago. Did Pamela or your son ever return to the places they had worked for any . . . any professional reason?"

"Oh, my dear, there's a simple answer to that question. Pamela was desperately in love with the man who owned that apartment. Everyone knew that. She was probably meeting him there. . . ." There was a rustling sound and Mrs. Henderson looked over Josie's shoulder at the door. "Oh, Sterling, you're home."

Josie and Gayle turned around to see an elderly man standing in the doorway. He was tall, thin, and elegant. His hair was gray, but his eyes were as blue as his son's.

"Gayle, you, of course, know my husband. But this is

Josie Pigeon, dear. She's interested in helping the police . . . well, in helping someone find dear Pamela's killer."

"May I ask exactly why you're involved, my dear? Since Francesca obviously does not know."

"I . . ." Josie glanced at Gayle, but the other woman was silent. "I'm good friends with the man whose apartment she was discovered in. I'm afraid the police might make a mistake, that they might suspect him."

"But then . . . ," Mrs. Henderson began and then stopped, looking to her husband for guidance.

"Pamela's death is probably exactly the sort of murder that happens all too frequently in these uncivilized times," Sterling Henderson stated. "An animal, a monster, had access to an apartment in a good part of the city and simply killed whomever he discovered there. My wife, my son, and I were discussing this just the other day."

"Yes," Mrs. Henderson added quickly, "so dreadful."

Josie glanced out the window into the storm and then back into the elegant, warm room and shivered.

TWENTY-SIX

THE SNOW HAD increased while Josie and Gayle had been talking with the Hendersons and they had used that as an excuse for their hasty exit when Josie realized they were going to learn nothing more. After Josie had assured Gayle that she could find her way back to Mentelle Park Apartments and thanked her for her help, Gayle had taken her packages and headed for the closest subway entrance. Josie had started walking.

Josie loved snow. The flakes reminded her of sledding on the highest hill in town when she was a child, of making snow angels and forts. Having stayed in good shape building and remodeling, shoveling show wasn't hard on her back and walking the beach in the winter was one of the special charms of living off-season at the seashore.

But, like so much else this week, a snowstorm in New York City was an entirely new experience. She had noticed before how the tall buildings channeled and increased the wind, but now the snow whipped around corners, momentarily stretching out in long tongues on the overhangs of buildings before falling to the ground in sharp chunks. The bitter cold stung her face, almost taking her breath away. There were already about six inches of snow on the ground. She passed a few industrious shop owners shoveling their walks, but the snow they shoveled into the street was almost immediately thrown back by a plow dashing by. Deep drifts were forming across cars parked at the curb. Their cabdriver hadn't been alone in his opinions; there seemed to be fewer cabs on the streets than at any time since her arrival in the city.

All the pedestrians were in a hurry. Some wore tall, fur-lined boots, and some were completely unprepared for the onslaught and slipped on the icy mess in thin high heels. She spied a man, sockless in his Gucci loafers, striding through the blizzard as though he was immune to cold. A white-coated waiter opened the door of a coffee shop and suggested she come inside and warm up with a cup of hot chocolate—for free, he added when she refused. But Josie hurried on, counting the blocks, anxious to get home, hoping Sam would be there to greet her.

And he was there, actually waiting in the lobby, chatting with Harold, looking very worried. Josie began to dash across the floor and fling herself into his arms, but she slid on the damp marble and, after a few seconds spent grabbing in the air for something to hold on to, crashed onto the floor, smacking her head against a marble pillar. Looking up, she saw Sam and Harold, surrounded by tiny colored, twinkling stars. She closed her eyes; the faces disappeared, the stars remained.

"I'll call nine-one-one."

"No. No. I think I'm okay." Josie tried to struggle to her feet, but firm hands held her down.

"This is all my fault, Mr. Richardson, I'd really feel better if you'd let me call for an ambulance."

"I'm okay," Josie repeated.

"I don't think an ambulance will get through this snow easily," Sam pointed out.

"But Lenox Hill is just a few blocks away. Maybe we could walk her there." Harold seemed determined to get Josie to the hospital.

"I'm okay. Really," Josie added when no one seemed to believe her.

"Perhaps we could walk her upstairs and let her lie down for a while," Sam suggested.

"Good. Yes. That's what we should do," Josie agreed. She would have shaken her head, but it really was incredibly painful.

"If she has a concussion, we should see the signs in the next few hours," Sam continued.

Well, that was a relief. "I do have a slight headache," Josie admitted.

"Look at her eyeballs," Harold suggested. "They shouldn't be dilated."

"Can we do this someplace else?" Josie asked. "This floor is awfully hard."

"Of course! Do you think you can walk or should we carry you?"

"I'd rather walk," Josie said very honestly. "If you could just help me get up."

It would have been much easier for her to get up by herself since Sam and Harold seemed to be under the impression that she was made of some sort of thin, fragile china. But she was on her feet in a few minutes. Harold insisted on putting a chair in the elevator so she didn't have to stand while she rode. Finally, a few minutes later she was lying on the couch in Sam's apartment, wondering if her mild headache actually might turn into something serious.

"Josie? I'm just going to put this on your forehead."

She sat up and the towel-wrapped bag of ice slid onto her chest. "What are you doing? That thing's freezing! Get it off me!" She grabbed it and tossed it onto the floor. "I was just beginning to feel warm." She sighed, sinking back into the couch cushions.

"Josie . . ."

Sam didn't continue and Josie looked up into his concerned

eyes. She remembered the worried expression on his face downstairs when she had finally made it to his building. "I'm sorry, Sam. I'm fine, but I had to walk here from . . ." She suddenly realized she didn't want to continue this part of the conversation. "It's really very cold outside," she ended.

"Did you leave Mother at her place and walk here?" Sam asked.

"I . . . yes. She should be home now," Josie said. "Her hair color is fixed," she added.

"Well, that's a relief. Would you like a glass of brandy? Or maybe some tea?"

"No, thanks, I'm fine. I have a bit of a headache, but nothing serious." She reached out for his hand. "I was so glad to see you when I walked in the door, Sam."

If she had expected anything it was that he would reply in kind, expressing relief that she had returned safely, but Sam seemed distracted, getting up and walking toward the kitchen. "I think some herb tea," he said, ignoring her.

"I really don't want anything." But Sam was filling the teakettle and Josie decided that maybe he was right. Maybe a cup of tea would be a good thing.

"So where did you and Mother spend the day? It couldn't have taken the entire time to have her hair done."

"No. Of course not. We went to this incredible sale. It was almost all clothing down . . . over . . . on the pier. At the Spotlight Sale."

"Oh, that's nice. Mother is always talking about going there. What did you buy?"

"Oh, well, I didn't get anything. I spent a lot of time looking . . . and holding clothing while your mother tried things on. It was the most fascinating place. Did you know that famous people, actresses and all, donate clothing and then their names are on the hangers?"

"And they charge more for those things?" Sam asked.

"I guess. To tell the truth, those things were designer

gowns and they seemed incredibly expensive—thousands of dollars for some of them—and it never occurred to me that where they came from had much to do with it."

"I'm glad you had a good day," Sam said, returning to her side with a steaming mug with a tea bag hanging out.

"It was interesting," Josie admitted. "How long do you think this snow is going to last?"

"I bought a small radio today. I was beginning to feel a little cut off from the world, frankly. It's in the bedroom. I'll go get it and we can listen to the news. A storm in New York pretty much captures the media's interest . . . but I wanted to talk with you for a minute."

Sam's voice and expression were deadly serious and, suddenly, Josie was afraid of hearing his next words. He put down the tea and took both her hands in his. "Josie, how do you think Mother is doing?"

It was pretty much the last thing she thought he would ask and, for a moment, she wasn't sure how to answer. "You mean, do I think she's beginning to become senile or something like that?"

"Sort of. Have you noticed any changes in her?"

Josie chuckled. "Besides her hair color?"

"I know I sound like a worried son, but this could be important, Josie. You've been with her almost every day since you came to the city. Think. Has she seemed strange? Or said anything strange to you? Anything at all?"

Josie thought. Carol and she had talked about Sam, about Pamela Peel, about decorating and clothing and hairstyles. She decided to tell the truth, some of it. "She is very worried about you," she answered.

"About me? In what sense?"

"Because Pamela Peel's body was found here. She . . . we've been thinking that whoever killed her wanted you to be the major suspect. And you know how Carol worries about you even when there's nothing to worry about."

"And she thinks that this time there is something real to worry about."

"Yes. Yes, she does," Josie said. "Sam, we're both really worried about you."

"I'm fine, Josie. It's Mother I'm worried about now."

"But there's no reason—"

"There is. I can't tell you everything, but there really is. Really," he repeated.

She didn't know what to say.

"Josie, you know Mother didn't like Pamela."

"How do you know?"

"Oh, Mother thinks she keeps her feelings hidden, but she's an open book to me. I always know how she feels about the women I date." And he smiled gently at her. "I knew how much she liked you the first time she came down to the island."

Josie smiled back. "It wasn't me she liked. She was crazy about Tyler and I was his mother, so she had to accept me."

"Well, whatever. But I am very, very worried about Mother. It may be only a matter of time before Mother is the primary suspect in Pamela's murder."

For just a moment, Josie wondered if this entire conversation was a hallucination caused by the concussion Sam was so worried about. Then she regrouped. Sam thought his mother had killed Pamela Peel. That's why he was acting so strangely. And, of course, his mother was acting strangely—because she was worried that Sam was the only suspect. She began to giggle inanely. "Oh, Sam, you won't believe . . ."

"I'm sorry, Josie. I don't see what's so funny." He leaned down and picked up one of her eyelids and peered inside. "Are you feeling okay? Maybe you should lie back down."

"No, I'm fine. It's not funny really. I guess I'm just a little relieved." She took a deep breath and regained her composure. "It's just that your mother is worried about you. That's why she's acting so odd. Well, odder than usual."

Sam rested his head in his hands. "Why? Why is she worrying about me this time?"

"She thinks you might be arrested for killing Pamela Peel."

Sam looked up and into her eyes. "She is the one person who knows I didn't kill her. She's the one person who can prove I didn't kill her. So why should she be so worried?"

"How . . . I don't understand. Why is Carol the one person who can prove you didn't kill Pamela? And, if that's true, why is she in such a panic that you might be arrested?"

"Josie, the only answers I have don't make any sense," Sam answered quietly. "At least," he added, his voice dropping almost to a whisper, "at least I hope I don't understand their meaning."

TWENTY-SEVEN

EVERY BABY HAS bad days, days when he cries for no apparent reason, days when he won't sleep, days when he makes the lives of those around him absolutely miserable. And those days almost always happen at the least convenient time.

JJ was having a really bad day.

So was his mother.

"Josie, I'd put him down, but he screams even louder," Betty said into the phone. "I hope you can hear me. I spent hours calling everyone on the list Carol made—before JJ began to act up—and I have three different companies who have worked for Henderson and Peel and seem to be willing to talk."

"What do you mean, seem to be willing?"

"I couldn't just ask what they knew about Pamela Peel. I mean, that would have been a little strange when I introduced myself as a prospective client, right? Oh, wait, JJ's taking his teething ring. . . . You know he's quite young to be teething."

"He's completely amazing in every way. Now tell me about these three contractors," Josie insisted. She had finally convinced Sam that it was perfectly safe to leave her alone and he had wandered into the bedroom to listen to the radio for news of the storm. The last time she'd checked, he was dozing on the bed. But Sam's restlessness would likely prevent him from sleeping too long and she wanted to talk to Betty without an audience.

"Well, I told all the companies that I would be hiring Henderson and Peel for a big job and I wanted to be sure that they were used to working with them."

"Good thinking."

"Thanks for that. There are days when I think my brain is beginning to bear a strong resemblance to Pablum."

Josie decided not to tell her friend that it was only going to get worse as JJ got older. "So give me the list and I'll let you go. Maybe JJ will fall asleep and you can take a long bath and get to bed early."

"Oh, Jon and I are thinking of bundling JJ up and going for a walk in Central Park. JJ loves being in his backpack and the city is so gorgeous in the snow."

"You must be talking about a different city from the one I was just walking in—the one where there's absolutely no place to put all this snow, where there are no cabs, where . . ." She remembered the waiter who had offered her free hot chocolate to warm up, and stopped complaining.

"I know. But look out the window when you get a chance. It really is gorgeous this evening. Oh, damn, JJ's losing interest in his teething ring. Listen, I faxed the list over to your place. It should be downstairs at the front desk. But don't hang up without telling me everything you've learned."

"That will be easy because I've learned almost nothing."

"That's not possible. You've been so busy."

"Well, not nothing exactly. I know a lot about how hairdressers stay in business; I know a little about how interior decorators work. I can tell midtown from downtown. And, thanks to Sam's mother, I am damn near intimate with some of the departments at Saks Fifth Avenue. But, as for finding out who killed Pamela Peel . . . well, that I don't know. But I am sure that Carol thinks Sam is going to be arrested for Pamela Peel's murder and Sam is afraid Carol will be."

"You're kidding!" Betty's words could barely be made out as her son's expression of unhappiness moved into high frequency.

"I'll call you as soon as I check out these contractors," Josie assured her and hung up without a formal good-bye. Sam was still snoring and she decided she could dash down to the lobby and be back before he noticed her absence. She rummaged in her purse for the keys Sam had given her. Then, locking the door behind her, she hurried toward the elevator.

Harold was wiping the floor with a huge fluffy mop and he looked up when the elevator doors opened and she stepped out. "Ms. Pigeon! Should you be walking around on your own? Symptoms of a concussion can appear hours after the initial injury."

"I'm fine. Really. But I was just talking on the phone with a friend of mine and she said she had faxed something here."

"Tell you the truth, I've been too busy to check the machine, but it's right in that room there if you wanna look for yourself. Your name will be on it, right?"

"I guess so," Josie answered, heading toward the heavy brass-covered door Harold had indicated.

It was his office, she realized once inside. Unlike the lobby, designed and decorated to impress, in here everything was unadorned and functional. There was a large computer sitting on an old gunmetal desk. Packages from FedEx, United Parcel, and the U.S. Mail were stacked on a bench in one corner. A huge bulletin board, covered with notes and diagrams, hung crookedly on one wall. A large coffeepot steamed away on top of a trio of filing cabinets. The scent of pepperoni wafted from old, greasy cartons squashed into an overflowing, black plastic wastebasket. A fax machine had been placed on upturned plastic milk cartons; its messages slid out onto the floor underneath.

"Welcome to my world." Harold stood behind her. "Did you find what you were looking for in the mess?"

"I think they're probably on the floor under the machine," Josie said, surprised by his presence.

"Well, don't bend down. You might get a head rush; don't want you passing out. I'll get them for you."

"Oh, thank you." Josie would have preferred to do this herself, but she didn't see how she could protest.

Fortunately, Betty had written both Josie and Sam's names across the top of the list of names and phone numbers.

"Mr. Richardson looking to remodel instead of move?" Harold asked, handing over the faxed message.

"No. I'm a contractor, you know," she added.

"No, I didn't. Who do you work for?"

"I own my own business," Josie said, feeling, as usual, the pleasure that statement gave her. "Island Contracting."

"Then why the list?"

"I'm looking for a . . . a carpenter who worked for me last summer," Josie improvised.

"And you think he may be with one of those companies now?"

"It's possible. A friend of mine who is living in the city now made the list. She thinks these companies are likely candidates." She glanced at the clock on the wall. It was almost seven P.M. "Thanks for letting me in here. I don't want to keep you from leaving for home, though."

"Oh, I'm not leaving anytime soon."

"I thought you went off duty at seven."

"Not tonight. Tonight I do an overnight. The night doorman lives up in the Bronx. Trains aren't running so he's stuck there and I'm stuck here. Not that I mind. These residents are my friends as well as my employers. I like to help them out in emergencies."

"Emergencies like murder investigations?" Josie asked,

suddenly realizing that Harold could be an untapped wealth of information.

"This is a first for me, to tell the truth. Not for Mentelle Park Apartments though," he added. "There was a man who found his wife in bed with his business partner. Shot them both dead and then turned himself in to the police. That was back in the fifties, though, before my time."

"Oh." Josie was quiet for a minute, looking down at the list Betty had sent and counting six contracting companies. "Do you know anything about any of these companies? Have any of them worked here?" she asked, remembering Betty's comment about the list kept by the building where she lived.

Harold took the list from her and read through it with a frown on his face.

"Well, I don't know about this carpenter you're trying to find, but I do know two of these contractors. Seems to me both of them have worked here." He scratched the back of his neck and continued. "Remodeling is big, real big, these days. Not like when I first came to work here. Back then, when someone didn't like their apartment, they moved. Then we became a condo building. Most of the buildings around either went condo or co-op, and it wasn't just a matter of finding a new place and getting your deposit back anymore. Now people had to buy and sell and they had to be approved by new boards and new residents had to be approved by the board here. It got harder and harder to move and it seemed a whole lot easier to just remodel what you had. Of course, remodeling always looks easier than it's going to be."

"You can say that again," Josie said, leaning against the desk. "My company works down at the shore, primarily on individual family homes, and a lot of the time we work off-season on summerhouses so the residents aren't directly bothered by our work. I can't imagine working on a small apartment like Sam's while someone is living there."

"It's not easy, I can tell you. Of course, there are people who manage to get their work done while they're at their summer homes up in Connecticut or out on the Island, but lots live with the dirt, dust, and workmen for the entire job. Never know with some of those people whether they're happy the job is done or just real glad to be alone again."

Josie chuckled. "I can't imagine Sam was happy to have the work going on while he lived here."

"Well, he always worked long hours and ate out a lot anyway. And he was dating that dead woman then and he stayed with her a lot too, I'd imagine." Harold looked down at the floor.

Josie was about to feel uncomfortable with this statement and then she considered that it might be significant. Was it possible that Pamela Peel had wanted it that way? Could she have given Sam the decorating job as a Christmas present hoping the angst of work would force him to move in with her, and possibly never move out?

"Although Mr. Richardson's job wasn't like most jobs," Harold continued.

"What do you mean?"

"Ms. Peel was real insistent that Mr. Richardson not see the job until it was complete, I remember that." He chuckled. "She had that work done in record time. Came in one day with a moving company that packed up his personal stuff and then took every damn piece of furniture out of the apartment. Got rid of it one, two, three. I always wondered what happened to the big old desk he had in the living room. Good-looking piece, made of real chestnut and inlaid like with a darker wood. It probably went off to Goodwill or the Salvation Army with everything else."

"Did the job take a long time?" Josie asked, thinking that if Pamela had wanted an excuse to keep Sam at her place, she might have been able to arrange for the decorating to take longer than was usual.

"Nope. Shortest job on record that I remember. Day after the place was emptied, it was all gutted. The actual construction took only a few days. She had so many workmen in there that they were complaining about bumping into one another. Then the decorating began. Those walls took four days to paint, I remember that."

"Are we talking about the gray walls that are there now?" Josie asked.

"Yup. There's an undercoat, of course. Then two layers of some special flat paint from the Netherlands, I remember that. Thought to myself back then that going to the Netherlands for that particular color paint was a real waste of time. Could of gone over to the Brooklyn Navy Yard and bought a few cans of the stuff they used to use on battleships, same dull gray. Anyway, there are two different glazes on the top of that foreign paint. Didn't turn out to be anything special is my own personal opinion, but you're the only one I'm sharing it with. . . . Sorry, I'll be right back. Someone's ringing the buzzer to get in."

Josie stared down at the names of the contractors, wondering if one of them might have worked for Henderson and Peel when they decorated Sam's place. She had just decided to ask Harold about that when he returned, a big smile on his face.

"It's the Hoges in Three-B. One or the other of them is always losing their key. This time they did it together. Gotta get the spare and hand it over." And he unlocked what Josie had thought was a fuse box on the wall. Three or four dozen keys hung there, all named and labeled. Notes hung from some hooks as well as keys. Josie stared. Betty hadn't known about this when she had checked on Mentelle Park's security arrangements!

Harold was barely back in the room when Josie asked her next question. "Who has access to those keys?"

If Harold was surprised by her blunt question, it didn't

prevent him from answering. "I'll tell you what I told the police detective who asked about access to the apartments the morning that Pamela Peel was discovered. There are three doormen. We have access to this room, which is usually kept locked, and we all three have a key that opens the key box and gives us access to those keys. We three are the only people who can let anyone into his place. Period."

"So the police thought someone might have used a key from here to get into Sam's place and put the body there," Josie said.

"They thought it, but I told them I doubted it."

"Why?"

"Look, Mentelle Park Apartments is not some fly-by-night developer's dream. We've been here a long time and we're gonna remain here a long time—by the grace of God—and it's not just the tenants who don't move. The employees hang around too. I've been working here for over twenty-five years. The night guy was here when I came. The morning man is our newest employee and he'll have been with us for a dozen years come summer. We do hire cleaners—companies to do the windows, someone who cleans the lobby twice a week—but no one has access to this room, or to these keys. And those outside people are bonded and never left alone. Mentelle Park Apartments is as secure as you can get in this city."

"What if I came here without Sam and told you I needed to get into his place?"

"I'd tell you the same thing I told that pretty young friend of yours. You don't get in without a key. Everyone knows keys are not given out by any employees. Now, as I told the policeman, you never know what residents might do."

"You mean who they might give keys to."

"Yup. That's exactly what I mean. They're not supposed to, but some of them have keys made for their significant others and sometimes those others don't stay significant for too long."

Josie reached into her pocket, pulled out the keys Sam had given her, and examined them. "It says do not copy. The words are printed right into the key."

"Yeah, and marijuana's illegal, but anyone can walk a few blocks and get that and most other illegal drugs as well. If you can make money selling it in this city, you'll find it sold somewhere. Might have to look, might not. But you'll find someone to copy that key easy. Most door keys have that message printed on them. Suspect most people just ignore it."

"What about Sam's tenant? Is it possible that he had keys made for other people?"

"I suppose so, but, to tell you the truth, Mr. Richardson's tenant was a real quiet guy. Worked long hours. Always came home alone as far as I knew. They checked with the night man, too, and I happen to know he said the same thing. Can't imagine that any keys were left around by him. Guess you'll have to look someplace else for the person who had a key to Mr. Richardson's place."

"I guess I will," Josie agreed, standing up.

"Sorry I couldn't help you more."

"Actually, you helped a lot," Josie said, leaving the office and heading back across the lobby to the elevator.

TWENTY-EIGHT

J OSIE HAD A lot to think about during the short elevator ride up to Sam's floor. What Harold either didn't know or had chosen not to tell her was that all these residents who were so actively remodeling had possibly—probably—given a key to someone who was working on their place. So there were two reasons for Pamela Peel to have been given a key to this apartment: love, her relationship with Sam; and money, the decorating job she had taken on.

The door opened on Sam's floor and Sam himself was standing there.

"Josie! I woke up and you were gone! Are you okay? How's your head?"

"I'm fine, Sam. I just went downstairs to . . . to see what the snow looked like."

"Snow looks different here than everyplace else?"

"Sort of." Josie wandered over to the window and peered out, putting her hands in her pockets and jingling Sam's keys.

"I talked with Betty on the phone and she said . . ." Josie had an inspiration. "She said it was gorgeous out and did I want to join her for a walk in Central Park. She said she and Jon do it all the time in snowy weather."

Sam smiled. "That's a good idea. If you're feeling up to it, why don't we both go?"

"That is a good idea, but . . . I have to go to the bathroom first. I'll be right back." Josie hurried toward her goal, stopping in the bedroom only long enough to grab the portable phone off the bedside table. She locked the bathroom door behind her and dialed. If only Carol was in . . .

She was! Without bothering to explain why, she told Carol exactly what she needed her to do and hung up, returning to the living room with a big smile on her face. "Ready?"

"Sure, just let me get my boots and coat. Damn," he added when the phone rang.

Josie reached out to pick up the receiver.

"Don't answer that, hon. Let's have a nice quiet walk in the park together. Who knows who might be on the other end of the line."

"But . . . but it might be Tyler! He might have a problem. I have to answer it." Josie picked up the receiver before he could protest further. "Hello? It's for you, Sam. Your mother. She says it's important," she added.

Sam sighed and reached for the phone, putting his hand over the receiver so the caller couldn't hear him. "I'll try to make it short."

Josie sincerely hoped he didn't manage to keep that particular promise, and she moved toward the doorway, picking up her still wet boots and damp coat. She sat down on the hard, black metal bench Pamela had provided, and prepared to reenter the storm.

She was not at all surprised when Sam put his hand back over the receiver and told her that he couldn't go out right now. She just kept struggling to put her foot into the soggy boot. "Josie, you're not going to go without me, are you? You might get lost."

"I only have to walk three blocks to the west. We're going to meet at the corner on Fifth." For a moment, she was distracted by the pleasure she felt at saying this. She was speaking just like a New Yorker! "They've probably already left home. If I don't hurry, they'll freeze to death. You know

Betty won't let Jon leave that corner until I arrive. She worries about me in the city almost as much as you do!"

Sam sighed. "Okay. I guess I have to do this. Under any other circumstances . . ."

"Don't worry. I understand," Josie assured him. "And I won't be long. Betty said just a short walk."

"Do you have my key? You'll need it to get back in."

"Yes. I'm fine. I'll just walk in the park for a bit with Betty and Jon then come right back here. And I'll stop at the deli on the corner and pick up something to eat," she added.

"It may not be open," Sam warned her.

"I'll find something. This is the city that never sleeps, isn't it?"

"Yes, but—"

"I'll be fine, Sam. Really!" Without allowing him more time to protest, she left the apartment.

Harold was busy with an elderly lady whose Pomeranian apparently needed to go out to visit the closest tree. Josie smiled and waved as she passed, heading out the front door and into the stinging cold. Once outside, she headed away from Central Park and right into the blinding snow. Fortunately she wasn't going far. Two blocks to the right, turn left and one and a half blocks more. She put her head down and walked, determined to make it to Pamela Peel's apartment in record time despite the weather. She didn't know how long Carol could keep Sam on the phone and she didn't want him to start to worry.

Some of the streets had been plowed and she had to climb over drifts of snow to cross at corners. Other streets had drifts down the middle. Unlike an hour or so earlier, there were people outside to have fun. A couple of cross-country skiers had taken over a lane on Park Avenue and were sliding along together, scarves flying out behind them. Families were walking and laughing, the children as thrilled as children always are by the opportunity to make snowballs and smash them into the backs of their parents.

Josie paused for a moment in front of the apartment building Carol had indicated just the other day. Would anyone notice that she didn't belong here? And what would happen if someone did? Well, she would just have to take her chances. She took a deep breath of the cold air and walked through the large entryway.

And discovered herself in an enchanting little park. The apartment building had been built around a center courtyard. There were large trees, shrubs, benches, and a frozen waterfall, all illuminated by thousands of tiny white lights. Children were building an igloo in a space that seemed to have been reserved for parking at other times. A uniformed guard stood by, watching three young men clear paths between the five doorways into the building. Josie smiled, waved her key chain in the air, and headed for the closest door. It wasn't locked and she found herself alone in a small foyer. To her right and to her left, glassed-in walkways had been built so residents could move around the interior of their common yard without actually going outside. Pots of blooming azaleas scented the warm, moist air. Josie spied a large copper rectangle dotted with a few dozen buttons; she hurried toward it. It was part of an old-fashioned intercom system. Josie read it through quickly. Pamela Peel had lived in apartment 5S—#3. She hurried toward the elevator.

Pamela Peel's apartment was easy to find and, Josie was relieved to discover, she had guessed right about the last key on the ring. It opened the door of 5S—#3. Once inside, Josie glanced at the walls, found the light switch, but waited until the door was firmly closed behind her to turn on the lights. With a flick of the wrist, she lit up Pamela Peel's home. Mindful of the neighbors below, she slipped off her boots and moved on tiptoe, careful to make as little noise as possible.

This was the place she had seen in the magazine article.

Only the brief glimpse she had spied in the pages had given no clue to the extent of what was here.

The apartment had been described as eclectic—a combination of all the things she loved, Pamela had said in the article. Her loves were incredibly indiscriminate. There were very modern pieces right next to what looked like antiques. A collection of Scandinavian glass was displayed on an ornate brass baker's rack. Handmade quilts hung on the wall beside another hideous abstract, which looked a lot like the one Pamela Peel had painted for Sam—only this one bore the name of an artist so famous even Josie recognized his name. There were three couches—two upholstered in matching chintz, the other covered with leather. There were six chairs and more occasional tables than most people would ever have an occasion to use.

There was a full dining room, an eat-in kitchen, a large bedroom done up almost entirely in lace and silk—Josie just glanced in and then left, trying not to imagine Sam doing anything in such surroundings—a white-tiled bathroom with yet another étagère filled with apothecary jars and white china dogs, a small kitchen that was so filled with decorator touches, it was impossible to imagine anyone turning on the stove for fear of starting a damaging inferno. Behind this Josie found another room, which she assumed was the maid's room. If there was a maid present, she was hiding beneath boxes and boxes of lamps, pillows, fabric swatches, and the like. Josie stood there in the open doorway and wondered just what, if anything, she had found here.

Discouraged, she wandered back down the hallway to the living room, smacking into an inlaid desk, too large for the small space it occupied. She started to walk around it and then had second thoughts. She'd had no compunctions about looking around Pamela Peel's apartment. Why stop here? Why not look in her desk? Josie started pulling out drawers and searching through them. After a few minutes, she decided that what she was looking for was probably at Henderson and Peel's office. She walked around one more time, discouraged and a bit depressed. Fascinating as it was to look into Pamela Peel's private life, she seemed to be getting nowhere. She had learned a lot in the last few days and her appearance had improved dramatically, but she couldn't prove that Sam hadn't killed Pamela Peel.

Disheartened, she decided it was time to go back to Sam's place. She put on her boots and coat and left the apartment, carefully locking the door behind her. She got on the elevator without paying too much attention to the man who was already there.

"Sam?!"

"Yes, Josie?"

It was obvious that only one of them was surprised. "Ah . . . ," Josie began.

"You've been in Pamela's apartment, haven't you?"

"Yes. I thought I might learn something there that would help you . . . keep you from being arrested for her murder."

"And did you?"

"No."

"Too bad."

"Do you think the police—"

"I don't know what the police are thinking. I didn't realize what you were thinking, to be honest. I've been so worried about Mother."

"Why? What's wrong?"

Sam looked down at her and frowned. "Listen, I don't know what might be open in this storm, but let's see if we can get some dinner. It's time we talked."

They left the building arm in arm, as much to keep from falling as for moral support. "There used to be a deli around the corner. I think the family that owned it also owned the building. They might have stayed open."

The deli was closed, but next door, a small sushi place's

lights were still on. Sam knocked on the door and two smiling young Japanese women waved them in.

"Sushi?" Sam asked.

"And soup. Good soup!" One of the women pointed to a blackboard where the menu had been written out.

"Two miso soup, two tekka rolls, two salmon skin rolls, and two yellowtail with scallion," Sam ordered, raising his eyebrows for Josie's approval.

"And tea," she added. "Hot tea."

The women hurried off and Josie and Sam sat down at a small table as far away from the window as they could get.

"Why are you worried about your mother? What's wrong with her?" Josie asked, getting to the point immediately.

"I've been afraid from the very beginning that the police will think she killed Pamela. All the evidence points to her."

"Why?"

"She was at my apartment the day Pamela was killed. She doesn't know that I know though, so don't tell her."

Josie was shocked. "You saw her there?"

"I saw her coming out."

"Where were you?"

"Returning from the storage area . . . you use the tradesmen's elevator to get there. I was just coming into the hallway and she was leaving my apartment. She headed toward the elevator and didn't see me."

"And you didn't call out to her?"

"I was busy and . . . well, you know how Mother can be. I didn't want to be held up."

Two little cups of steaming green tea were placed before them and Sam cupped his hands around his before continuing. "Remember you showered before we left for the theater?"

"Yes, but—"

"Well, while you were in the shower, I went down to the storage locker in the basement. When I came up, Mother was leaving my apartment."

"She was inside while I was in the shower?"

"Yes, and, I'm afraid Pamela could have been in there too. That might have been when Pamela was killed."

"But, Sam, why do you think that? She could have been killed while we were having brunch with Betty and Jon. Or while we were at the theater in the evening."

"Then why hasn't Mother admitted that she was in my place that day? Why would she be keeping that fact a secret?"

"But Sam . . ." Josie didn't know what to say so she snapped her mouth shut. Maybe it was true. Maybe Carol had killed Pamela. Maybe Carol had been working so hard to prevent Sam from being arrested because she knew he hadn't killed Pamela because she had done it. Josie thought for a moment. "Didn't Harold see her?"

"Yes."

"Did he tell the police?"

"No. They didn't ask. He didn't tell. If they ask, though . . ."

Josie nodded. "Of course. He couldn't lie to the police."

Sam smiled for the first time since sitting down. "I don't know about couldn't, but I told him that he shouldn't. He's crazy about Mom, so he'll protect her as long as he can. But I don't know how long that will be. I didn't tell Jon about all this, but he's like you. He's afraid the police are beginning to get anxious to find a suspect. If only *New York* magazine hadn't put Pamela on their cover. She was always well known in her professional world and a small, wealthy segment of the population of the Upper East Side, but that story made her famous. And the police can't ignore the murder of a famous person. Makes the media ask too many questions."

"Sam, I have a question."

"What?"

"What did the desk that used to be in your living room look like?"

TWENTY-NINE

L ATER, WHEN JOSIE was explaining what had happened to Tyler, she realized that running into the desk in Pamela Peel's apartment had been a turning point. She had been looking in the wrong places and, more important, at the wrong things. In fact, everyone's attention had been directed in the wrong place. Instead of running all over the city, she should have centered most of her attention on Sam's apartment.

Josie and Sam hadn't had to return to Pamela's apartment for them to be pretty sure that the desk which had occupied the place of honor in his apartment before Pamela Peel had decorated it had become an annoyance in her hallway.

"It's not like Pamela to have furniture blocking what she called 'the flow.' I would imagine that it wasn't supposed to stay there for very long. She always had so much stuff in her apartment and she was always rearranging it," Sam said, dipping his spoon in the steaming miso soup. "And, of course, it wasn't there when I was . . . well, was there."

"It may have been in storage," Josie said. She wanted to check out a few things before she told Sam, or anyone, what she thought had been going on. She sipped her soup. It was warm and delicious, but she had more questions. Some she wanted to ask, some she had to ask.

"Why did you ever get involved with Pamela Peel?" Josie asked.

"Well, she was smart, beautiful, well educated . . ."

"From the way you talk about your life in the city, it's always seemed to me that you could say that about almost every woman you dated."

"That's true. There are a lot of wonderful, single career women in New York City. A whole lot."

Their waitress placed a beautiful tray of sushi in the middle of the table and they stopped speaking for a moment to admire it.

"So what was different about her? Why did that relationship last longer? Why was it more serious than the others? Were you in love with her?" Josie asked the fourth question and held her breath, waiting for his answer.

"I've been asking myself that same thing for the past few days," Sam admitted slowly. "And I think I've come up with the answer. Inertia."

"In . . . What do you mean?"

"I mean that Pamela came after me and I stood still—for a long time. And then, of course, after a few years I started moving. And I moved right out of the city."

"Are you telling me you didn't love her?"

"Josie, to tell you the truth—and I am ashamed to admit this—I didn't even like her."

"Are you saying that to make me feel better?"

"I'm saying it because it is true. Sad and true. Pamela Peel loved two things: money and fame. I was involved in a big case at the time, lots of publicity and notoriety. She came after me because of what I had. And I was exhausted, tired of the round of getting to know a new woman every few months, all those first dates with the same questions and so many times the same answers. I didn't run after her; all I had to do was stand still and let her catch me. And I did. And then we became a couple. We argued a lot, but I didn't have the sense to see that it was because we were completely incompatible. I didn't realize that until she decorated my apartment. It was *so* not for me. The first night I spent there, I woke up to go to the bathroom and was suddenly struck by what a depressing place it was. I knew I had to get out. And thinking about that forced me to reevaluate my life, and eventually led me to retire and move to the island."

"So, if you hadn't been involved with Pamela Peel, you might never have changed your life," Josie said, deciding she would ask him about this money he had had another time.

"And if I hadn't changed my life, I might never have met you," Sam added, taking the thought to its logical conclusion.

"Yes, I suppose that's so." Josie dipped a tekka roll in soy sauce and raised it to her lips. "But she really was a talented decorator, right?"

Sam didn't seem surprised by the question. "Yes, definitely. Henderson and Peel won all sorts of major awards and they were getting many of the best jobs in the city."

"Yes, but was that because of Pamela's talent or Shepard Henderson's? Or did they work together as equals?" Josie asked.

"The money was Shep's and the talent was Pamela's. She always said so and he was a little drunk one night when we were all having dinner together and he confirmed it. Said he couldn't run the company without her. Why?"

"Because I think that's why he killed her."

"He . . . Josie, are you sure?"

"I think so. I just don't have any proof."

"Are you saying that Shep Henderson killed Pamela because he wanted to destroy his company?"

"No, of course not. He killed her because he was afraid she would destroy the company. In an odd way, he was probably trying to save it."

"I'm sorry, Josie, but I don't understand."

"I don't understand completely either. But I'm hoping that I will tomorrow. Can you wait that long?"

"What's going to happen tomorrow?"

"I'm going to talk with some of the contractors who worked for Henderson and Peel. I'm hoping at least one of them will have a few answers."

"Which you will pass on to me immediately."

"Yes. I promise." She put down her chopsticks long enough to reach across the table and squeeze his hand.

"Of course you're going to have one big problem . . . just like the rest of the city."

"What?"

"Getting from one place to another," Sam said, staring out the window at the still falling snow.

It was a relief to be honest again. The next morning, Josie found herself smiling as she climbed over snowdrifts and squished through the gray slush-filled streets. Last night she had called the three contracting companies, and identified herself. She hadn't pretended to be getting ready to go on a diet; she hadn't claimed to want a different hair color. She was an out-of-towner, she owned a contracting company, and she was looking for information. She had been simple and to the point. And the answers had been too. The owner of the last company she had called seemed particularly amenable to talking about Henderson and Peel. All Josie had to do was be at their work site at seven A.M. Josie had agreed, set the alarm, and gone to bed, ignoring Sam's protests that the city would be completely impassable in the morning. Finally, he gave up trying to talk her out of going and insisted on going with her.

Although it was still dark when they left Mentelle Park Apartments, the number of people on the streets amazed Josie. The storm had passed and a massive cleanup had begun. Snow was being shoveled from sidewalks and piled up wherever a few square feet could be found. Bulldozers were filling large dump trucks with snow, to be driven away and dumped into the rivers surrounding Manhattan, Sam explained. Cars whose drivers had ignored the No Parking Snow Route signs were being towed away. Corner coffee shops were open for business and Josie stopped and bought half a dozen cups of coffee and a dozen glazed doughnuts. "You're not the only person who knows the way to a carpenter's heart," she explained, handing her purchases to Sam.

"Just as long as one of those cups of coffee is for me."

"You can have as much as you want." Josie was forced to watch where she was stepping on the slippery sidewalks, but at least her feet were now encased in familiar work boots. Her old clothing, which Carol had deemed so inappropriate for city wear, had turned out to be the only practical choice this morning.

The address she had been given was only a few blocks away. Josie had assumed they would be heading into yet another ornate lobby with yet another uniformed doorman, but this place turned out to be one of a row of brownstones. It was easy to find the one they were searching for. A gigantic snow-covered Dumpster stood on the street before it. The sidewalk had been cleared as well as the stone steps leading up to the doorway. As they mounted the steps, a young black man pulled one of the tall French doors open and exited, bumping one of Josie's shoulders as he brushed by. "You better get upstairs with that coffee. She's in a piss-poor mood this morning," he said, without slowing down.

Josie looked up at Sam, grinned, and shrugged. "Sounds like we're expected." She walked into the house and immediately felt at home. The walls had been stripped down to their lath and plaster bones; the ceiling was in need of serious repair. More than one of the newel posts on the ornate stairway leading to the second floor needed to be pulled off, rerouted and put back in place. Drop cloths were on the floor and the dust in the air was that peculiar combination of plaster, sawdust, and ripped Sheetrock. It had been less than a week since Josie was on a work site. She was surprised how happy she was to return.

"We're looking for Ava Edgar," she said to two men struggling with a coping saw standing in the middle of what had once been the home's formal parlor.

"She's upstairs. Turn right when you reach the landing. And watch what you're doing. Some of the steps are damaged, the handrail is a disaster, and God knows what might fall from the ceiling any minute now."

Josie grinned and hurried up the stairs with Sam at her heels. They found a middle-aged black woman, her salt-and-pepper hair braided into dozens of tiny spikes barely contained by a bright orange bandanna. She was perched precariously on one sawhorse, her feet resting on another. She had a large sheath of papers in one hand, a pen in the other, and a frown on her face. She looked up when Josie and Sam walked into the room.

"Don't suppose either of you knows anything about contract law," she stated.

"Actually . . . ," Sam began, holding out his hand for the papers.

"He does. He's a lawyer," Josie explained, a grin on her face. "You must be Ava Edgar."

"And you must be Josie Pigeon. Do you always travel with your own personal lawyer?"

"Sam's a good friend."

"I also function as coffee and doughnut carrier," Sam added, handing over the bags of goodies.

"Then you're a gift from the gods," Ava Edgar said, grabbing a cup of coffee and starting to peel off its lid. "Now what can I do for the famous Josie Pigeon?"

"I . . . why famous?"

"I just got the impression that you are a woman of many talents. At least that's the way your son and his friend talk about you."

"My son? How do you know Tyler?" Josie was completely confused.

Sam looked up from the documents he was reading and answered Josie's question. "You've met him with his friend Tony, right?" He waved the contracts at Josie. "Ms. Edgar here is remodeling this house for Taylor Blanco. I gather he's stopped in this week to see how things are going?"

"Actually, the big producer is too involved in professional problems to come look at what is going to be his wonderful new home. Seems the film he's working on takes place in the early spring in New York City, but not in the middle of a major snowstorm. He has people running all over the city searching out indoor locations so they can keep working until the snow melts. But his fiancée—Toni with an I—has been over every chance she gets. And she brings the young men with her. The crushes those boys have . . . whew, it takes me back to my childhood to just see the expressions on their faces. But if you didn't know I was working for Mr. Blanco, you're not here to see me about him."

"No, I'm looking for information about Henderson and Peel."

"Well, Pamela Peel, to be a bit more exact," Sam broke in.

Josie shook her head. "Actually, I have a few questions about both of them."

"So have a doughnut and shoot. I can only break for a few here, so let's not waste any more time."

"Is the company good to work for?"

"Not bad. Better than some, worse than others. There are always problems working for partners. That's why I like owning my own business. Everything comes from me. But sometimes Henderson didn't seem to know what Peel was doing and vice versa. He did all the paperwork—which would be nice—and she was more hands-on. She would come around and tell us what to tear down, what to save, what to trash. He would walk clients through jobs, explaining what things were going to look like when they were done, smoothing things over when the schedule wasn't being adhered to exactly. She brought in lots of other subcontractors—paperhangers, painters, and such—while he visited with prospective clients explaining things completely wrong much of the time." She shrugged her muscular shoulders. "Must have worked for them. They were getting more and more popular."

"Did you ever see them angry with each other? Arguing over anything?"

"Can't say that I did, but they weren't together too much of the time, at least not when I was around."

"Did you like her?"

"I liked working for her. She knew what she wanted and she expected the people who worked for her to do what she asked. She was easy to work for as far as I was concerned. She wasn't sweet. She wasn't friendly. But she was professional. You know how it is."

"Yes, I do." Josie took a deep breath and asked the big question. "Was she stealing?"

Ava smiled. "Oh, so I'm not the only one who noticed."

"Noticed what?" Sam asked.

"Things disappearing . . . well, maybe not so much disappearing as getting lost in the shuffle. Like . . . see that mantel over there?" She pointed to a heavily carved oak mantel leaning up against a wall. "We're replacing that old-fashioned thing with a beautiful work of art, an amazing chestnut mantel, hand carved by an artist in Surrey, England."

"And what will happen to that one?"

"It will be sold. May not be fashionable this year, but next year maybe that type of thing will become real popular and worth a whole lot of money. But that's not my problem. The architect or decorator will take care of it. When Pamela Peel took care of that sort of thing, the owners never saw a penny of the profit from the sale. Same with furniture, I'd bet, although that's not my field and I can't say that I could prove it."

"And did Shep Henderson know about any of this?"

"Oh, no. That man never had to worry about money and he gave the impression that he was above such things. Once I heard him disparage another firm, said they were always worrying about nickels and dimes and not paying enough attention to the big picture. So I think as long as he looked at the big picture, Ms. Pamela Peel could steal whatever she wanted from right out under his nose. Is that the type of thing you're interested in?"

"Exactly what we needed to know," Josie answered. "Thank you. We won't take up any more of your time."

"Yes, thank you," Sam added. "I didn't really have enough time to go through these papers, but I'd be happy to come back another time."

"You're a nice man. Tyler said you were, and he was right. Thanks, but no thanks. I'll call my lawyer and he can just figure out a way to get through the snow from Riverside Drive and do what I pay him to do. Lord, you'd think we were living in the Alps instead of New York City to hear that man talk."

Her cell phone rang and Sam and Josie thanked her again and made a hasty exit. Sam noticed the frown on Josie's face as they made their way back down the precarious stairway. "What's wrong?"

"Sam, you know how you always keep a copy of any contracts you go over for me?"

"Sure. Standard procedure. I want to make sure I have a copy available if any questions come up in the future."

"Do you do that for everyone or just for me?"

"Everyone."

"Pamela Peel too?"

Sam stopped walking and looked down at Josie. "Yes. What are you getting at?"

"Did you keep them in your apartment? In those file cabinets Pamela hated? Then in the window seat?"

"While I was living there, yes. Then I moved them to the basement when I moved, but . . ."

". . . but Pamela didn't know that," Josie ended for him.

"She was looking for those old files when she was killed." Sam spoke slowly.

"She was looking for them when Shep Henderson killed her," Josie added. "And he probably came to your apartment to find the files as well. It was just bad luck that they happened to be there at the same time.

"Does this all make sense to you?" she asked when they were back on the street.

"You think Shep Henderson found out what was going on and killed her?" Sam answered her question with a question.

"You don't think that's possible?"

"I suppose. But there must have been a catalyst. Something must have changed. Something must have made Shep Henderson go from being ignorant of the situation to becoming aware of it, to feeling that he had to kill her before she destroyed Henderson and Peel."

"Oh, that's easy. It was that magazine article. Look carefully at the photograph on the cover. Pamela isn't just surrounded by the things she loves, as the article says. She's surrounded by the things she stole. And it's entirely possible that the people she stole them from read *New York* magazine as well, don't you think?"

THIRTY

"I HOPE YOU don't mind me saying this, but Pamela Peel was an incredibly shallow woman." Josie Pigeon picked up the pink drink their waiter had just placed on the table in front of her and sipped, glancing around at her companions. Sam, his mother, Jon and Betty, and Josie were having cocktails at the Rainbow Room.

Sam was studying a bottle of wine as though he had never seen one before. Carol was smiling in what she probably thought was an encouraging manner, her new (used) Hermès bag sitting prominently on her lap. Betty and Jon were both leaning forward, attentive expressions on their faces.

"You see, I thought she would be . . . well . . ." Josie suddenly discovered that she couldn't go on.

Fortunately, Sam got the point. "You thought she would be more like you," he said, nodding up at the wine steward as he handed back the bottle.

"Yes. I guess I did. Anyway, once I realized how much she cared about money, I started seeing things more clearly."

"Fine, but what exactly did you see?" Jon asked.

"She was making money on the side, selling off furniture from various decorating jobs out of her apartment, skimming money off various contracts, even doing work on her own using Henderson and Peel's name to get those jobs."

Betty looked up. "You're kidding!"

"Nope. Sam's desk was in her apartment. That was the

first clue. Sam said she hated that desk so she certainly wasn't planning her own decorating scheme around it. And Ava, a contractor Sam and I met this morning, verified what I was thinking." Josie paused and looked out the window at the twinkling skyline. "She said Pamela sold off bits and pieces from decorating jobs. She also said that Shepard Henderson paid very little attention to the day-to-day running of the company. Apparently he didn't know anything about what was going on. Or not until he saw the photograph on the cover of *New York* magazine."

"Shepard Henderson killed Pamela Peel because she was stealing some of the profits of a very profitable business?" Jon asked, sounding doubtful.

"No, he killed her because he was afraid she was going to destroy Henderson and Peel with her need for extra money. He knew that he might not be the only person who noticed that Pamela's eclectic décor was a mélange of their clients' possessions. And some of the other people who noticed just might be the clients to whom those possessions once belonged. And Henderson and Peel is a very small company. When one person is a problem, it reflects on the entire company." She paused for a moment and remembered the discussion about this very thing during her pedicure earlier in the week. "Besides," she continued, "this wasn't the first time—"

"Mother and Betty are both looking confused, Josie, and Jon . . . well, Jon doesn't know you as well as the rest of us and he's not used to your rather convoluted way of thinking. Perhaps you should start at the beginning of the story," Sam suggested.

"I don't know where the story begins. I do know that Pamela was the talented one and Shepard Henderson had the money and the contacts—and that they both were desperate for the company to be successful. Pamela because she wanted all that success can bring in this city. And Shepard because he was trying to prove to his parents that he didn't have to follow in his father's footsteps to be a credit to the family name.

"Owning your own company is wonderful and frightening," she continued, talking about something she knew well. "Shepard Henderson and Pamela Peel had to depend on themselves to get where they wanted to be. But they didn't define success in the same way. For Shepard Henderson it was being a successful company. He didn't seem to need more money. But for Pamela it was money, money, money. She wanted to live in expensive buildings, eat in the right restaurants, go south in the winter and to Europe in the summer. She wanted her hair and nails done weekly whether she could afford to tip or not.

"I got the first clue about what could be going on when Sam explained how decorators make money. Their billing practices leave a lot of loopholes for someone to add on extra charges, skim money off the top, whatever. And I think Pamela took advantage of this from the very beginning."

"I don't understand why you think so," Jon said.

"Because Pamela Peel, according to everyone who worked with her or for her or knew her, never got up on a ladder in her life."

"I'm sorry, but I think you lost me there, Josie," Sam admitted.

"Not long after Henderson and Peel was founded, Shep Henderson gave Pamela Peel a gift certificate for two months of twice-weekly sessions with a personal trainer. He told the company that provided the trainers that Pamela had hurt her back in a fall off a ladder. But everyone agrees that Pamela never climbed ladders, never did the physical work that many decorators do. The made-up fall was just an excuse to give her a present that would keep her at home for a certain amount of time each week while he examined the company's books without her interference. And I think he discovered that she was stealing from the company and insisted that it stop. And, for a while, it probably did. Pamela was smart; she didn't want to go back to working for people who took advantage of her looks and not her talent. She needed Shep Henderson.

"But Pamela was also greedy and a snob. She trashed the people who worked on her at Elizabeth Arden when she decided to leave and didn't need them anymore. And she adopted a wealthy older woman, calling her aunt. But hanging out with the rich and famous wasn't enough. She wanted far more than she could manage on her share of the profits of the company. So she tried to get extra cash another way. She left her chic, spare apartment and changed her style. Suddenly she was into eclectic furnishings. Because, of course, if you steal a bit here and steal another bit there and hang on to all those bits until you sell them off, eclectic is what you end up living with."

"You know, you're probably right about that," Sam spoke up. "That apartment never made any sense to me. It was so unlike Pamela. She was a very talented decorator. She could create modern interiors as well as traditional ones. She designed very feminine spaces as well as very masculine ones. But, while the period or style of the furnishings may have been different, some things were the same. Pamela loved order and perfect color schemes. Hell, we broke up over a brown chair."

"You what?" Josie, Carol, and Betty asked simultaneously.

"We broke up because I wanted to put a brown chair in my gray apartment," Sam said after a momentary pause.

"The chair you have in the corner of your living room at home on the island? The chair you always sit in to listen to music and read? That brown chair?" Josie asked.

Sam nodded. "That brown chair. I saw it in the window of a shop down in SoHo. It cost an arm and a leg. Hell, it cost two arms and two legs and the shop owner assured me it was the latest design from Paris, so I thought Pamela would like it. I didn't buy it for its looks, of course. It was—it still is—the most comfortable chair I've ever owned. Anyway, I ordered it and then forgot about it. It arrived a few months after Pamela had redecorated my place. I rearranged a bit and managed to put it in a corner without interrupting what Pamela would call 'the flow.' And then I forgot about it. Until Pamela saw it."

"I gather she didn't like it, dear?" Carol asked.

"I think you could say that she hated it. I suspect my neighbors on either side as well as above and below me could tell you just how much she hated it. She screamed and yelled and generally made the biggest stink anyone could possibly make over one single chair. I broke up with her that night."

"You broke up with her," Josie repeated, absolutely amazed. "Why didn't I know? Why didn't you tell me? I thought . . . I know you told me that the feelings were mutual, that you just stopped caring about each other and broke up."

"Pride." Sam said the word as though it explained everything.

"But you broke up with her. She didn't break up with you," Betty pointed out.

"I broke up with her because of her reaction to a chair I'd bought. Only a fool would say that. Only a fool would have a long relationship with a woman who would go nuts over a chair the wrong color. Only a fool would have such an odd wake-up call."

"I don't think so, dear," his mother broke in. "Pamela was beautiful and charming, and she was after you from the first time she saw you. You were busy with some important cases and, perhaps, just a bit into the beginning of a midlife crisis. Dear Pamela took advantage of your particular situation the way she did all others. You simply fell into that relationship and it took something rather odd to make you realize that it wasn't working. I wouldn't blame you at all."

"Thank you, Mother. But I blame myself."

Josie remained silent, relieved by what Sam had just said, but disturbed as well.

"So you were telling us about the new apartment and Pamela's new method of making money," Betty reminded Josie, picking up her husband's sidecar and taking a sip. "Yummy."

"She sold things and used her apartment as a place to store them. There's really not that much to it," Josie said. "She could have made extra money that way for years and years if she hadn't agreed to allow the photographer from *New York* magazine into her home to take pictures. I'll bet Shepard Henderson went crazy when he saw that cover."

"I'm sorry to be so dense, but how did Pamela and Shep Henderson both end up at Sam's place?" Betty asked.

"Sam kept copies of Henderson and Peel's contracts there. And probably some of those contracts Shep Henderson didn't even know about. Pamela did those jobs on her own, and made all the profit. Anyway, I think Shep wanted to see the copies Sam kept to make sure they matched up with the ones kept back at the office. Pamela, of course, wanted them herself. She was probably going to destroy the evidence. You see, when she ran into Sam that first day he was in the city, he told her he was going to sell. She knew she had to act if she wanted to get rid of the contracts."

"Get rid of them?" Betty asked. "You would have destroyed them?" she asked Sam.

"No. I would have sent them back to Henderson and Peel."

Jon nodded. "Standard procedure," he explained to his wife. "But what I don't understand," he continued, "is how they both got keys to Sam's apartment."

"Sam gave Pamela one for her personal use and she had

one made to give to the workers who needed to get in and out during the time the place was being redecorated," Josie explained. "The second key was probably kept in Henderson and Peel's office—available to Shep anytime he wanted to use it."

"So they ran into each other at my place . . . And Shep killed her and hid her body in the window seat," Sam said slowly.

"Yes, that's what I think happened," Josie said. "It worked out well for Shep because there was no reason for the police to suspect him and maybe more than a few reasons for you to be a suspect. Of course, all that changed when you dropped off those old contracts with a friend at the police department. Shepard Henderson moved right to the top of the shortlist of suspects."

"Jon says he was arrested this afternoon," Betty spoke up. "After you and Sam went to the police with this story," she added to Josie.

"Yeah, word down at the office is that Sterling Henderson has been buying up all the high-priced defense lawyers he can find," Jon said.

"I should have known it was him," Carol said. "I ran into him on the sidewalk after I left the building that afternoon. I should have realized he was waiting for everyone to leave so he could head on upstairs."

"You were there? At Sam's apartment that afternoon?" Jon asked.

Sam answered the question. "Yes, she was."

"How do you know that?" Carol asked, surprised.

"I saw you. And if you had just told me that you were there . . . I didn't even have to know why you were there . . . if I had just heard from you that you were there, I wouldn't have been so horribly worried, Mother."

"And Sam would have answered my questions about what

he was doing that day," Jon added. "And I wouldn't have been so worried about what he was hiding."

"I saw Mother coming out of my apartment," Sam began.

"Sammy, where were you?" his mother asked.

"Sam was using the tradesmen's elevator to come up from the basement storage area," Josie explained.

"It wasn't that you were there that bothered me, Mother. It was that you didn't tell me you were there. At first, I just thought it was one of those things. After all, I know how much you like to take care of me so I thought that perhaps you had been dropping off something you had cooked. But there was no food in the place, and, when you didn't mention it, I thought it was odd, but figured I'd understand eventually. But then we found Pamela's body, and I kept wondering what you had been doing in my place and, well . . ." Sam stopped, looking sheepishly down toward the floor.

Josie grinned. Sam looked adorable. "So why were you there?" she asked Carol.

"I was there to drop off some pâté and a bottle of champagne. I was just trying to make sure this week went as perfectly as possible for the two of you. But then I heard the shower running and just left without leaving anything behind." She looked across the table at her son and scowled.

"Frankly, Sammy, I've waited long enough to be a mother-in-law. For the last week, I've been doing whatever I can think of to get you married to the best woman you've ever known!"

EPILOGUE

JOSIE AND SAM were sharing his comfortable brown chair. The windows were open to cool breezes coming off the ocean, blowing away the heat of the August day. The television was on, a video in the VCR, and they both leaned forward watching intently as Tyler, looking incredibly grown-up in his tuxedo, escorted a gorgeous blond bridesmaid down the church aisle.

"He looks so handsome, doesn't he?" Josie asked, sighing.

"Like mother like son," Sam answered, kissing her shoulder.

"You're so sweet," Josie said, jumping up to turn off the set as picture turned to snow. "It was nice of Taylor Blanco to send the clip of the scene from the movie that Tyler is in, wasn't it?"

"It was even nicer that he and Toni with an I asked both Tyler and Tony with a Y to usher at their own wedding down in Santa Fe—and to send them tickets and make arrangements for them to spend the weekend at a nearby dude ranch while the celebration is going on," Sam added.

"Yes. It was." Josie walked over to the sliding doors that would lead to the new deck that Island Contracting would build as soon as the busy summer season ended. "And you know, I've been thinking."

"And?"

"And now that Tyler has had all this practice . . . you know, playing an usher at a wedding in a movie and then being an usher at a real wedding . . . well, we wouldn't want all that training to go to waste, would we?" She turned back to Sam, a smile on her sunburned face. "I was wondering, Sam . . ."

"About what?"

"Well . . ."

"Take your time, Josie. You know I don't want to rush you. I've never wanted to rush you."

Josie took a deep breath and plunged in. "I was wondering if you'd like to marry me." She smiled.

He returned her smile and got up to join her before answering. "I'd love it," he answered, putting his arms around her. "I've just been waiting for you to ask."

Don't miss these other Josie Pigeon mysteries by Valerie Wolzien!

MURDER IN THE FORECAST

With a signed contract for remodeling the grandest old house on the island, contractor Josie Pigeon figures her summer is made. But before she can lift a hammer, she finds her new employer— wealthy New Yorker Cornell Hudson—murdered on the premises with a strip of drop cloth twisted tightly around his neck.

When Hurricane Agatha sweeps away both the house and the body, Josie would like to forget she ever saw them. But she cannot. Now, through rain and wind, and through a past that refuses to die, Josie pursues the truth—and nails down a killer who is tougher than boards. . . .

Published by Fawcett Books.
Available wherever books are sold.

THIS OLD MURDER
A Josie Pigeon Mystery

When the production crew for Courtney Castle's Castles invades contractor Josie Pigeon's job site to shoot a PBS remodeling series, Josie's fifteen minutes of fame seem imminent. Unfortunately, the confusion of taping compounds the chaos of construction, and Josie is soon ready to kill.

Which is why, when a bludgeoned body appears on the premises, Josie is a top suspect. That's when she decides to make her own suspect list. But the more Josie hammers down the facts, the closer to home she hits. . . .

**And look for Wolzien's delightful
Susan Henshaw mysteries!**

AN ANNIVERSARY
TO DIE FOR

Susan and Jed Henshaws' anniversary celebration
promised to be a night to remember . . . for all the
wrong reasons. By evening's end, Ashley Marks
became the ultimate party pooper. She was dead,
apparently poisoned, her body hidden beneath a
pile of gifts on the bed in the Henshaw's room.

Following a cold trail of clues, Susan tracks down
a killer whose roots may be buried deep in
Ashley's past, along with deadly secrets. . . .

**Published by Fawcett Books.
Available wherever books are sold.**

DEATH AT A DISCOUNT
A Susan Henshaw Mystery

As her wealthy friends knew, Amanda Worth
wouldn't be caught dead in a discount store. But
she was. Susan Henshaw found her in a dressing
room with a Hermes scarf knotted murderously
tight around her elegant neck.

What possibly could have lured Amanda to the
grand opening of the new outlet mall? Susan shops
around for the answer and discovers that in this
pristine Connecticut suburb, murder is suddenly the
fashion. And one size fits all. . . .

Published by Fawcett Books.
Available wherever books are sold.